Skin and Bone

Brand of Justice
Book 5

Lisa Phillips

eBook ISBN: 979-8-88552-172-7

Paperback ISBN: 979-8-88552-173-4

Published by: Two Dogs Publishing, LLC. Idaho, USA

Cover Design by: Sasha Almazan and Gene Mollica, GS Cover Design Studio, LLC

Edited by: Christine Callahan, Professional Publishing Services

Chapter One

A warm summer breeze drifted through the open car windows. Kenna hunched down in the driver's seat and kept still. Earbuds in.

Kids played in the pool—a boy and a girl. The parents drank beer at a round table while the water reflected flickering, dancing light onto the side of the motel. A reclining cowboy spun above the parking lot, permanently tipping his hat to weary travelers looking for a place to stay, while the sign marked MOTEL below him made the full rotation.

The little girl squealed and screamed at her brother to quit splashing. Followed by a loud, "Mooooooooom!"

"Knock it off! Both of you." The dad.

Kenna stared at the door to room 8, periodically scanning the parking lot.

Music blaring from bass-boosted speakers cut through the night air as a car rolled in. Black paint and blacked-out windows. Some kind of low-slung Mercedes. The driver pulled up in the lane in front of Kenna, and the music cut off. The passenger door opened, and one leg emerged first.

Tanned skin, slender, with a tattoo on her thigh. A red high heel hit the pitted asphalt of the parking lot.

"Remember what I said." A man. Low and lethal, his voice rang with authority.

"I remember." She had a slight accent, and this wasn't her comfort zone, but she'd toughed out worse things. "I got it."

"I don't want no mistakes like last time," he grunted. "I'll be back in an hour."

She climbed out. Leather skirt, big hair. Big hoop earrings. She didn't falter once striding across the cracked parking lot to the door of room 7, like she was walking on flat ground in slippers. Or bare feet.

The door to 7 opened before she got there. Mister big belly—white tank and tan pants with his receding hairline—waited for her. He stepped back, and she sashayed inside.

Kenna shifted on the reclined seat and ran both hands over the knees of her jeans. *How long is this going to take?* She needed to get up, and the sensation made her antsy, but she had to sit here. Wait.

The kids splashed and yelled. The parents drank. Light from the pool reflected in a kind of dance across the white stucco side of the motel building.

Finally the door to number 8 opened, and Ben Landry stepped out. Kenna grunted, dialing the phone connected to her earbuds while she stared at him.

The call connected. "He's out?"

"Yes, Maizie." Kenna pulled the lever and raised the seat so she could see a little better. "He just left. And get this, he's wearing jeans and boots."

"Anything else?" The teen's voice held steady most of the time.

Because the plan was *working, thank you very much.* "Well, he's wearing a shirt if that's what you're asking. A vintage T-shirt by the look of it. I wouldn't be surprised if he has one of those semipermanent tattoos on."

"Can I get one of those? Just for research. I know what I want."

Kenna pressed her lips together.

"It's already in my cart. I got a coupon in my email. Can I put it on your company card? It's a business expense, right, if it's for research?"

Kenna blew out a long breath. "Don't use the card. It can be traced, and it needs to be dormant for a while."

"Right." A shadow cast something dark on Maizie's tone.

"Use the *other* account. Remember?"

"Oh yeah." The tone was gone.

"Pick out something for me, too."

"I have it! It's *so* cute," Maizie said. "It's a dog paw print."

"How is Cabot?"

"Upside down, asleep, paws twitching."

Kenna smiled. "The target crossed the street. Looks like he's heading to the bar that's a block down." She pushed the car door wide and climbed out, pocketing her phone in the back of her jeans and sliding her holstered gun on the back of her belt. Lock pick kit. A tiny can of pepper spray in her front pocket. Car keys.

She strode to room 8 like she was supposed to be here and used the lock pick out of sight. Seconds stretched like minutes, and by the time she got inside, a bead of sweat ran down her back.

She closed the door and pushed out a long breath. "Got it."

"Are you gonna teach me how to do that?" Maizie asked.

"It does come in handy if you ever lose your keys."

"Craig got a second set for the trailer, and he let me hide it wherever I wanted. No one knows where it is."

Kenna frowned. "Craig?"

"Stairns."

She blinked. "Huh."

"Elizabeth calls him Craigey, but I don't think I'll go that far."

Kenna chuckled. "Pretty sure I'm gonna stick with Stairns. Craig is just weird." Her former Special Agent in Charge from back in her FBI days had always been "Stairns" or "boss man."

Now he was a volunteer employee—she didn't like labels —who did research for her. Stairns lived on nine acres in Colorado in the middle of nowhere. His wife, Elizabeth, was a licensed therapist who saw clients online. Both were supposed to be retired, but neither seemed to have slowed down.

These days the airstream that had belonged to Kenna's late father was parked on the side of their expanse of back-yard, occupied by a teenage girl with no parents and no name but the one she'd given herself.

Maizie.

Kenna supposed the girl was her ward—or wanted to be. The goal was to keep Maizie safe until she felt like she could strike out on her own. When she felt safe and in control of her life. Sure, Maizie wanted to do that with Kenna now, like they were partners, but they'd all agreed the girl needed time. And all that was aside from the fact there was a spotlight of atten-tion pointed their direction from Washington, DC.

Kenna had shot the FBI director a couple of months ago and taken down a dangerous and highly connected CEO. One who had kept Maizie prisoner her entire life.

Hence the motel room Kenna currently stood in.

She went to the closet and found a suitcase. "He unpacked."

"Do people...usually?"

"Sometimes. I don't settle, so why would I put my things in the drawers? You just have to take them out when you leave." Kenna paused. "Maybe if I was staying somewhere for a couple of weeks, or longer."

A thump hit the wall of the neighboring room.

She rifled through the drawers and found everything organized. Dress shirts still in clear bags like new clothes ordered online. More vintage T-shirts. She pulled open the next drawer. "Huh."

"What is it?"

"He's got a priest uniform in here." She went to the closet. "Two suits, one black and one gray, and dress white military uniform hanging up. The nametag says MUELLER."

"I told you the name Ben Landry was a fake."

Kenna left the closet undisturbed and looked for any other personal items. "He's got a leather briefcase. Soft sided, like with a flap that lifts up and a buckle." She put one knee on the motel carpet and opened it.

Fingerprint collection would be messy. Any other way besides the powder that got on everything would be finnicky. Maybe DNA? That could take weeks, but she needed to know who this guy really was.

She'd met him as part of the Vegas group Intellectus, a private group who were formed to solve cold cases and other mysteries. Two members were dead, and the other two—an older man and Ben Landry—had disappeared before she found Maizie.

After that, Kenna had exactly one goal. Keep the teen safe.

Only, in order to do it, she had to figure out who Ben Landry was and if he'd had any ties to the CEO, Maizie's captor. Kenna needed to give the girl peace long enough for her to have a shot at healing. That meant making sure every part of this was over. That no one would ever show up because they knew who she was. Maizie would never have to think about any of it again.

She could have a normal life.

Never mind there were missing pages in one of her father's journals that Intellectus had given her. She planned to ask Ben where those were when she finally sat down with him. Whether he was connected to Maizie or not, she would get an answer to that question.

"Anything?"

The question jogged Kenna out of her thoughts. "I need sleep. My mind is drifting."

"I got in the motel surveillance system. Their computer is laughable. I could've hacked it blindfolded. Anyway, if Ben comes back, I'll give you a heads-up."

And with no way to get out other than the front door, even that might be too late. "Thanks."

"You're welcome."

Kenna smiled to herself. "Okay, what do we have—uh... who needs four wallets?"

"He's a thief?"

She started flipping them open. "The photo is the same every time." Kenna slid out her phone and swiped up for the camera. She took a picture of each one, with the name and driver's license in view. "All different states, but he seems to stick west of Nebraska."

"Okay...they're loading." Maizie had access to Kenna's photo drive, so that her images synced automatically, and she didn't have to waste time sending anything. "I'll run these. See if any of them is his real name."

"Copy that." Kenna found a white envelope containing a

gold-embossed invitation. She didn't read it, just took another picture for Maizie.

Another thump hit the adjoining wall. Things were getting interesting in room 7, but she wasn't going to joke about that with Maizie when the girl had been through horrors most people didn't even want to contemplate. Captive her whole life by a man who thought they should die together so they could continue to be married in the afterlife.

At least, that was what he'd said before Kenna stabbed him.

Step one in Maizie's new life.

Step two was to avoid being compelled to testify in a hearing where she would be obligated to tell the truth to the Department of Justice. Usually not necessarily a bad thing, but she didn't want Maizie to have to show and give a statement. She didn't need to be treated like a suspect.

Step three happened to be what she was doing right now during step two, eliminating every loose thread of this threat. Making Maizie safe.

Instead of a thump, she heard a crash next door.

"What does multiple IDs mean?"

Kenna straightened and decided to check the bathroom. It wouldn't be the first time she'd found a dead body in a bathtub but wasn't how she wanted to spend her night. "Last guy I met with this many IDs was a serial killer. Unfortunately Ben fits the profile. He seems to assimilate like a pro, because when I met him in Vegas, he was all slick like this yuppie guy from the Hamptons."

Maizie made a noise.

"You okay?" Even though she knew the teen was *not* okay.

"I don't like that place."

The Hamptons. Kenna simply said, "Copy that." And vowed never to bring up that spot in New York State ever again. "Ben could be anyone. We need his birth name, and then we can track where—and who—he's been since then."

"And where he's going. Apart from generally heading north." Maizie sighed. "These fake IDs are pretty thin. The one I made for you is *much* better."

Kenna smiled.

"You could just wait until he comes back and then ask him where the journal pages are." That wouldn't be the only thing she asked. Maizie continued, "I could hack a federal database and run his picture."

Kenna headed for the door, listening to the noise coming from the neighboring room. The ambient setting on her earbuds gave her plenty for her ears to process even if they altered her spatial awareness a little in a way she had to compensate for. Maizie had insisted on contact, and Kenna needed it to be hands-free.

When she'd ditched her watch and cell phone for burners, she'd gone low-tech. A few weeks ago Maizie upgraded her. The phone wasn't one Kenna had ever used, and given how it acted, sometimes she was pretty sure Maizie had messed with it. But that was what happened when a genius came on board with the team.

Kenna sighed.

"What is it?"

"Nothing." Just that her solitary life wasn't looking so solitary these days. She had more friends than she knew what to do with, colleagues who meddled more than they should, and a dog she missed—who was currently keeping Maizie company. Both of them were recovering so that was fine. "How about we avoid drawing the attention of the feds by hacking a database, yeah?"

"If they find me, then I deserved to be caught."

Kenna rolled her eyes. "It's a risk."

"Maybe if I was an amateur."

"Let's keep the illegal activity to a minimum, yeah?"

Maizie sighed. "Okay, *Mom*." She dragged the word out so that it dripped with sarcasm.

Kenna said, "You've been watching teenage sitcoms again, haven't you?" She wanted to laugh, but they both knew Maizie did that when she had nightmares. Kenna did as well, though with a totally different kind of soothing entertainment.

Maizie didn't like scary stuff, not even cartoons.

Another thump from next door. Then someone cried out, a low tone, but it could've been a scream.

"That doesn't sound like fun."

"I can watch something else," Maizie said. "I just..."

"We'll get to teasing. Later. But that comment wasn't for you." Kenna strode to the door. "You can watch whatever you want as long as it makes you feel better not worse." There were some other qualifiers but not what they had time for right now. "Something is going on next door." She explained about the guy who'd dropped off the woman and seeing her go inside.

"Is that...normal?"

One day Maizie wouldn't have to ask that question, but by then she would understand how many things that should never be...also seemed so commonplace. "It's not usually something I'd get involved in."

A man screamed.

Kenna said, "Is the coast clear?"

"Yes. He hasn't shown back up."

She left Brad's room and moved to number 7. Kenna backed up, braced herself, and kicked beside the door handle. It swung open.

"Wow!" Maizie said. "I'm taking a clipping of that."

Kenna stepped inside. "I've been running with a weighted backpack."

The woman turned in a crouched position, holding a broken wood chair. Blood on her face and hair. Her front. Her legs. The man lay on the carpet, past the point of being able to defend himself.

"Maizie, call 911."

The woman screamed like some kind of possessed thing. Thralled by the rush of beating a man half to death. She dropped the chair and ran at Kenna, who reached back for her gun and brought it up in time to clip the woman on the underside of her chin with the momentum of her swing.

The woman's head snapped back, and she crumpled to the ground.

Someone behind her screamed. "What did you do?!"

Kenna let out a sigh and turned to the guest. Beyond her, police sirens sounded in the night.

So much for staying below the radar.

Chapter Two

"That was when she ran at me, and I clipped her with the butt of my gun." Kenna motioned to her hip since it was close enough to her holster and she didn't want to twist around. She'd put it away as soon as she could and didn't intend to ruffle feathers more by drawing it.

Especially not when a uniformed Reno PD officer stared at her. Gave her a nod of recognition. "Out cold?" he asked, unruffled by the blood everywhere in the room as though he'd been doing this a while. Silver temples. Lines on his face that weren't from laughing. Ring on his finger. Kids probably.

Living a life Kenna might've lived, if things hadn't taken the turn they did where she lost everything.

Left with what she made for herself.

She shivered, just so he'd think she was rattled and tipped her head. "The other guest asked what I was doing, and I asked her to call for an ambulance."

The vehicle had already pulled out of the lot, speeding toward the hospital with lights and sirens. They'd rushed away so fast she figured it wasn't good. But with the guy in the state he was in when she kicked the door down, it had been hard to tell.

"You think that guy is gonna make it?" She didn't want the cop to think she knew too much about this kind of thing. Maizie had made her private investigator license cards for her new ID, but actually using them was a whole lot different than just having a fleshed out fake identity.

All so she didn't pop on the radar of whatever federal employee had been tasked with finding the woman who shot the FBI director and bringing her in so she could explain the whole case to them. She applauded their need to know there weren't any loose ends. That everyone connected to Rushman and involved in his behind-closed-doors business got the justice they deserved for victimizing innocent people.

She was going to leave most of that to Jax, since he was the FBI agent involved. Given he was not dead and not dirty, he should be someone they believed. Kenna planned to keep Maizie far away from it all. Far from being forced to testify, or Kenna from going to jail because she refused to tell them where she was—or who the teen was.

No way whoever was unpacking the case against Michael Rushman didn't notice the same teenage blonde showed up so many places. Photos. Files. Video. Surveillance. Even on the staff list at Rushman's company, with its government contracts and cutting-edge technology. Thanks to Maizie, who'd been unofficially working there since she was a preteen.

If push came to shove, Kenna would do time for contempt. She wasn't above lying, but she also had no intention of putting Maizie in the spotlight.

Kenna knew what that felt like all too well, and no way would she subject Maizie to that fear. Her memories. People who crawled out of the woodwork to see her, for whatever sick reason.

"Hard to say." The cop rocked back to his heels, then forward again. "If he does, it'll be because of your quick thinking, Ms. Shearson."

"I'm just glad I could help." She kept her fingers tucked in the pockets of her pants, hoping he didn't see the scars on her forearms.

She needed to get used to the fake ID name, *Clara Shearson.*

That and the cop seeing her scars would lead to more questions than she wanted to answer—and the possibility he might figure out who she was. She needed to lock it down.

Keeping a tight lid on the risk gave her peace. Sure, it looked a lot like ironclad control, but given it allowed her mind to let go a little of the worry, it certainly felt like peace. Never mind what Ryson had said.

And she was teaching it to Maizie. Showing the girl that she could have peace even after everything she'd been through.

Live your life. Because the past doesn't control you.

"Did you need anything else?"

The cop glanced over to stare at the door to the room where the incident had happened. "We've had a rash of incidents like this lately, johns who were shaken down. Beaten for the cash in their wallets—and their IDs stolen. We figure someone is recycling them for fakes or selling the information online. We'll chat with the woman when she wakes up and get to the bottom of it. Thanks to you."

She didn't know why he told her all that, except maybe she gave off the aura of someone who knew what they were talking about.

Kenna nodded. "No problem."

The suspect she'd clocked was cuffed in the back of the squad car, being babysat by this cop's backup. But not where

Kenna could see her from here. She figured the woman likely had some choice things to say—not that she'd get the chance.

"Did you see anyone else around that might've been with her either before or after?"

Kenna shrugged, just to give herself a second to decide whether to tell him. "I just arrived. Haven't even checked in yet. But I did see her get out of a car a bit ago. It was a dark Mercedes."

"And when you went to check in, that's when you heard the commotion?"

Kenna would have to account for the time between. "I was so tired from driving I shut my car off"—she motioned to the car that didn't belong to her. But then, a dead man didn't need his vehicle back and the tags were good—"I just passed out. Took a little cat nap, you know?"

"Who was driving the Mercedes?" he asked.

"I didn't see his face."

"Okay, thanks for your time."

"I hope this solves it. I'd hate for anyone else to get hurt."

"Me, too." He wandered off.

Kenna figured the case was closed, though there was always a chance this had been a copycat. Or an unrelated incident. Maybe a single occurrence that got out of hand. Then again, given what the man in the car had said—that she'd better not let it end up like last time—it seemed to be a recurring thing.

But this wasn't her case.

Kenna tracked lost and missing people. Victims who had seen the darkness and needed a shot at a second chance. Usually she brought them back to their families, or got them safe, and then let them live their lives. She wouldn't be a reminder of the worst time in their lives, even if they'd survived.

Maizie needed more than that.

But the same underlying idea was still true. She needed a shot at a second chance just like any other victim. Kenna refused to believe the teen had been captive too long that she'd never have normal. It wouldn't be an easy road. Nothing worthwhile ever was. But they were all going to fight.

She'd made that promise to Maizie. When the teen felt like she had no strength, Kenna would help her—and vice versa.

"Heads up."

Kenna turned away toward her car. "Copy that."

She wasn't surprised the line was still open, even if Maizie had been the one to alert the cops first. Anonymous tip. However she did that, Kenna was grateful the night had gone the way it did.

What she didn't need now was for things to go from bad to worse.

Kenna passed a couple of people, stepped off the curb, and headed through the parking lot rows of cars to hers. Sure, she could have given it up after Vegas. After the mobster who gave it to her died. But she liked it, and Kenna had barely any personal possessions.

She'd lived in trailers most of her childhood.

College dorms. Apartments. Even a townhome, during a dark time when she'd been an FBI agent in Houston before Salt Lake City. Not something she liked to talk about. Then RVs, a class C that she was shot in. A camper van that was set on fire—she was still mad about that.

She needed some kind of housing soon. Living in motels was getting old pretty quickly.

"Tell me when you're in."

Kenna shut the car door. "Go ahead."

"Ben is coming back, and he's almost to the corner."

Maizie paused. "At least, I *think* it's him. The video is pretty grainy. You should still get out of there before he sees you and that car."

"Yep." The guy would see her at some point, but it would be when she chose it. At least as much as she was able to control the situation.

She needed the missing journal pages if she was going to figure out what Santino had said about her father investigating her mother's murder. Kenna didn't remember the woman and didn't know really anything about her.

The whole thing made about as much sense as Joe Don Hunter, a friend of her father's and sheriff of a small town in Northern California, having an autopsy in his safe. He was dead, so she couldn't ask him what that had been about.

Same as Santino.

If there were leads to find, everyone who could tell her anything was dead.

So it was hardly a case.

Especially when there were things to do that had leads—and a teen to help.

She pulled onto the street and headed north to find a rest stop where she could get some sleep, then take a shower in the morning.

"Did you leave the tracker in his bag?"

"Yes."

"Good. We need to find out what this invitation is about."

"What are you..." Kenna remembered the envelope in Ben's bag. "The other photo?" She gripped the wheel. "What is it?"

"Here we go. 'Loading, please wait,'" Maizie quoted. Her voice trailed off, then she continued, "'You are hereby invited.'"

"To what?"

"Doesn't say. It's literally like, 'The Gathering Place. Midnight.'" Maizie hummed the way she did when she was figuring something out. "There's no phone number, no idea who these people are that produced this, though maybe I can find a printer. If you had the original, it'd be easier. Maybe there's something on the back."

Kenna knew it wasn't recrimination. Maizie was right, it would be easier to figure it out if they had the card. But that would tip their hand to Ben that he was being watched. That someone had broken into his motel room. "There was nothing on the envelope."

"And the invitation isn't even addressed to Ben specifically. It's just generic, so we can't use it to figure out who he is. Or was. Or should be."

As far as Kenna could tell, Ben Landry wanted to be everyone—or no one. To fly under the radar. But there was a reason he'd joined a mystery-solving group before she even arrived in Vegas. Then when things heated up, he split. To do what?

She needed to know what he was up to. They'd located him after he used a credit card in the name Ben Landry, and now Kenna had been following him for three days.

"So we have a time, but no date and no idea what it is." Kenna frowned. "Run the IDs I found, and I'll take a look at the photo of the invitation when I stop."

"You don't know that it's going to be something scary."

"Irrelevant." Because Kenna figured it probably was exactly the worst thing she could think of. Why else be cryptic about what he was being invited to? Why use a generic term for the location, and no date? She would have to follow Ben more, see where he went at midnight every night for the foreseeable future.

Until she figured out what it was.

Maizie stayed quiet for a second. "I know you're trying to protect me."

"Yes, I am." Kenna hadn't bothered to hide that from the teen. "Obviously, I am." She literally had no other objective right now. "So until we know what this is, you'll stick to running IDs. Got it?" The silence on the other end of the phone line gave her an answer. "This is how it's going to be."

Maizie sighed.

"I'll figure out what 'The Gathering Place' means, and which day at midnight it's talking about, and whether it will help us keep you safe."

Kenna would out her presence here to Ben before she let Maizie even get near something that could remind her of what Kenna had saved her from.

Some might consider it a kind of divine calling. Kenna wasn't sure, but she did know there was more to this world than what she could see or touch or hear. Her father had believed in God in his own way but rarely stepped foot in a church.

She talked to God. Mostly they had a détente she wasn't sure how to break. She just knew there had to be more to all of this than what she understood right now.

"Because it could be part of Rushman's operation," Maizie said, her voice subdued.

Kenna swallowed. "We don't know that. He had that whole online thing, and it was all digital. This is paper."

"Maybe it's a wedding."

"Maizie—"

"I know," the teen said, "I'll stick to running IDs."

"Please let *me* worry about it."

"Because you think I can't handle the pressure?"

"I don't want you to *have* to. That's the whole point." Kenna pulled into the parking lot of a grocery store with the lights on. Open twenty-four hours. If she had to wait around to see if Ben went somewhere at midnight, she was going to need caffeine.

Maizie said, "You can't fix or change what happened."

"You know that out of literally everyone, I'm the one person who knows that without a doubt." Kenna stared at the dark parking lot. "You get some distance from it, and then one day...it's like it walks back into the room and hits you all over again."

Maizie said nothing.

"There's nothing you can do about it. The past will always be there." Kenna's stomach clenched. "The day that happens—because it will—I want you to be on a firmer footing than you are right now. So you can take the hit, and you don't fall."

Chapter Three

Kenna stepped out onto the back porch. Every time she did, it hit her. With a glass of lemonade in one hand, she took a moment to sip just so she could stare at it. Not only did they have her staying here for Stairns' Fourth of July celebration, she had shorts on. Bare feet. They'd told her to disarm, but she'd kept a couple of small things out of sight.

Her father's airstream, up on blocks, looked like it had been on the right side of Stairns' yard for years.

Maizie and Elizabeth, Stairns' wife, had planted flowers all over. The girl had an awning out over the door that provided shade on this side of the trailer.

She sat on a blanket at the bottom of the steps with Valentina Ryson, watching baby Luci toddle on those chubby legs and then topple onto the grass.

Maizie scooped her up and blew raspberries on the baby's bare belly, making her laugh before she set her back down. Maizie didn't smile, but the look on her face was the closest thing Kenna had seen to enjoyment since she'd met the girl.

Ryson was over at the grill, flipping burgers.

Elizabeth had a client call, so she was in the house.

Stairns came out onto the porch with a sweating beer bottle, followed by Kenna's dog with her limp. "Salad is all mixed. We're about ready to eat."

Kenna bobbed her head. "Good." Cabot, her mutt, sat beside her leg and sighed down to lay her head on Kenna's foot.

"Have you been inside the trailer yet?" he asked.

"I'm sure it looks nice. Elizabeth helped her get set up."

"Sure," Stairns said. "Elizabeth didn't really understand all the computer stuff, wires, and monitors, but she helped pick out the rest so Maizie has somewhere to be comfortable. We hope. But that wasn't what I was talking about."

Kenna sipped her drink. "Then what?"

"That was your father's trailer. Your trailer." He shifted beside her. "You lived in it for years."

"Doesn't mean I need to go inside now and see how small it is compared to what I remember. Or how much it changed."

"It's your history."

"And now it gets to be Maizie's second chance. Her fresh start. Dad would agree that's a good idea." Why wouldn't he? Her dad had been all about solving mysteries. She geared more toward saving lives in the process of solving a mystery. Recovering victims and returning people to their families. "Besides, she needs to know that's her space. I'm not going to go trapsing around in there unless she invites me inside."

Her phone buzzed in her pocket.

She dug it out and looked, but it was only a text with a coupon.

"He on his way?" Stairns asked.

Kenna stowed the phone. "Not yet."

He clapped her on the shoulder. "He'll be here."

Ryson wandered from the grill with a plate of burgers. "Are we talking about Jax?"

She shot him a look.

"What? I'm married. I need gossip."

Stairns snorted. "I'll go tell them lunch is ready."

Kenna watched him stop ten feet from the blanket, getting a read on Maizie and how she was with the older man. She held some tension in her shoulders. Maizie might never lose that wariness, and that was fine. There were plenty of people in the world who should never be trusted. The teen would figure out Stairns was the kind she could relax around. His daughters had been here over the weekend, and the simple way they were with their father, their husbands, and their children was proof enough.

Family life wasn't something Kenna had ever had much experience with. It had mostly just been her and her father, but she could see why people liked it.

She slid out her phone again and looked at the screen.

"He said he'd call when his plane landed, didn't he?"

Kenna started. Cabot lifted her head.

Ryson clapped her on the shoulder. "Delays?"

"No more than usual."

"He'll be here."

"I know." She spun to Ryson and glared.

"So then let's talk about something else." He shifted to let Stairns and Maizie pass, then kissed his wife and his baby. "We'll be there in a second." Then to Kenna he said, "Walk with me."

Kenna followed him down the porch steps onto the grass. Cabot stayed on the porch, watching.

"I just wanted to say this before we get into eating and hanging out."

"You mean before Jax gets here." She folded her arms.

Was this about her burgeoning relationship with the FBI agent?

"I just..." Ryson glanced at the expanse of Colorado sky above them for a second. "You're doing a great job with Maizie, letting her feel safe. Keeping things tight so nothing bothers her."

"Something will, eventually. It's inevitable."

"You're teaching her good boundaries. And how to keep the memories at bay so they don't incapacitate her."

Also something that would likely happen at some point. No plan was foolproof.

"But here's the thing. And don't take this the wrong way."

Kenna frowned.

"Control isn't the same as peace," Ryson said. "And healthy boundaries are great, but don't guarantee you peace, either."

"You think I don't have peace?"

The others came out onto the porch and sat around with their plates.

Ryson scratched at his chin. "Remember last year, when you told me to go to church?"

"I don't know if that's *exactly* what I said."

"'Talk to someone.' Well, Valentina and I found a church. I got baptized a few weeks ago, and I've been going to classes. Learning what the Bible says."

"And so now you think I'm doing things wrong?"

"I know you're searching for something. Trying to find peace."

Kenna shrugged. "I'm doing fine."

"I know you think that. Or you want to believe that." Ryson frowned. "Maybe you just have to realize you're not fine. But I'd hate to see what kind of situation you have to get yourself into in order to reach that place."

"I'm *fine.*"

Ryson shot her a look. "You do a great job. There's no one else in the world without a degree and a whole lot of trauma counseling training who could do half the job with Maizie you're doing. You've been there. You've walked it, you know what it's like to be a captive."

"Not the half of what she went through."

"But you get it."

"Elizabeth is the one counseling her," Kenna pointed out.

"And you're the one making sure she has space to heal. A place to do it. People she can trust. Then you leave and work your cases, live your life. All of it orderly and in the right place. No mess. No intrusion. No emotions you don't want to feel. Just iron clad control of everything."

"There's nothing wrong with knowing what I want."

"But is getting it giving you peace?" Ryson stared at her. "Do you actually rest?"

She wasn't about to tell him the best sleep she'd had in the past few years was the single night in a motel room in Vegas where Jax slept on the second bed. Knowing someone else was there to watch her back—someone she trusted—allowed her to let her guard down in a way she didn't usually. Ever.

"If you're looking for peace, you need to know it's a fruit of the Spirit."

Kenna shook her head. "And what does that mean?"

"Before I give you the answer, mull it over. Think about it, and I'm here if you need to ask me anything. I want to help."

"I don't need—" She pressed her lips together, not wanting to get defensive.

"If you don't get your spiritual life in order, you can't have real peace. And you can't pass it on to Maizie." Ryson laid a hand on her shoulder. "When I figured that out, accepting what God had done. For *me*. Then I understood what peace with God, and the peace *of* God was."

"I've read the Bible. I know what it says." She listened to sermons sometimes, along with worship music. Mostly on the radio when she was driving. "I don't think I need to make some kind of pledge or whatever."

"Good, because it's not a fan club. It's a family."

"I already have a family." Didn't he know that's what this was for her? The people she'd invited into her life, the ones she wanted to stick around. Every piece of it was a risk she would lose one of them the way she seemed to lose everyone, but she was taking a chance, wasn't she? He had to appreciate the risk she took every time she let someone in.

He yanked her over, and she slammed into him. He hugged her against his side. "Yes, you do."

"And they're as annoying as families are supposed to be."

Ryson chuckled. "Just think about what I said, okay? Do some soul-searching between cases. Tell me if you're satisfied with where you're at."

"Well, I *was*." Now that he'd said something?

Ugh. Families were so annoying.

Chapter Four

"Which house?" Kenna eased off the gas. "I don't see Ben's car in any of the driveways, or at the curb."

"The GPS location where he stopped is a little farther down. Maybe four houses," Maizie said through the phone line. "Keep going."

"Assuming he's not looking out his window right when I pass by in this completely obvious car."

"So ditch it and get another one."

"No. I like it."

The teen chuckled. "Are you gonna let me borrow it after Stairns teaches me how to drive?"

"Maybe." Kenna rolled slowly down the residential street in Helson, Washington—close to the US–Canada border— where Ben had gone when he left the motel that morning.

"That house." Maizie paused. "To your right."

"Okay." Kenna scanned the windows—blinds closed. "There's a detached garage on the far side. Maybe he parked in there."

She needed to find a motel in town she could stay at while they figured out why Ben was here, what the invitation had been for, and *who* he was. Once she'd cleared him from being connected to Rushman, she would put this place in her rearview.

Find another case.

"There's another house to check out," Maizie said.

Kenna didn't need to stay where Ben could come out and spot her. She wanted to control the moment he realized she'd been following him for a week now. "What house is it? Did you find the Gathering Place?"

Maizie rattled off an address.

According to Kenna's maps app, it was right beside a lake. Across the other side of town. "Are you going to tell me what this place is?" she asked.

"Are you going to trust me?" the teen countered.

Ryson's words about control rang through Kenna's mind, so she kept her mouth shut all the way to the place. "So it's a house." She pulled the car onto the driveway.

"It's a short-term rental. And it's where Clara Shearson is staying."

"I can find a motel."

"You can also go inside this house. With your things."

Kenna did the mouth-shut thing again, and typed the code Maizie gave her into the lockbox on the door. "How big is this place anyway?" She twisted the handle and listened for a second before she entered the house. "And how much is it costing me?"

"Big enough you won't be staring at the same four walls for the next however long."

Kenna glanced back at her car at the curb, then dumped her duffels in the hallway. "Speaking of which, how long did you book this for?"

"Two weeks."

Kenna frowned. "Is this a vacation?"

"Why not? *I'm* on one. Why shouldn't you be?"

She strode down the hall. The place smelled like lemon-scented cleaner. How long had it been since she was in a house—let alone when she'd actually stayed in one? "This isn't a vacation for you, Maze. Quit waiting for the other shoe to drop."

Kenna set her phone on the counter and listened to the silence.

The house, and the phone line.

She spotted the view between vertical blinds over the patio door. She swept the whole thing back. "Wow."

"What?"

She frowned at the subdued tone of Maizie's voice. "The view out the back. It backs up to a lake."

"I thought you might like it."

"I do. But motels are fine."

"I'm living in your house."

"The airstream isn't really my house," Kenna said. "It's where I grew up, mostly. It's not where I need to be now. It's for you to make into a place you can feel safe."

"I know."

Kenna slid the patio door open so fresh mountain air could fill the house.

A breeze ruffled the trees on the back lawn, one on either side. Between them the still water of the lake. On the other side, a stretch of mountain lifted higher than she could see. Someone rode a jet ski or motored a boat around. She could hear the hum of an engine but couldn't see who it belonged to.

"It's beautiful, Maizie."

"I thought you might like it better than a boring motel and gas station food."

Kenna chuckled. "I guess I should figure out how to cook. It's been a while."

"Do you want groceries delivered? I can do that."

"I'll hit the store." She stretched her arms above her head, then had to push in one earbud threatening to pop out. "Where's Ben?"

"Still static at the house where he parked. But that only means his car and his stuff are there. He could've left on foot like he did last night."

After the motel incident, Ben hadn't come out of his room all night. Kenna had spent that time in her front seat, across the street, keeping watch. Early this morning he'd hit the road, and she followed him all the way to the town of Helson, Washington.

"Maybe whatever's happening is going down at midnight tonight."

Kenna continued wandering through the house, looking at the neat rooms. A little dated, but freshly painted and clean. The whole place had been decorated like a mountain cabin. Bears on the comforter. A deer's head on the wall in the living room. Wood burning stove. Old oven.

"Any idea if there's somewhere in Helson that could be the Gathering Place?" Kenna got her stuff and dumped it in the bedroom, not really sure where to put things. Or if she should sit on the living room couch or on the bed like she usually did in a motel.

"Nothing on Maps, but I'm still looking." Maizie paused. "The town has a pretty sordid history. You might need to ask Stairns because I need to get into FBI files, and he told me I shouldn't do that without asking."

Kenna wanted to chuckle. "Tell me about the sordid history?"

"Thirty years ago, a few weeks before Waco, the FBI

executed a search warrant on a group called Children of the Morning, here in Helson. Their compound is about five miles to the north, and it's been abandoned since."

"I've never heard of it."

"The whole thing was pretty brutal, with tear gas and a lot of gunfire. The feds busted in and there were members who fought back—a select few lower-level males. Several members of the group were found dead from poison, but they were all adults and mostly women. The kids were found shut up and trapped, and the FBI managed to get them out. They were in a cistern filling with water, but the agents broke it open and freed the kids. They even managed to resuscitate a few of them."

Kenna stared at the lake through the screen door. "How have I not heard about this?"

"According to this website, Waco and what happened there overshadowed everything. Since that siege went on for weeks." Maizie paused. "The one in Helson was considered a success. Plus, it was done in one day, late the year before. Between Christmas and New Year. There were a couple of people arrested, and a few of them killed themselves before the warrant could be executed. The gunmen were either arrested or killed, and the FBI saved those kids. Then Waco happened, and there was such an outcry no one wanted to know about survivors or anything good the Bureau did."

"Can you send me all the files?"

"I'll have Stairns get them for you. I'm just reading information off the internet."

"Thanks." Kenna let out a breath.

"I'll call if Ben moves."

"I'm gonna go for a run."

"Copy that." The call ended.

Kenna pulled out the earbuds and put them back in the case so they could charge, and so her ears could take a break. She could listen to music, or an audiobook, while she ran, but the worst night of her life started with a run so she needed her wits about her. Exchanging the fear for strength, or at least confidence and self-assurance, was a new part of her life.

Small ways to take back the control.

Not the same as peace.

Ryson's words had been rolling around in her head for a month now. She'd done some internet searches about the fruit of the Spirit. Christians seemed pretty divided on that, so she'd read Galatians where it talked about it.

Far as she could tell, there were ways of doing things that she'd have to give up. An exchange that seemed to be what God wanted for her, but she'd never felt that way about faith. She'd never done more than amassed knowledge about the Creator in an informational way so she could analyze why some people believed so fervently while others were adamant none of it was true—and every shade between.

Kenna felt like she needed to have some kind of "experience" or decide to trust God. Right now she had work to do. It could come in handy with this case, and it was certainly tempting to ask God to take care of Maizie. But Kenna also needed to do some things herself. To make sure she could trust it had been done.

That the girl was safe.

She'd do what she could, and let God take care of the rest. Did it work like that?

Kenna slipped her feet into beat-up tennis shoes and skipped the weighted backpack. Phone in the side pocket of her leggings that held it tight to the outside of her thigh. Knife. Pepper spray.

Even in cooler mountain weather, it was hard to disguise a gun in a running outfit that didn't have any give to it. She left her pistol behind in a lockbox and used a key from the kitchen hook to lock the patio door once she was outside.

Kenna started with a walk along the sandy edge of the lake. Letting her muscles warm up while she got the lay of the land. Maybe the road went around the lake, but the beach didn't seem to have a corresponding path.

Far down the other end of the oval, about half a mile away, someone walked a black dog off-leash. The person looked like a lady, wearing jeans and a T-shirt. Hair pulled back in a ponytail the way Kenna had done with hers.

She picked up her pace and started to run.

Nothing connected Rushman to Ben Landry. Yet.

Just as nothing connected the invitation to the Children of the Morning. Yet—if it ever would, in either case. Ben Landry might be one of those children the FBI had rescued. He definitely fit the profile of a victim of trauma, displaced from everything safe. All the support he'd had ripped away in a mass of fear.

Kenna let the rhythm of her footfalls keep pace with her breaths. Her muscles started to settle into the *thump-thump*, and she managed to speed up a little, since she didn't have her weighted backpack on. Given the state of her forearms she'd been left with, it made sense to have as much leg strength as possible.

She'd been working on her arm strength as well. But most likely, she'd never be able to hold a weapon up and aimed for more than a few minutes.

She hit the end of the beach, where the lake angled around to the left. In front of her was a grassy area. Kids park. Benches and shelters with tables. Beyond the recreation area was a parking lot. On the other side of the lake were tents and campers.

She headed away from the lake onto the asphalt and went away from the house for a mile or so, then turned and headed back. The asphalt street had no lines, barely wide enough for a car on both sides. Huge trees towered over her.

Not a bad place to live.

Certainly better than the concrete jungle, and another dingy motel room. Not that scores of people hadn't occupied the vacation rental over the years, but it just seemed homier—a place to make tea and sit watching the lake.

A guy with a jacket on, and a gray beard, walked two corgis off leash. As she passed, he called them back to him and both bounded over.

Kenna skirted them and spotted a For Sale sign a ways up on the far side. She passed it and spun around... and nearly tripped over her feet. She had to get her mind to comprehend what she was looking at in order to stop.

Kenna bent forward, breathing hard, and stared at the sign. The Realtor's picture, her name, blond hair teased out like Dolly Parton—the bounty hunter Kenna had met months ago in Hatchet, New Mexico, with her tiny dog Tilly, living in an RV.

Now she was here? And her name according to the sign? Bianca Wynn.

Kenna blinked. *What on...*

Her phone rang.

She figured it was Maizie asking why she'd stopped and if everything was okay. Instead, the name STAIRNS lit up on the screen.

"Hey. Tell Maizie I need a deep dive on Dixie Cabrera. With the name Bianca Wynn." She told him about the sign.

"Sure, but you and I need to talk as well."

Kenna started walking toward the house. "What is it?" Had something happened to Maizie? "She okay?"

"She's working. It's the file for Helson, Washington."

She waited.

"One of the agents..." Stairns paused. "There's not really any easy way to say this, but...your father is listed. FBI Special Agent Maxwell Banbury."

Kenna swallowed.

"You'd have been about three at the time your father participated in serving the warrant on the Children of the Morning."

"He was here."

"He's the one who saved those kids."

"Of course he was." Did he think her father would've done anything else? He'd been an agent for years before her mother gave birth to her—and was killed shortly after. Max Banbury had quit the Bureau and gone into private investigative work all over, even internationally. He'd raised her on the road and never said one thing to her about her mother's death being anything to look into. No mystery.

Nothing.

"You have history with that town, Kenna."

"Doesn't sound like it to me." She gripped the phone. "Sounds like my dad did. And he probably didn't even stay more than a couple of days. It's not like he left something for me to find. Or some*one*."

"It has to be connected to this case."

"All I'm doing here is figuring out how Ben Landry connects to anything involving Rushman, and if he knows about Maizie. That's all."

"If you say so." Stairns hung up.

Kenna stowed the phone, turned around, and jogged back the way she'd come. She caught up to the corgi guy and rounded the end house to the lakeside. She pounded sand to the house and let herself in, breathing hard.

This whole thing was just Ben—his real ID and an invitation she barely cared about.

There *was* no case.

Chapter Five

"You're at the compound?"

Kenna put the car in park, her phone on speaker in the cupholder. She stared at the chain link fence in front of her, a gate padlocked with a chain securing the entrance. She'd have to walk from here.

"Why are you at the compound?" Maizie pressed.

Kenna glanced at the clock. "I've still got a couple of hours until midnight. Ben hasn't moved, right?"

"Not as far as I can see, but still with the GPS signals versus him walking out the door and going somewhere on foot. His bag and his car wouldn't move."

She dug her earbuds out and stuck them in. "Can you hear me?"

"I think it's *you* not hearing *me*. What's going on?"

"Nothing," Kenna said. "I'm good."

Kenna pushed out of the car and left it parked at the gate. The compound was situated in the hills above town. No one around, just darkness and the swish of trees in the summer night breeze.

Who would know if she peeked around and got a look at a place her dad walked?

"So you're taking the case?" Maizie asked.

"What case?" Kenna went to the trunk. "The invitation?"

"I mean, there's probably a case somewhere in this whole situation even if no one is missing and the local Helson newspaper website says nothing about strange deaths or murders. Do you usually have to dig this hard for something to happen?"

Kenna dug out a flashlight. She pocketed her keys and checked the gun she'd slid onto the back of her belt, at the small of her back. Boots. Knives. She needed to look into something palm sized, or a small revolver she could put in an ankle holster. She had night vision goggles, but the flashlight would do just fine. "I'm just gonna walk around. And no, I don't usually have to dig so hard for something to happen. Or an open case."

"The website hasn't had any activity, but maybe it's unsurprising that no one has filled out the contact form when it's been all over the news that you killed the FBI director."

"So I'm persona non grata now?" Better than talking about what she was doing at the compound—and after she'd told Stairns it meant nothing.

"I don't know what that means."

Kenna clicked on the flashlight and headed for the gate. One side was wedged forward at the bottom, the padlock chain pulled tight, open enough someone could squeeze through—which was what she did. "I'd have thought you'd be going to sleep, given you're in Mountain Time."

"I want to wait up and see if tonight is the midnight on the invitation."

Kenna figured that statement wasn't unlike the answer

she'd given Stairns. Denial. Evasion. A whole lot of pretending nothing was going on. Were these the healthy habits she was teaching Maizie to deal with her past trauma?

She winced, heading up an asphalt drive covered in potholes. The car never would've made it up here without cracking an axle.

"So you'll share your fitness tracker's sleep data with me?" Kenna said.

"I turned it off."

"Yeah, I didn't want to know either." But it had been Elizabeth's idea for Maizie to log her sleep, her emotions, her thought patterns, her eating. Exercise. All of it. Kenna had done something similar when she walked out of the hospital. Getting back into a routine had helped her find an equilibrium within all that grief. "But I sleep better than I used to."

"Cabot heard your voice."

Kenna smiled. "Hi, doggy!" She reached the front door, which might've been locked at one point but didn't seem to be now. Though the handle turned, the door was wedged shut by something inside. She needed another entrance.

"She's wagging her tail."

Kenna traipsed around the outside of the building. "Do we actually have any indication Ben Landry was part of the Children of the Morning?"

Maizie let out a long breath. "He's the right age to be one of the children found by the feds—including your father."

"Stairns told you?"

"It's good, right? He was good?"

Kenna realized how it might seem, so she said, "Yes, he was a good man. No one's parents are perfect, and in a lot of things he did the best he could. Or he did what he thought he needed to. But when you're a kid you see things through those child eyes. You don't always understand what was going on."

She'd certainly realized that in Vegas. Almost nothing had been what she'd thought—and Maizie was the one who had suffered.

"I'm tracking what the FBI and then Child Protective Services did with the children. Most were adopted out. I'm tracing names, trying to find out what happened to them."

"Good. How many boys, how many girls?"

"Seven girls. Six boys. The youngest was a baby, and one of the girls held on to him. The oldest boy was fifteen."

"Okay." Kenna couldn't imagine what it had been like to be trapped. "Where did the FBI find them?"

"Back of the property," Maizie said. "There's the main building, which you're walking around now. Behind it is a giant grain silo. And a shop, according to the plans."

"Probably where they kept equipment."

"Okay, there are two other buildings, and then a water tower. They had the kids in a basement under the grain barn. It's connected to the main building by tunnels—none of which were on the plans, so the FBI ended up getting surprised by that."

"It's shocking they didn't lose more people."

"One agent was winged, but no one was killed."

"Probably because the bulk of the group were dead or shut up when they raided. The few that fought back were dispatched quickly. They probably only wanted to buy time for the kids to die, and they were going to die in a fiery gun battle."

"Why would they do that?" Maizie asked.

Kenna stared at the land behind the main building, darkness beyond the beam of her flashlight. The rustle of trees a whoosh against the ambient speakers of her earbuds. Looming shadows of buildings and the water tower.

She needed to answer Maizie's question. "Strength of

belief. In this case, in the wrong thing. They were willing to die for what they believed in."

"That's supposed to be a good thing."

"People twist everything. Humans take all the good there is and warp it into something that can be misused or can hurt others."

"So we're supposed to leave each other alone?"

Kenna sighed. "Some people think you just find others who believe what you believe, and you band together. I keep my world tight, so I don't have to deal with the crazies. Except when it's about a case."

She hardly knew how to explain what was wrong with the entirety of humanity, the history of religion and how it had affected the world, and all the major conflicts in a few minutes.

She figured she'd keep it to this specific situation, since that seemed to work for her. Even if Ryson didn't think the control she exercised over her life just to stay sane was enough to give her peace.

Wasn't it working—at least to an extent?

Maizie continued, "In the case of the Children of the Morning, it wasn't about their religious beliefs, or their right to live the way they wanted to. It was about them not having the right to break the law. Hurt people."

She knew it was a sticky situation. The man who'd held Maizie for years had the right to hold true to what he believed—but not when that meant victimizing a young girl for years. If the leader of the Children of the Morning was anything like David Koresh, she didn't want Maizie looking into it.

Kenna wandered across the dark grass to the water tower. "You have enough to do running Ben's IDs and looking into the kids. Don't worry about what they went through. A lot of them probably don't even remember. I can read my dad's case notes."

"Is that why you're out there? Because you get to be somewhere he was?"

She hadn't chosen to find this place. "I was led here. I'll look into it." Ryson probably thought God was the one who'd brought her to this place rather than it being about chasing leads in a non-case.

She'd rather worry about what she could see right in front of her, but as much as she wanted to ignore her dad's involvement, she would walk away wondering what she might've found.

Kenna heard voices behind her. She clicked off her flashlight and turned.

A yellow beam flashed across a frosted glass window inside the building.

"Gotta go, Maze." She hung up, but left the earbuds in and drew her weapon just in case.

Kenna made her way to the back door and tucked the flashlight under one arm so she could turn the handle. Unlocked. Whatever had been wedged behind the front door wasn't the case back here.

The door led to a back hall, dirt and leaves on the linoleum.

She clicked the door shut, then held the flashlight under her gun hand. Just in case. At a certain point she'd have to ignore the screaming pain in her forearms. But until then, she could search and know she'd be able to protect herself.

Whoever was here.

She stopped at the T-junction in the halls. Glanced right. Light flashed in one of the side rooms. The whole place smelled like an animal had come in from the cold and died somewhere, maybe in the walls—hopefully.

The idea of being trapped somewhere in here didn't sit right. Probably no sane person would walk around in a place like this, and she had a perfectly legitimate fear.

"Just grab something and let's *go*," a girl said.

"It has to be a pamphlet." The second person was a guy, maybe late teens. High schoolers in the abandoned compound. Summer evening. They could be planning to get up to all kinds of things, but it sounded like the girl couldn't wait to leave.

Kenna walked to the door to the room they were in. Looked like a classroom—where the Children of Morning schooled the young ones?

Yep, two teenagers.

The girl had on a tiny pair of shorts and a shirt that had been cut off just above her belly button. Long blond hair, perfectly styled. She cocked her hip. "Can we just *go* already?"

The guy had dark hair, hanging down over his ears. He swept it back with one hand and looked through the shelves. "They won't believe us if it doesn't have the creed. We won't get paid. You wanna go to that concert, right?"

The girl didn't seem super impressed by the prospect of being here much longer, even for a date night.

"She's right," Kenna said.

They both spun to her and gasped.

"It's time for you both to leave."

The boy sized her up. "Who are you?"

"The person telling you to leave."

"You're one of them, aren't you?" the girl wailed. "You're gonna murder us on the lawn and string us up as a warning."

"I think you've been watching too many horror movies." Kenna lowered the gun but not the flashlight. "I'm not going to kill you, but you shouldn't be here." The guy started to argue, so she said, "Bet or no bet, you're not getting paid tonight. Go home."

He strode toward her.

Kenna had no intention of backing down.

"I don't see a badge." He shoved her shoulder back with a jab of his fingers and strode out into the hall. "I'm gonna check the barn."

The girl just stood there.

"Come on. Let's go outside." Kenna didn't know what else to say. She needed to stop the guy from getting into trouble or getting hurt. "Should've brought my stun gun from the car."

"That was your car?" The girl eased past her, eyeing Kenna like she might confirm the girl's suspicions and get out a machete. "The black one?"

"Yes." Kenna led them down the long hall to a side door different from the one she'd used to get in here. "What's your name?"

"Annabelle."

"You live around here, Annabelle?" Kenna pushed the door open and saw the boy's flashlight disappear into a door across the grass. He'd gone inside the barn.

"Yeah, we moved here a couple of years ago from Seattle. I miss the city." She brushed hair back from her face and ran her fingers through the front, smoothing it back into perfect place. "Small towns suck."

Kenna smiled. "What is he looking for?"

"A souvenir." Annabelle sighed. "It's the deal. Find one and bring it back. You get all the money in the pot."

"Have you guys been together long?"

"Just this year." She shrugged. "Jordan is the football captain, I'm a cheerleader."

"So why this place?"

"You don't know about the compound?" Annabelle turned to her, wrapping her arms around her bare waist to ward off the night breeze. Kenna spotted what looked like a doodle in pen on the back of her hand, just below her thumb. A tiny flower with four petals. "Everyone in town thinks it's haunted by the ghosts of all the people who died here."

"I know a little about the Children of the Morning."

"People in town are crazy. They won't even say the name." Annabelle shook her head. "Like it's like...cursed or whatever. They think the ghosts snatch people who go missing and they're never seen again. They say if you come out here at four in the morning when it's misty, you can see a girl walking through the trees in a nightgown. I don't know if I believe that part. But my neighbor—his cousin went missing. His mom prays for his cousin every night. She thinks he was some kind of child sacrifice."

"So they're never seen again, and they're killed? By the ghosts?"

"That's what people believe." Annabelle shrugged. "They all grew up here. I'm just an outsider, so what do I know about how things are. At least, that's what they all tell me." She shook her head. "I don't drink the tap water. Or open my mouth when I shower. I brush my teeth with bottled water. Cause whatever they're drinking? I don't want it."

"Sounds like a smart choice." Kenna started forward. "Let's go check on Jordan, okay? Just in case."

Annabelle shuddered. "If you say so."

Kenna believed there was a spiritual world—because if she didn't, then she wouldn't believe God existed. But she refused to believe ghosts performed child sacrifices. There was enough evil in people that the world didn't need vengeful spirits for that.

She pulled the door open to the dark barn, shining her light inside just as a cracking sound ripped through the structure and Jordan screamed.

The sound disappeared down, followed by a crash.

Chapter Six

"No." Kenna grabbed Annabelle and held her back from going inside the barn, or whatever this structure was. "It's not safe."

The girl wailed. "He fell! He's probably dead! We have to help him!"

Kenna didn't point out that if he was dead, he wouldn't need help. Then again, she could've also explained the risk inherent in sneaking into an abandoned compound after dark to get a souvenir. "Helping him means you don't get hurt and we end up with two injured victims. Got it?"

Annabelle blew out a breath.

"Good." Kenna pulled out her earbuds and slid them in her pocket. "Okay, you've got a phone?"

The girl nodded again.

"You're going to call 911 and tell them what happened, and where we are. We need an ambulance or Life Flight to get Jordan out. And help, maybe even equipment, to get him out of where he fell in."

"He's not saying anything. Shouldn't we be able to hear him?"

Kenna couldn't worry about the unknown. Right now she needed to get in there and find out what the situation was—then she would know. Facts led to a plan. Plans saved lives. "You're going to go to the gate and meet the emergency services people when they get here. You're going to show them where Jordan is, so they don't waste any time trying to find us. Got it?"

Annabelle jerked her chin.

"Get on the phone. Now."

The girl pulled out her cell, and Kenna listened while she stepped into the barn. Her flashlight beam lit on an old broken-down tractor, more rust than metal. Other equipment and tools. Crates and pallets. Sacks of grain spilled open. So there were probably mice in here. Birds in the rafters. Spider webs.

Kenna shivered. She kept going, forcing her feet to move because she wasn't trapped. Didn't need to stay where she was, because it wasn't her in danger—it was a teen boy. "Jordan!" She called his name as loud as she could. "Can you hear me, Jordan?"

In the center of the wooden floor, a number of two-by-four planks had splintered, leaving a hole in the middle.

Kenna pulled in a long breath. Down there would be dark —and all too reminiscent of her own nightmare.

You're not the one in danger here.

There was risk, sure, but she could hear Annabelle behind her talking to the dispatcher.

The floor creaked.

Kenna stopped. "Jordan!"

Nothing.

She took another step. There weren't many more she could take before she hit a broken one and risked another collapse of the floor—which would send her plummeting below.

Kenna got down on her hands and knees to displace her weight. She got two or three feet farther along, toward the hole.

"Hey, lady!"

She twisted around. "It's Kenna."

"Okay." Annabelle was a shadow in the doorway. "They said it'll be half an hour. The helicopter isn't available. It's faster to send the people in town that volunteer, but they've got to drive up here."

"Thirty minutes. Okay." Kenna made a decision. "Go check the main building for supplies. We need a first aid kit, preferably. If all you can find is towels, or sheets, that works. Can you do that for me?"

"Okay." Annabelle sounded hesitant.

"You can stay here with me, but if it's gonna be thirty minutes before they arrive, we might need to help Jordan."

"Okay, I'll go look."

"Be careful," Kenna said. "Stick to the ground floor and above, okay? No basements."

"Okay." The girl disappeared from the open doorway.

Kenna turned back to the hole and crawled forward. She stretched out on her stomach and looked over the edge, pointing her flashlight down. He wasn't too far. Probably a cellar below the barn.

Jordan lay on a pile of splintered two-by-fours. Blood on his side where his T-shirt had ridden up when he fell. Eyes closed.

Scanning his head, she couldn't see a head injury. She shifted the flashlight to his hips, then his knees and feet. One leg lay at an odd angle, and the bone stuck through his thigh. "Compound fracture." She needed to pack that so he didn't bleed out before the first responders could get here. Kenna edged forward so both arms and her shoulders were over the broken end of the floor. She shined the flashlight around trying to find...

There.

Around her one o'clock, so the right side in front of her, she spotted what she'd been looking for—wooden stairs in the corner of the cellar, which was about half the size of the barn and looked pretty much empty except for some stalls. What they'd been used for by the Children of the Morning didn't matter now. So long as there was no one down here.

Kenna scooted back and stood, then picked her way around stuff to the stack of pallets over where she roughly figured the cellar door was. Figures the feds never found it, given they hadn't moved a stack of wood to find what was underneath. She tossed them one by one, trying to ignore the pain in her forearms that sparked every time she forced them to bear weight.

She'd survived, the way Jordan was going to—if she had any say in it.

She supposed Ryson would probably pray to God that the kid survived. But why did she need to do that when she planned to get down there, do everything she could, and see what happened? Whether the kid lived or died would be an empirical fact, not a matter of spiritual interpretation. If God was in control, then He would take care of the outcome. She dealt with concrete things.

Life and death.

Moving and standing still.

Action and reaction.

Kenna kicked aside the last couple of pallets and looked at the hatch. She knelt, tugged at the padlock, and sighed. "Darn."

"Ma'am?"

Kenna spun around, reaching for her gun with one hand and lifting the flashlight with the other. The beam lit on a guy she pegged right away as a local cop. She didn't unclip the strap holding her weapon in the holster.

"Easy." He started toward her.

Like she would relax?

If she did that, she could have two male victims on her hands. Or one victim and an assailant.

"Careful," Kenna said. "It's precarious." She shined the flashlight on the floor so he could see as he made his way around the hole. "Any way we can get a padlock off the door to the cellar?"

He had white-blond hair and eyebrows. A slim build. Jeans and a buttoned denim shirt. "Bolt cutters." He looked around, his jacket shifted, and she spotted a badge on his belt. Local police department, not federal or a sheriff. "Over there." He headed toward what he'd found.

"Did you hear the call over the radio?"

"I live nearby, so I figured I'd get here first." He paused a beat. "What's your name?"

"Clara Shearson."

"Right. I'm Detective Thomson."

"Good to meet you," she said. "Got a first aid kit?"

He shrugged. "Just me."

"Did you see a teenage girl, the one who made the call, on your way in?"

"Nope. Just you in here." He brought the tool over. Long-handled garden shears she wasn't sure would do the job. "And there's an injured kid down there?"

"Yes. He fell through the floor, though I didn't see it happen. Annabelle and I were by the door outside." She shifted out of the way, prying the pepper spray out of her front pocket. Because Kenna not only avoided enclosed dark spaces but also disliked strangers—whether friend or foe.

"Let's see what's what."

"I already looked over the edge."

He snapped the padlock and broke it. "And?"

She described the boy's injuries.

"We should be able to lift him back up here. You couldn't reach him from the edge?"

"Too far." And she couldn't haul up that much weight with just her arms, anyway. But she didn't need him to know.

He opened the hatch door.

She caught it and leaned it open against a beam on the wall, then turned her back to the corner so he wasn't behind her and she could see him go down the steps. Unknowns were in front. Never behind her where she couldn't watch for the threat.

He nodded. "I see what you mean about his leg."

"The girl went for bandages, or some fabric. I should go find her if you're good with him." Kenna crouched at the opening and looked down. "Do you want the flashlight? I can throw it to you."

"Come down here. You can help me carry him, Clara."

She scooted to the edge, dropped her feet in, and got low enough her head was inside. "I need to make sure Annabelle is okay."

"This one won't be if we don't get him out."

"Can you have dispatch call her phone back and find out if the girl is all right?" Kenna said. "Then I won't be worrying." She was the one who'd sent Annabelle to find supplies but still felt uneasy about the risk.

He palmed his phone and made the call. The tenor of his voice more than what he said told her he was who he said he was—and had no ulterior motive here. Empathy crept into his tone as he explained to the dispatcher what he needed.

Maybe he just had issues with this place and the people who'd lived here. Or kids coming up here getting into trouble. Or he was a quiet person.

He said, "Thanks, Bev," ended the call, and turned to Kenna. "She's going to contact the girl and let me know."

"ETA on the ambulance?"

"Ambulance should be here in ten. So let's get this kid out of the cellar and upstairs."

Kenna eased slowly down the stairs, shining the flashlight around down here. "Do those look like cells to you?"

"Are you a cop? Or you were once?"

Kenna crouched by the kid. "We could remove his shirt and wrap it around his leg."

"I got it." Thomson pulled off his jacket and slid it under the thigh where Jordan's bone protruded from his leg. He wrapped the sides around and tied the sleeves in a knot. "Not perfect but it'll do for now."

"I want to look around down here." And avoid explaining why she was useless carrying a heavy load.

"You look familiar."

"We've never met, Detective Thomson. I've never been in Helson before." And she doubted he'd remember her father even if they'd run into each other. Kenna had been three when the FBI raided the compound. She had no idea where she'd been—or who took care of her—while her father was gone on this operation. Maybe he'd been working out of the Seattle office, and that was why she loved cooler weather and mountains.

She pressed two fingers to the teen's neck and found a steady pulse. The blood on his side looked more like road rash —probably from the splintered wood when he fell.

Kenna looked at the time on her phone and saw she had a weak signal down here. Hopefully, Annabelle was all right in the main building. At least Jordan had a shot at being okay. She spotted his phone in his front pocket. The EMTs or whoever could call his parents. "Do you know this kid?" She shifted back in her crouch and stood, shining the light around again.

"Football star. St. Clair, something like that."

"Jordan St. Clair?"

"That sounds right." The detective shifted about.

"You're good to carry him, right?" She stepped away and looked at the first stall. "These are definitely cells. I don't think I wanna know what those Children of Morning people did down here."

Except that her usual curiosity meant that wasn't entirely true.

The FBI had found the kids in a cistern, and no one had been left down here. There were no bodies. Each stall was empty. One entrance and exit. Dirt walls. The cells had concrete blocks dividing them as makeshift walls, not even stacked to the ceiling. One at the end had been knocked over or pushed or had fallen over the decades.

Something rustled in the dark. Kenna whipped her flashlight over and saw something scurry from the light.

Then she shifted her beam to a dark opening at the far end. A symbol had been carved into the dirt above the door. The same four-petaled flower Annabelle had on her wrist—except on the wall it looked like two eights, overlaid at right angles to each other.

Thomson said, "I'll get him upstairs."

"Okay." She didn't linger long enough to get caught down here alone before she headed back up. Why would Annabelle have that same symbol on her wrist? Probably just a teen who'd latched onto local lore since she moved here, or she'd simply copied what other girls did. More than likely it had nothing to do with a dead cult.

"You didn't answer my question about whether you've been a cop."

Kenna followed Thomson outside, where he laid Jordan down. "It's a complicated answer."

"Seems like a yes or no to me."

"It's not something I like to talk about."

Plus, telling him the name she'd given him wasn't real would lead to uncomfortable questions about the fact she'd killed the FBI director and hadn't shown up to any of the interview requests. She'd given her statement to the district attorney for Clark County, Nevada. Rebecca Rodriguez had delivered that statement along with her own in person.

What more was there to say?

Rebecca knew nothing about Maizie's identity or her location.

"If you did feel like talking, it would probably answer why you look familiar." His phone rang. "Are you an APB that would've come across the wires?"

"I hope not."

He grinned and answered his phone. After a few seconds he said, "Thanks."

Jordan was super pale. Kenna checked his pulse again and laid a hand on his chest so she could feel him breathe. Hopefully, he didn't have hidden injuries that took his life before he could get to a hospital.

"They called the girl. No answer."

"I'll go look for her." She straightened. "Make sure she's all right." After all, Kenna was the one who told her to go off alone. She used the side door they'd exited from and called down the hall. "Annabelle! Can you hear me?"

A breeze ruffled her hair so there was a door open at the other end somewhere.

Kenna propped the door back with a rock from the ground outside. Just in case. The constant vigilance she felt the need for weighed down everything she did, piling exhaustion on her shoulders. The idea of letting go of her peace of mind and how she obtained it, trusting a God she would say she believed in but didn't really know, wasn't something she could get into now.

When someone's life could be at stake.

Kenna unsnapped her gun and pulled it from the holster. "Annabelle?"

She cleared the ground floor room by room. In the entryway where she'd come in when she first arrived, someone had left the door open. On the frame, level with Kenna's head, she found a smudge of blood she didn't recall being there before.

She stepped out onto the concrete front stoop, where an ambulance pulled up behind her car, lights flashing.

But she didn't see anyone.

The girl was gone.

Chapter Seven

Hours after Maizie sent her a text that Ben hadn't moved for the midnight meeting, Kenna poured herself her fourth cup of coffee. Probably fourth, anyway. Definitely not way more because it was nearly six in the morning and she hadn't slept yet.

She'd resorted to pacing the break room of the Helson Police Department just to stay awake. The minute she sat, she would be half asleep. So she walked by the round table with its coffee cup stains and the ratty couch to the fridge under the counter and the sink full of dirty mugs.

The small department in Helson, Washington, had maybe twenty officers covering twenty-four hours of the day, across the area. Two detectives, one of which was also a sergeant, a captain, and the chief.

She'd seen them come and go through the night. Not everyone, but she'd watched the group that assembled have a briefing and then head out as a group to search again for Annabelle, but not before someone floated the idea of calling state police for their K-9 to come out.

The call for that had been made.

And yet she'd been asked to remain here. For hours—after they'd ascertained the girl wasn't at the compound she'd been parked here.

Kenna had hit the point where she wanted to ask *why* she was still here. Then Detective Thomson passed by the window that separated the break room from the bull pen, followed by a haggard-looking couple. Midforties, nice clothes but rumpled. The woman clutched her purse against her side. She had the same coloring as Annabelle. This woman was undoubtedly the mother. Annabelle's father or stepfather spotted Kenna in the room and did a double take.

"Is that her?" He strode right in. "Was it you?"

Kenna didn't even know what to say.

The wife came in behind him, and Detective Thomson just watched from the doorway. Kenna figured then that he'd stashed her here for exactly this reason—to see her reaction to the parents' grief over their missing daughter when Kenna was confronted by them.

Kenna held her composure on a tight leash.

Did he really think he was going to get her to break down and confess? If she'd taken Annabelle, why would she have complied with his request to come here and then voluntarily stayed for hours? After she realized the girl was gone, the EMTs had shown up and taken Jordan away on a stretcher. She and Detective Thomson had searched the whole place inside and out. Every inch of it.

No sign of Annabelle.

She lowered the mug to the counter behind her. "Has there been any news about Jordan?"

The dad blustered. "Now you're worried about one of them, when you're the reason my child is missing!"

The mom started to cry.

Kenna could hardly argue against his assertion, since in a

way it *was* on her. She'd told Annabelle to go look for bandages, sent the girl off on her own and unprotected. But how could Kenna possibly have predicted the teen would go missing?

They hadn't found the girl's phone anywhere, but maybe the detective had asked the parents for access so they could locate her GPS. But if they had, then they would know where Annabelle was by now.

"I'm concerned for both of them." Kenna used her FBI victim-interview voice. Calm. Steady. "And I've been praying that Annabelle is found quickly, and safe." She shifted her gaze. "Detective Thomson?"

His expression didn't change from the same assessing frown. The lines on his face were more pronounced now, as were the dark circles under his eyes. "Jordan was still in surgery last I heard."

The dad shifted, the stance of his shoulders aggressive even if he didn't get near her. "Don't pretend you care when you probably stashed her somewhere."

Kenna wasn't going to be accused. "Where could I possibly have put her that we didn't look? Detective Thomson was there with me."

The dad turned around to the cop. "You checked the trunk of her car, right? And wherever she's staying?"

"Ms. Shearson couldn't have possibly taken Annabelle anywhere that we didn't find her while we were apart. There wasn't time." Thomson didn't dispute the car, though. He'd had her open every door and the trunk so he could check even though it was fruitless.

"And the car?" The dad grasped the back of a chair at the break room table, his fingers flexing so his knuckles turned white. "The black one was hers, right?"

Kenna had the keys in her pocket. Thomson had allowed

her to drive it back to the police department in town while he'd followed her—and probably run the plates. That meant he'd likely discovered it didn't trace back to her, but to the daughter of a deceased man who'd been a resident of Las Vegas or Santino himself.

The Nevada plates alone wouldn't have told the whole story, but the registration likely did. Unless Santino had it under a different name.

If he hadn't put together who she really was yet, it would only be because he'd been looking for Annabelle and talking to the parents. And it was merely a matter of time before he figured out the truth.

An officer approached Thomson from the bull pen behind him. "Tom."

The detective held up a finger. "Her car has been thoroughly searched. It's unlikely Annabelle was ever in it." He glanced at the uniformed officer and lifted his chin. "Mr. and Mrs. Wakefield, if you'll go with this officer, he can take you out to join the search."

After they'd filed out, Thomson looked at her. "Leave the coffee and come with me." He led her to an interrogation room—big surprise—and had her sit. "I just need to clarify a few things in your statement."

Right. So he could find an inconsistency, trip her up, and be able to go back to the parents and everyone else to tell them she was guilty. Case closed. "You're recording this?"

"Yes." Thomson studied her.

"But I'm not under arrest?"

"Depends. What did you do that would warrant me arresting you?"

Kenna nearly smiled. "What do you want to talk about?"

She leaned back in the chair since as he probably knew already, she'd been in rooms like this more times than she could count—though usually not sitting on this side of the table. As a kid, when her dad had been working cases with local police departments, she'd slept on the couch in break rooms. One time she even laid a blanket and pillow on the table of an interview room just like this one.

Did he really think this would set her off balance?

Maybe he didn't know who she was.

"Eager to get back to your home, or your motel room?" The guy looked as tired as she felt. He had no idea where she was staying right now.

"This what you want to do to try and find this girl, Detective? It's a waste of your time and mine."

"I'm thinking this won't be a waste of time." He leaned back in his chair, adopting the same stance she had. Relaxed. Unfazed by the attention and the pressure. "Low and behold the car you're driving is registered to a dead man. A guy whose body was found in a house in North Las Vegas the same night the FBI director was killed. Oh, and it was in the same neighborhood. The shooter? Kenna Banbury, famous private investigator." He leaned forward slightly. "Do you have a twin sister, Ms. Shearson?"

"I have nothing to do with Annabelle's disappearance, and no idea who took her or why." Just so they had that straight.

"There's a national alert out for you, not quite an APB but close. I'm supposed to contact an FBI agent at the Washington, DC, office if I spot you. The alert was sent to *everyone*. Every department, every agency, every field office. Which is likely why you're here, using an assumed name."

Kenna studied him. "Is that what you're going to do? Call the FBI and rat me out?"

She'd admit, it was preferable to...say, going to jail for

murder, or abduction. Or suspicion of either. She didn't want to be arrested. At least, not if she could help it.

She didn't *want* to talk to the feds in DC. But if push came to shove, she'd quit avoiding them and do it.

After she made sure Ben Landry had nothing to do with the man who held Maizie captive.

"That all depends on what you say to me in the next few minutes, Ms. Banbury."

She couldn't exactly argue that assuming a fake identity had been for her protection, but it hadn't been to hide a crime. She just wanted some alone time—and the chance for Maizie to be left alone by people in authority.

Kenna blinked, longer than necessary. Then took a long breath, trying to wake up her brain with fresh oxygen. She was going to hit a wall if she was up much longer without adrenaline to keep her going. "So ask me a question."

"And you'll answer truthfully?"

Because she had no other choice, and he'd turn her in if he didn't like her answers? "Let's not make commitments we might not be able to keep."

The corner of his mouth curled up. "Annabelle babysits my son."

"No one expected her to disappear. Least of all me." Kenna wanted to grieve for the girl and her parents, but how would that help find her? They didn't even know if she was dead. "Did the blood at the main building correspond to Annabelle's blood type?"

"Test results aren't back yet."

"Any sign at all of what might've happened to her? More cellars, or tunnels? A place she could've been stashed?" There were a limited number of explanations for what could've happened to her.

"I'm the one asking the questions, Ms. Banbury."

"Kenna is fine."

"Tell me, why you were there last night?"

"I didn't know the two teens until I ran into them. They were snatching a souvenir...so they could prove to their friends they were in the compound." She said the last part like it was a question.

Thomson lifted his chin in acknowledgement.

"They told me their names. I chatted a bit with Annabelle. Jordan headed for the barn alone and fell through the floor." She sighed. "Is he going to be all right?"

"He'll be less all right if we don't find Annabelle."

"I'm happy to help any way I can." Only because she didn't like the idea of a young girl being scared and alone—or terrified and not alone. "Whatever you need."

"When I should rightfully report your presence here to the FBI?"

"Look..." She watched her index finger tap the tabletop for a second. She'd grabbed a thin sweater and hooked the sleeves over her thumbs, so at least he couldn't stare at her scars. He'd had her leave her gun in the car despite the open carry law here—this was still a police station. She wasn't officially on a case or helping out. "I can't stop you from calling them. But my father was an FBI agent during the raid of the Children of the Morning compound, so I opted for the chance to walk through the property while I had the time."

"Max Banbury." Thomson stared at her.

She tipped her head to the side. "I haven't read the files, so I don't know exactly what he did."

"Why are you in town?" he asked.

She had to try to shrug a shoulder. "Taking a break, staying at a short-term rental on the lake."

He frowned. "I thought the local council made that illegal." He pulled out his phone. "Booked under the name Clara Shearson?"

She shrugged. "Probably. My assistant made the booking."

"I'll find out and swing by if I need anything."

She gave him the address, so she'd complied with at least something. "Who do you think took Annabelle? Or do you think she just walked off?"

"I guess her leaving of her own accord is definitely possible, but nothing in her life so far suggests she had issues with anyone."

"She gave me the impression she didn't really feel like she fit in here."

His shoulders bobbed. "My wife would know more than me, Annabelle talked to her when she came over to watch Elijah. I need to ask her, but she's heading in shortly with coffee and breakfast. After that I'm headed back out to walk the grounds in the daylight with everyone else."

"I hope you find her."

"Me, too."

"Anyone local you've had your eye on lately you think might've snatched her?" Kenna wanted to know if he had a suspect, and was only keeping it to himself because she wasn't a cop. She wanted to see his reaction even if he wouldn't give her all the details.

"I don't think it was one of the ghosts, if that's what you're asking."

"There are multiple ghosts? Why not Bigfoot?"

Thomson flushed. "Stories are rampant. People hear screaming late at night. Folks go missing." His gaze darkened. "The previous chief? His son never came home from basketball practice one night. He was seen walking away from the school, and never reached his house. No one ever saw him again."

"Any other cases like that?"

Thomson shrugged. "Similar, but not the same. That's just life in an odd part of the state, where there are too many memories, it's like they've seeped into the ground water. People in town want to forget what happened. The rest of the country did when Waco went down."

"Failure is a much better story than success. People want to talk about government overreach, and use of force, more than they want to know that agents saved a bunch of kids no one else ever cared about. Kids everyone thinks were brainwashed."

"If you're asking if I think Annabelle is connected to that, I can't see any reason she would be."

Kenna wanted to ask for the cold case files. Maybe Maizie could get them for her. But that would mean getting involved in more than just Ben Landry and what that invitation was about. All she needed to do was find out if he was connected to a dead man, Michael Rushman. Other than that, what was happening was none of her business.

Or so she wanted to tell herself.

The door opened. "Hey, honey." A blonde waltzed in, a lunch box in one hand and a hot cup in the other, her hair teased out to max volume. Full makeup even though it was barely dawn. "Elroy said you're just..." She stopped short at the sight of Kenna and choked.

Dixie Cabrera.

Thomson turned. "You okay, Bee?"

Chapter Eight

Thirty minutes later Kenna was in her car pulling out from the police station parking lot. The phone rang on speaker in the cupholder as she drove right behind a certain blonde. Proof that it wasn't just her in Helson with an assumed name. The local Realtor, Bianca Wynn, was a certain bounty hunter.

One who knew something about Annabelle's sudden disappearance?

Kenna planned to find out.

She followed after the gray van she was surprised to see Dixie driving, following in a way that wouldn't bother to disguise the fact Kenna was behind her. If Dixie didn't notice the black Impala behind her, she was either massively distracted or she'd lost nearly every instinct she had as a bounty hunter.

Here in Helson, Dixie—Bianca Wynn—was the wife of police detective Steve Thomson. Kenna didn't get whether it was a job, or something real, or a bit of both.

The phone call finally connected.

"It's me." Stairns' voice echoed up from the tinny-sounding phone speaker.

"Is Maizie okay?"

"Rough night. She didn't know where you were, and you weren't answering the phone. So we checked your GPS. It helped to see you were at the police station but not much. Everything good?"

Kenna gripped the wheel. "Yeah, I'm good." She told him about Annabelle, and why she'd only replied with a thumbs-up to Maizie's message about Ben. Other than that, she hadn't wanted to bother the girl with what was going on until she knew more. And the risk of being overheard—or having her messages looked at after a judge issued a warrant for her phone—wasn't worth possibly incriminating herself.

She'd opted to play it safe, and where did that get her?

"Where is she now?" she asked.

"Talking to Elizabeth, having tea," he replied.

"Tell her I'm fine." She blew out a breath.

"It's tough, huh."

"What?" Kenna shook her head. She took the turn Dixie did, keeping a few car lengths behind.

"Being a parent," Stairns said. "Even under normal circumstances, you'll tear your hair out with a teenage girl."

And this was far from a normal circumstance. Not to mention the other piece. "I'm not her parent."

"Because she never had a real one she could count on. Not ever in her whole life."

Kenna sighed. "I know."

"Until you."

I didn't sign up for this. Except that maybe she had. But the girl was seventeen. "Does she need a mother?"

"Don't worry about any of that. Just keep doing what you're doing, it's working. She smiled the other day."

They both knew well enough that healing wasn't linear. More like a rollercoaster. "Tell her to call me as soon as she gets a second."

"Will do," Stairns said. "Anything you need from us?"

"A copy of the FBI case file, and a rundown of each child recovered and where they are now. In fact, same for everyone listed as a member of the Children of the Morning who survived."

"You think one of them is connected to this young woman's disappearance?"

Kenna thought for a second. "If not, they're connected to the invitation. Maybe." Loose, but she'd based a lead on less than this. "There's definitely something going on in Helson."

"And the police? Will they let you help find her?"

"I'm working the Ben thing. If they need help, that's fine but I've got other fish to fry."

"Copy that," Stairns said. "We'll get to work."

"Just keep Maizie out of the cult stuff, okay? She doesn't need the nitty gritty details."

"I'll send that file your way."

Kenna followed Dixie into a residential neighborhood. Going home, most likely. "Thanks."

"Get some rest." Stairns hung up.

Kenna parked behind Dixie, who'd stopped at the curb. The conversation hadn't been much of anything, just "Bianca" who Thomson referred to as "Bee" dropping off his breakfast burritos and fresh coffee from home. Apparently, the bounty hunter Kenna had met months ago in New Mexico had been domesticated.

Dixie had clammed up after she realized who her husband was talking to. Thomson had asked her if she was all right, and she'd brushed off his concern, citing the teen's disappearance. She'd told him she had a full day of work, and since Annabelle was supposed to watch Elijah, that meant she had to take him with her. She'd assured him that was fine.

The whole exchange was maybe two minutes, most of which she ignored Kenna as though she was inconsequential—something that wasn't going to happen now.

Kenna slammed her door, slid her phone into her back pocket, and strode toward Dixie. She needed a shower, a nap, and a meal, but nothing energized her the way determination did. "Wanna tell me what this is?"

Dixie slid the back door of the van open. "Come on, honey. Let's go get our things together."

A boy of about twelve slid out, his eyes glued to a game console in his hands. His running shoes hit the asphalt, and he started around the car.

"Careful, Elijah," Dixie called after him.

The kid didn't pay her any attention.

"He's a special kid."

Kenna just stared at her.

Dixie slid the van door shut. "I suppose you want a cup of coffee?"

"I'd rather have an explanation and then just leave, but I could use coffee."

"Come inside. But we'll have to keep our voices down. Elijah might not seem like he absorbs much of the world outside his head, but he's surprisingly astute." She turned from Kenna and strode down the front walk to a townhome in a row of townhomes. Just a generic family neighborhood without much personality, a far cry from the swanky RV with its chrome accents and her tiny yappy dog.

"Where's Tilly?"

"I don't wanna talk about it." Dixie glanced over her shoulder, and the grief in her eyes arrested Kenna.

"Sorry for your loss."

"And Cabot?"

"Surgery for cancer. She lost her leg, but she lives with friends and enjoys a quiet life in the country." And Kenna missed her every second. She needed to ask Maizie to share more pictures.

Dixie led her to the kitchen, a small space hemmed in by cupboards and a breakfast bar, where she went to the coffee pot. The refrigerator had an LED screen, and the oven looked brand-new. But given how little Kenna used real kitchens, she didn't know how to assess appliances.

"Listen, Dix—"

"It's Bianca."

Kenna stuck over by the breakfast bar where she leaned her belt buckle against the edge of the stone countertop and planted her hands flat on the surface. "Explain that. 'Cause last time I saw you..."

"We don't know each other. Not then, and not anymore."

"Then it's nice to meet you, Bianca Wynn married to Detective Thomson, which makes no sense."

Dixie—fine, *Bianca*—filled a French press with boiling water from an electric kettle. "I kept my name when I married Steve four months ago."

"Shotgun wedding?"

"I wasn't pregnant." Bianca folded slender arms. "If that's what you're insinuating."

Kenna lifted both hands. "Sounds more like a solid cover story."

"I fell in love."

"And Elijah?" Kenna thumbed over her shoulder, even though she had no idea where the kid had gone.

"His mother died years ago. I met Steve in Tacoma. He was on vacation and taking Elijah to a few doctor's appointments." Bianca lifted her chin. "I saw a chance to settle down and not be alone, and I took it. He's a good man. Elijah is a sweet kid. I have a life here, a business. We go to church."

"You're not working a job?"

"I haven't worked as a skip tracer since we met." A dark note flashed over Bianca's expression. "After Peter attacked me, I needed to lay low for a while. Around the time I thought about getting back into it, I met Steve."

A serial murderer, Peter Conklin had almost seemed sweet on Dixie, for a moment. They'd gone back to her RV so he could clean up when he showed his true colors. Kenna had found Dixie bleeding from a deep knife slice on her thigh, and days later Kenna had killed the guy in a hotel in Albuquerque.

She looked at Bianca now. "So you chose quiet and safety."

Bianca shrugged. "Is there something wrong with that?"

In an effort to control her environment and keep the fear at bay? Kenna didn't know what Ryson would say about it. "I don't think there's anything wrong with making sure you're safe."

She'd done the same thing. Now Kenna was teaching Maizie to do the same.

Bianca handed her a cup of coffee. "Are you going to out me to my husband?"

"Depends if he calls the feds on me." Kenna took a sip. "This is good."

"You want me to make sure he doesn't, or otherwise you'll tell him who I really am?"

Kenna might've made that deal. If she were another type of person. Vindictiveness had never sat right with her. "No. I won't tell him unless—and only if—doing so would save someone's life." She would never promise to lie indefinitely. "But if you could get him to *not* call the feds, that would be great."

"I'll have to tell him we know each other."

"Maybe you won't. See how it goes." Kenna sipped some more. Elsewhere in the house she could hear someone playing the piano and tilted her head to listen.

"It's Elijah."

"Wow."

Bianca beamed. "He's a prodigy. On the spectrum, but math and music? No one is better." Her face softened the way a mother's might. She genuinely cared about this kid, rather than him simply being her husband's child from a previous relationship. "One of his teachers thinks Steve should send him to a special school, but we don't want him away from us that long."

Kenna glanced around, looking at the small touches of a home. Bianca wasn't so far removed from Dixie—she'd toned down nothing. But the loss of her dog, and the misjudgment both of them had committed with Peter Conklin, had changed her. The way finding Maizie had changed Kenna. "It's good to see you happy."

Bianca sipped her coffee with a smile.

"Annabelle was your sitter, right?"

She hunched her shoulders up. "She was supposed to watch Elijah this afternoon. I've got an open house I can't miss, so I'll have to take him with me."

"Anything she said or did lately that might give you the impression she had a beef with a friend? Any problems with people she knew?"

Bianca sighed. "She got along fine with her friends. I think she was still settling in, but hard not to be included when you're cheerleading captain."

Kenna had zero idea about high school other than movies but didn't give that impression to Bianca. Not that she'd ever fit with the homeschooling crowd either—at least not what it had been fifteen, nearly twenty years ago. "What about her parents?"

"They didn't understand her. She was planning on Virginia for college, or Hawaii."

"So as far away as possible?"

Bianca nodded. "Sounded like it. The chance to branch out."

"Did you see her outside her nannying for you?"

"At church. She's in the choir." Bianca sighed. "No other reason. Did you look into their financials? Maybe it's a business thing and whoever took her is going to ask for a ransom."

Kenna nearly grinned, even though it wasn't funny so she hoped that wasn't what would happen to Annabelle. "Does Bianca Wynn watch those kinds of shows and movies?"

"Steve does. I overhear things. And my book club are suspense fans."

"As long as you don't read any of my father's books."

Bianca grinned. "How do you know we haven't?"

Kenna winced.

"We watched the movie together after we read it."

She nearly put her head in her hands, her face flushed so hot.

"The movie was better, oddly enough."

"I know," Kenna said. "It's because the misery is over quicker."

Bianca laughed. After a second, the sound hollowed out and she sighed. "I hope they find Annabelle. She's a sweet girl."

"Me, too."

"Is that why you're here?"

Kenna shook her head and explained about Intellectus, the mystery solving group, and Ben Landry with his multiple IDs. Before she got to the invitation, Bianca cut her off.

"Someone from Vegas is *here?*" Bianca's eyes widened with the fear Kenna had seen in Dixie months before. "Why?"

Kenna pulled out her phone and showed Bianca a picture of Ben Landry. "Ever seen him before?"

She frowned. "Never. That's him?" She took a photo of Kenna's phone screen with her device.

"We could just exchange numbers."

Bianca shook her head. "We don't know each other."

"Then I should quit drinking coffee with you in your kitchen," Kenna pointed out.

"Yeah, you should go shower and take a nap."

"Ain't that the truth." She set the mug down and pushed away from the breakfast bar.

The piano music that had been drifting through the house stopped abruptly.

Bianca frowned. "He doesn't usually end before finishing the song."

Kenna took a step back and motioned with her hand. "Show me."

The blonde went first. Four inches shorter than Kenna, she strode through the living room and down a hall to a back porch sunroom with an upright piano against one wall, a yard through the windows that was all green trees and landscaping. An oasis that would've made Kenna want to stick around and take it in.

Except Elijah wasn't here.

"Why is the door open?" Bianca raced for it on her heels, onto the paving stones of the patio.

A young boy cry came from the far end of the yard.

Kenna reached for the gun she'd left in the car. She tugged on Bianca's elbow. "Call your husband." Then raced across the yard, pumping her arms and legs as fast as she could.

Bianca called out, "Ten o'clock. The gate!"

She figured out what that meant and angled toward the left corner, where a gate was nestled back in the huge bushes nearly disguising the path. The gate stood open.

Kenna crouched to draw out her knife, smashing a flower under her boot so the scent of it wafted up to her nose and then raced through the gate.

Down the tiny alley, barely wide enough for two cars to pass each other, she spotted a blonde dragging Elijah toward a van. The boy struggled, confusion on his face.

"Stop!"

The blonde turned. Annabelle.

Elijah screamed.

Kenna raced for them.

The missing girl ran toward the van and jumped in the passenger side. Kenna caught up to Elijah and wrapped her arm around his shoulder. "It's okay."

Her words were swallowed up in the revving of the van engine as it sped away.

Chapter Nine

Kenna set the laptop on the table on the back porch. "Can you still hear me?"

One side of the screen displayed Maizie and Stairns, in two different windows—their backgrounds different. He was in his office in the house, and Maizie was in the airstream.

"Yeah, it's still connected fine." Maizie's gaze shifted like she was looking at something else on her screen. "Your signal is good since I boosted the Wi-Fi there."

Kenna opened her yogurt and sat back in the Adirondack chair. "It's nice out here."

"Beats being at the police station all night, too." Stairns' brows lifted.

"Yes, it does." And after talking to Bianca, followed by saving Elijah from kidnappers, she'd finally been able to take a shower and a nap. The sunset to the west, at the end of the lake, glowed orange across the sky. She stared at it for a second.

"You okay?"

She shrugged in answer to Stairns' question. "Elijah is good. Detective Thomson is on the case. I gave my statement."

There was clearly something going on in town, and given it was the missing teen Annabelle who had tried to take him from their house, the whole thing was right up Kenna's alley. But first she had to take care of something else.

"What about the children who survived the raid?" Kenna asked. Stairns had sent over the case file, so she'd spent an hour after the nap reading. "Can we track where they ended up?"

Maizie lifted her chin. "Out of the seven girls and six boys, we have nine alive and four deceased. I tracked them through the CPS database and follow-up local news stories on where they are now as well as a couple of social media groups where people talk about the Children of the Morning."

"And?"

"I'm still confirming Ben Landry's original identity, but I think he might be one of them." Maizie winced. "The kids had no birth records. They never saw doctors outside whatever care they were given by members of the Children of the Morning."

From the file she'd read, her dad's statement had mentioned how malnourished the kids were overall. A couple of the boys had shown evidence of being beaten. One of the girls, a preteen, had a broken arm that hadn't been treated.

Stairns said, "One pretty vocal survivor who likes to troll the discussions and correct people's statements about what the group was like—that they weren't crazy, they were just devout—is giving me issues. She's local, but I can't get past her identity. Looks like an alt account under a fake name tied to an email address that goes nowhere."

"Send it to me," Maizie told him. "I'll dig a little."

Stairns said, "Did you get anything from year books?"

Maizie shook her head. "The ones we need go back too

far, they aren't digitized. But they might be at the local library there."

Kenna set her empty yogurt container beside the laptop. "What about the house where Ben is staying?"

Maizie nodded. "It's registered as being owned by William and Martha Jones. They adopted a child they called William Jones Junior, which CPS has on record along with county adoption records. I guess they didn't want to keep any of it a secret."

"And he just happens to be staying at the house?"

Stairns frowned. "You think little William went home?"

Kenna leaned more toward the fact Ben Landry chose multiple names having an origin point in being a child with no legal name. Maybe he didn't want to be who he was but found it easier to be whoever he chose to be. "But why would he be here? Except to respond to the invitation."

Maizie said, "Are you going to find out?"

"I think I'll pay Ben a visit at the house tonight. Before midnight. Find out what he came home for."

It would at least cross off one unknown here in town. Striking off the easiest thing—finding out whether Ben had ties to Michael Rushman—would close one case and free her up. Annabelle was out there somewhere. The kid, Elijah, might be targeted again. Kenna needed to be free to pursue leads even if the police department in Helson intended on solving the case.

"Keep us posted." Stairns didn't say anything else.

From the look on Maizie's face, the girl wanted to add a comment.

"I'll be okay," Kenna said. "Can you get me the information for whoever in town worked the case with my father?"

"You want to ask them about the group?" Stairns lifted his chin. "They might be able to confirm who the children are now. Or any other members who might be up to something in Helson."

"The current police chief might've been an officer back then. I can look." Maizie's fingers already swept over the keys.

Kenna said, "See if you can find anyone who is no longer serving." She didn't want anyone who might connect who she was the way Detective Thomson had. She also had no intention of distracting whoever was looking for Annabelle with the past if it turned out not to be relevant.

Annabelle—and whoever had been driving that van—might simply have been trying to take Elijah because of how she felt about the child. It could be they thought he was being mistreated or kept from achieving his full potential.

Both of which she'd floated with Detective Thomson.

Neither he nor Bianca had known of any reason Annabelle might have to think she should take care of Elijah rather than his parents. They'd been completely surprised when Kenna told them that it was the missing teen who'd tried to kidnap their son.

Maizie scrunched up her nose. "Maybe the former police chief. I'll see if he's still around."

"Thanks." Kenna heard the oven beep in the house. "My dinner is ready, so I'll let both of you go, all right?" They nodded. "Find out if there's any connection between Annabelle and the Children of the Morning."

"Will do." Stairns left the chat.

"Need anything?" Kenna asked.

Maizie shook her head.

"Call me if you do." She gave the girl the chance to say something if she wanted. Just in case she had something on her mind.

"Okay. I will." The way Maizie said it, Kenna believed her.

"I'll call you after I talk to Ben."

Maizie nodded, then signed off reluctantly.

Kenna took the laptop and her trash inside. She ate in silence, nothing playing on a screen while she looked at the lake through the patio door. Giving time for her mind to work the problem in the background.

Ben. Annabelle. Elijah. They might be connected or only linked in some ways but not others. But the fact that all three were in Helson meant something.

So far all she had were a load of questions.

The person she wanted to talk over them with hadn't responded to her messages in a couple of days. She'd decided not to be needy—generally a good idea, and more attractive in the person you liked. They were using an app Maizie had assured her wasn't something that could be hacked. Since Jax was currently working the aftermath of the Michael Rushman case, and figuring out precisely how far his influence reached, she should leave him to it.

They all wanted Maizie safe.

The FBI would root out any infection that had spread from Rushman's sickness out to other people he was connected to. A few people in Washington had already owned up to being blackmailed by him. Business leaders and politicians had owned up and immediately put all the blame on Rushman, which considering he was dead seemed handy. The FBI director's life had been torn apart, and news programs constantly ran stories about how Rushman had leaned on the director to do his dirty work and ensure his company's government contracts remained in place.

Now the company was being broken up and sold off piece by piece, making Kenna wonder if Maizie still had a hand in the inner workings. Maybe she'd kept pieces of the business, or intellectual property, for herself.

Kenna cleaned up and geared up. She braided her hair, then headed for the car. It didn't take long to drive to the address where Ben Landry had parked the other day and seemingly never left.

She strode up and knocked on his door.

The entry light inside clicked on, and she started moving forward. Ben opened the door with Kenna already stepping in, backlit so that his face was in shadow. Kenna shoved the door back before he could figure out what was happening, and Ben stumbled back.

He started to bluster.

"Save it." Kenna slammed the door closed behind her. She didn't have any weapons out and didn't move toward him. "I have questions, and you're gonna give me answers. And then we're going to leave each other alone after that."

"Kenna Banbury." He glared at her. "Get out of my house." Ben Landry was a good-looking guy, at least for social media standards. He probably managed to con more than one person on his appearance alone.

"Nope." She shook her head. "You have information I need."

"So you can make something out of nothing like you always do. Get people in trouble when they're only trying to mind their own business." He came at her then. "Get out of my—"

Kenna grabbed the pressure point in his wrist. It didn't take much strength to squeeze enough that sparks would fly up his arm, his nerves set alight.

He hissed out a breath.

"I'm not leaving, William."

"Don't call me that." Ben's expression shot daggers at her.

"Let's talk." She strode past him into the living room, then turned back to face him. "You are William Jones Junior, right?

I don't know the name you were given at birth, but I'm guessing you're older than you look being as you're a survivor of the Children of the Morning."

He stared at her as though if he had a weapon handy, he'd launch himself across the room and kill her.

"But that's not what I' m here to talk about." Kenna showed him both her hands, fingers spread. "I'm reaching for my phone, nothing else." She drew it out and flicked to her photos, showing him a picture of Annabelle. "Do you know this girl?"

"I know she's missing. It was on the news last night."

"I'm surprised it made the broadcast."

"Must've been a slow night." He shrugged. "But they always report on the Children of the Morning, or anything to do with them. It's the only thing that puts Helson on the map. Though, I figure you disagree it was a ghost."

"Not hardly one of those." Kenna just needed her presence there kept out of it. "But I'll figure out who did it." She waved the phone. "You know her?"

He shrugged. "Why would I have? I don't live here."

"What is the Gathering Place?"

His body jerked, a flinch of his shoulders. "How do you know about that?"

Lest he think she'd broken into his motel room to read his mail, she said, "I've heard it mentioned around town."

He sighed and ran a hand down his face, probably trying to compose himself so he could be impassive. "You're going to mess everything up."

"How's that?" Kenna said. "You think I'll intrude on your secret meeting? Are the survivors having a reunion?"

He'd composed himself enough he didn't react to that. "Stay away from my business."

"Tell me what it is, and I'll see what I can do. How does that sound?"

"I hate who they are. I hate being part of them."

"So you come home to visit? Seems like it would be better to avoid Helson entirely."

"You know who I am?"

She shrugged. "I can guess." And her top choice was that the guy was some kind of con man, or grifter.

"Things got too hot after Vegas. Too many people asking questions, so I came home to lay low." Ben waved a hand. "I'm packing boxes."

She'd noticed the cardboard that had been broken down in a pile. Boxes he could tape back together and fill with the stuff here. "You're moving out?"

"Helson will be officially nothing but a memory. The folks are gone, so what's the point of keeping this place? Something I got recently reminded me how much it's like a noose around my neck. Well, I'm done with it."

"I know a good Realtor in town if you want to sell the place."

He looked aside, then said, "I hate them. I got out as soon as I could. I don't know what they're doing."

"But me being here could mess it up?"

His jaw flexed. "I'm gonna hand all of it over to the cops."

"Tell me now, and you can stay out of it."

"No." He shook his head. "I got the idea from you, but it's *my* mess. I'm gonna clean it up. The PD here needs to know that the Children are up to something."

"They're still active?" she asked.

He nodded in response.

"The survivors like you?" she added.

He gave her a shrug.

"Tell me who they are." She moved a couple of steps

closer to him. "I'll keep an eye out. Make sure no one gets hurt."

"It's probably too late for that. But I've been gone so long I don't know who they all are."

"Would you recognize them, or their names?"

"It's been like twenty years." His eyes darkened. "I didn't talk to them after that guy saved us."

"He was my father."

Ben stared at her.

"Let me help make sure no one gets hurt. That invitation was a request for you to join whatever is going to happen?"

"Fine. Yes."

"So when is it going down?" Kenna asked. It couldn't be an anniversary, as the raid had taken place in early December while there had been six inches of snow on the ground. Nowhere near the summer.

"I'll get another mailer with the date," Ben said.

"And when you get that, you'll tell the police?"

"I figured I had to get evidence, or they won't believe me."

"Does it have anything to do with the teen who went missing, and the fact she tried to kidnap a boy this morning?"

Ben frowned. "You're on the case?"

"Loop me in, I'll close it for you."

He stared again. "Kenna saves the day? I guess you want all the accolades." He shook his head. "You're unbelievable. Rolling into town like you can fix everything. You probably think if you save someone here, you can make everyone forget you killed the FBI director. I bet you were part of Rushman's thing, and this is nothing but misdirection."

"Goodbye, William." She strode past him out into the hall. "Have fun fixing your problem alone."

He clearly didn't think he needed her help.

Whether that was true or not remained to be seen.

Chapter Ten

Kenna grasped the brass handle and pulled open the heavy door to the church building. The tenor voice of the preacher rang through the entry, the vestibule.

No one sat behind the desk in the corner where an ancient computer monitor took up most of the counter space below the bar. Beside it, between the desk and the doors to the sanctuary, hung a huge board. Notices, announcements, and flyers posted all over.

Despite the gospel the Children of the Morning had preached, folks seemed to still want to hear the Word.

She headed for the double doors to the sanctuary just as noise erupted on the other side. People talking, moving. The doors swept open toward her, and Kenna sidestepped to look at the flyers, keeping half her attention on the crowd spilling out of the end of service. Her gaze caught on a flyer for a local counseling group. Survivors of trauma, people dealing with grief, and those who needed to talk through the things they'd been taught to believe in order to move on from religious abuse.

Seemed like something survivors of the Children of the Morning might attend—or facilitate if they felt so inclined.

"Kenna."

She glanced over and spotted a familiar face. "Bianca, good to see you." She then scanned through Elijah, and her assessment catalogued the expression on the detective's face. "How are you all?"

Thomson gave her a single nod. "We're doing well. I'm heading back to work after lunch to check in and see where we're at searching for Annabelle."

Kenna normally would've asked what leads they had. He might know who she is, but the hunt for the teen wasn't for her to intrude on their case.

"You know, the two of you never actually explained how you know each other." Thomson turned his head to watch Elijah hurry over to where a lemonade station had been set up. The preteen ran back, and Thomson gave him a dollar so he could donate for a drink. "How long have you been friends?"

Because they'd been married for a few months, and yet *Bianca* hadn't mentioned once that she knew the infamous Kenna Banbury?

At least the man she'd come here to see hadn't exited the church yet.

"Kenna helped me out a while back." Bianca slid her arm through her husband's elbow. "With my brother. I told you about him."

Thomson nodded. "March."

Bianca said, "There was nothing she could do, but we talked over how sad it was."

Thomson eyed her. "When the case wraps up and things quiet down, we'll get your RV out of storage and go somewhere."

"I know." She kissed his cheek, but her expression remained unconvinced that things would ever "quiet down."

Kenna figured that was likely a healthy assessment of being the wife of a cop. She decided to steer the conversation where she needed it, not just so they could move along, and the detective could get back to work. "Did the two of you see Ron Arnold in service?"

Thomson frowned. "I believe he's still seated. But why do you want to talk to the old police chief?"

Kenna shrugged, settling on the lowest common denominator. "He met my father. I'm always curious to talk to people who did and get to know the man he was."

That seemed to satisfy him well enough.

Bianca touched Kenna's arm. "Come over for dinner later. Steve and I need to ask you something."

Thomson looked at his watch. "Actually, if you could swing by the house in about an hour, that would be great."

Kenna frowned. "Okay, I'll see you then."

They left the church as a family, and she peeked into the sanctuary. White walls, wood beams. A high ceiling to direct the sound of singing up to the heavens. Rows of pews with bright-red cushioned seats, Bibles in the pocket on the back of the seat in front.

On the wall, someone had painted a verse in gold script.

For You, Lord, have not forsaken those who seek You.

Kenna would describe herself as a "seeker" even if she wasn't sure what that meant exactly. Ryson's encouragement meant letting go of the control she had over her life, giving it up to a God she didn't completely understand yet—or trust.

Whichever one of those came first, this would be about taking a step at a time.

She slid out her phone and saw there were no new notifications for the app she was using to talk to Jax.

She could use a talk right now.

A single man sat in the third row. The preacher in his white robe spoke with a woman in a knit shirt and knee-length skirt, her graying hair pinned back in a bun. She looked enraptured with whatever he said to her.

The seated man stared at his hands, fingers entwined on his knees. Gray hair, lines on his face and the papery skin of age. Tan slacks. A checkered shirt with pearl buttons. A cowboy hat lay on the seat beside him, untouched, a Bible peeking out from under the brim.

Kenna strode down the row in front of him, turned, and sat sideways on the seat facing the aisle. He didn't look up, but he knew she was there.

The preacher and the woman continued their conversation.

Kenna set her arm on the back of the pew so the sleeve of her thin sweater stretched at the shoulder. "Ron Arnold?"

He lifted his head, and a flicker drew two bushy gray brows together. "Who are you?"

She stared for a second, wanting to start where she wanted to start—and it had nothing to do with Annabelle. "Do you remember an FBI agent here to serve the warrant on the Children of the Morning?"

Across the front of the sanctuary the woman broke off her conversation and gasped.

Ron said, "Malcolm Banbury."

"I'm Kenna." Her stomach clenched. "Malcolm was my father."

"Was?"

"He passed away a long time ago."

Ron stared at her. "Your father?"

"That's right."

"Huh."

Kenna had to ask, "Is there some kind of thing here...such that you don't mention *that name*?"

She'd wondered if it was supposed to be hush-hush, and residents didn't want to be reminded of what had gone on up the hill at that compound. But this man had been an officer with the Helson PD at the time. He hadn't had the luxury of ignoring it or brushing it under the rug.

The pastor said something to the woman, who left. He came over and sat in the pew in front of Kenna, thankfully not blocking her in. He also sat turned toward Ron so they could talk as a group. But was it to ensure Ron was counseled, or to get him to confess?

Ron's jaw flexed under loose skin. "Folks don't want to think about those people, or what went on at that compound."

"Ignoring something, or pretending it isn't there, doesn't make it go away."

The pastor just listened.

Ron said, "You sought me out. What do you want?"

"I want to know what *you* want." Kenna studied him. He seemed almost broken, but the case had been a success. So what did he have eating him now?

Ron stared at his hands again. His chest rose and fell. Years ago he'd have been barrel-chested and thick in the shoulders. Did he raise a son who took after him? A legacy he could be proud of, like being there when the Children of the Morning were disbanded. All that corruption, and abuse, had been broken to pieces and cast wide.

Prison. Therapy. Foster care for the kids. Hospitals and

psychiatric facilities for everyone else not charged with a crime.

"I want this to stop eating at me." He lifted his face, his light-blue eyes in the center of that craggy face almost gray as though the color—the life—had been leached out.

"It's been over for years," she pointed out. "What's still eating at you?" If something was going on, the police department either didn't want to acknowledge it or were oblivious. Neither was optimal. "Unless you don't think this is over."

Ron stared at her. "It's never been over. Not when ghosts still walk the mountains. Haunting the compound. Haunting me."

The pastor said, "Brother, there is darkness in the world, and the spiritual is real. If you're being oppressed by it, there are things we can do."

Kenna had expected him to brush it off as not real. This pastor believed in...what, demons? Spiritual beings that tormented people and caused them to nearly go mad. "I'm not sure I completely believe that's what it is. But then, in my experience, memories and fear are enough to drive a person to their breaking point."

Ron gave a half shrug. "Maybe that's what it is."

"A teen girl was taken or ran off from the compound after her friend was hurt, and a day later she's trying to abduct a preteen boy from his house." Kenna might have stopped it, but that didn't mean it wouldn't happen again. "So you tell me, what is it about this town, and that compound, that puts everyone on edge and has a teen girl acting so apparently out of character?"

The pastor said, "Annabelle was troubled when she arrived here. Her parents wanted her to speak with one of our ladies, get some counseling, but Annabelle never showed up."

"Why Elijah Thomson?" When neither of them said

anything, she continued, "I know she was their nanny, but did Annabelle ever express concern for him, or pay him too much attention?"

The pastor shook his head.

"Any connection that you know of between her and the Children of the Morning?" Kenna glanced between them.

The pastor shook his head.

Ron said nothing.

"If I asked for the names of every one of those children, the survivors, and anyone in town connected to the group, would you give that to me, Ron?"

After a few moments silence, he said, "I just want it to be over. I don't want to get back into all that."

"Any idea why Annabelle would kidnap that boy?" She glanced between them again.

Ron shook his head.

The pastor gave a shrug of one shoulder.

"I believe there's a series of cold cases here locally," Kenna said. "Things that can't be explained, or mysteries that went unsolved. Could I bring the files over and talk through it all with you?"

Ron said, "I thought you were just going to ask me about your father."

Kenna nodded. "That, too. You met him. I only have a child's perspective of who he was. You saw him as a colleague."

"A fed." Ron huffed.

Kenna smiled. "They aren't all bad."

His chest shook with a chuckle.

"Will you help me look into this? Perhaps finally put it to rest."

"That's a young person's game."

"I should probably also mention at this juncture that

everyone I've met in the past few months whoever knew my father is dead now."

His brows rose.

"Not by me." She lifted her hand from the pew so he could see her palm. "But it's not without risk."

He chuckled aloud this time. "Solve cases, and possibly die? Sounds like a good time."

"So you'll help me?"

"Bring the files. I have some of my own." Ron sighed. "We'll talk."

Kenna nodded. "Thanks." The guy probably understood more about this town than anyone.

"Anything I can help you with, Ron?" the pastor asked him.

Like all pastors, he seemed to be...not passive. More like benign. Or at least, nonthreatening, which was probably good. No one wanted someone that strode in and hit everyone over the head like they knew better. This guy's approach was more like a counselor. Someone who asked questions and pointed a person in the right direction but didn't just tell them what to do or what to think.

Given Kenna's history with therapists, and the friendship that was distant but which she'd say had survived, she didn't latch onto people who wanted her to open up.

Ron took in a long breath that expanded his chest to the size it had likely once been, then blew it out slowly. "It's peaceful in here."

"Good." The pastor studied him with a gentle expression. "But you know the peace comes from in you. It's not in a location."

"It's not in me at home, or out at the compound."

"I thought it was a fruit of the Spirit," Kenna said. "That's what someone told me."

"And His Spirit is in us," the pastor said. "If we're born again. We already possess everything we need."

"I don't think I do." Kenna's life would be better if she did. "At least, not right now."

"The best time to change that is right now." The pastor nodded in long contemplative lines. "That's what I always say. Whatever time it is, it's the right time."

Something in Kenna hesitated to accept that. Did she really have time for this? In the end she said, "Thank you, Pastor. I'll think about what you said." To Ron, she said, "I'll come by with those files."

He lifted his chin.

Kenna left them to talk and drove over to the Thomson residence. Her head swam with thoughts of ghosts, and the Holy Spirit. Not exactly everyday stuff, but here she was. Cold cases. Ben Landry. Annabelle. Steve Thomson's son being in danger of someone trying to take him again —but why?

She parked outside the Thomsons' house and just sat for a minute to let her thoughts settle. She wanted to talk to Jax, but he was apparently even busy on a Sunday. Or not in a spot where he could call or text, even on an app that couldn't be traced or hacked.

Kenna pushed away the insecurities and got out.

Thomson opened the door, a tiny drop of something yellow on his church shirt. "Come in. Want a sandwich? Bianca makes the best Reuben sandwiches."

"How is Elijah doing?"

"I'm not sure he'll ever be your biggest fan, since you were there when he was so scared." Thomson led her to the living room, where Elijah played on a handheld game console. "And he hasn't spoken about what happened, not even to his occupational therapist yesterday. But he seems to have settled."

"Has he played piano yet?"

Thomson shot her a look, as if impressed. "No, he hasn't."

Kenna shrugged. "I'm sure he will when things settle down again."

Bianca drank from a glass of iced tea. "Sandwich?"

"Maybe in a minute. What did you guys want to talk about?"

Thomson turned and leaned his lower back against the breakfast bar where Kenna had stood talking to Bianca only a day before. "We want to hire you."

Kenna frowned. "For what?"

"You know what you're doing," Bianca said, "so we want you to be here to protect Elijah."

"When I'm at work, doing my job," Thomson added. Which, given his tone, he didn't believe to be also Kenna's job. He didn't want her trying to follow police leads. "While I'm there, we want you to be here. On protection detail."

Chapter Eleven

The dark expanse of sky stretched above them and down to meet the mountains around the Stairns family property, lights sprinkled across the dark. The stars added an ethereal glow Kenna didn't often stop to appreciate.

"It's beautiful." She shifted in the Adirondack chair, her head leaned back.

Jax entwined his fingers with hers and rested his hand on the arm of her chair. "It's definitely something I don't take the time to stop and appreciate nearly often enough."

"I'm glad you could come."

"Me, too." He squeezed her fingers.

When she glanced over, his gaze was on the fire flickering in the pit Stairns had built out in the middle of the yard. Something in his body language let her know his thoughts weren't completely here. They might also be back in DC on the case, and the wrap up of the Rushman thing being splashed all over the news.

She didn't ask. He didn't explain. They just sat beside

each other by the fire, enjoying quiet moments after the Fourth of July fireworks. Eating too much food. Drinking her body weight in ounces of lemonade Maizie had made with far too much sugar.

"She seems good." Jax lifted their hands to motion at Maizie, under a blanket on a chair across the fire. Cabot lay at the girl's feet, gently snoring.

Everyone else had gone to bed, but Kenna didn't want to leave the teen alone out here. And she liked being out in the open.

She sighed. "I'd settle for better, not just good. Or even just a few moments of peace for her. Because when has she ever had that?"

"She has it," Jax said. "Because of you. Because you didn't back down."

"She found me."

"Because she has that same kind of strength you do. You both survive."

Kenna didn't know what to say.

"The tough part will be learning to *live*."

She sucked in a breath. "I thought that's what I was doing." And he was going to tell her it wasn't good enough?

"You are. With stuff like this. Giving her things she never had, pieces of home and family. The way you give them to yourself when you think it's safe to allow it in."

He saw too much. He had since they met. Why had she let *him* in?

Kenna started to pull her hand away.

"It's safe, Kenna. You're safe." He lifted her hand and kissed it. "You'll always be safe with me."

She managed a chuckle. "I think you're the most dangerous out of everything."

"Being scared isn't a bad thing."

"You think she'd agree?" Kenna motioned at Maizie, glad the girl was asleep.

"There's a big difference between healthy fear when you understand the weight of something and so you care about the outcome, and terror that seeps into your blood so you never know a moment without it."

"Yes," she could admit out loud. "There is."

In case Maizie wasn't totally asleep. The girl had kept Jax at a polite distance all day, but he respected it. He'd been friendly with everyone, like he fit in. In turn they'd demonstrated that they trusted him. Here and now, in the dark, would be where the truth emerged for the girl.

"Maizie is not you. She has her own story," he said. "You've been walking this road for much longer, proving how capable you are." She felt a warm finger trace the scar on her arm. "Maizie might need something different."

"But she gets to choose what that is." Except hitting the road with Kenna to find the lost and solve crime. She didn't want the girl in danger until she had a more solid footing.

"And until then, we'll make sure she's safe." A note of something in his voice interrupted their moment.

"What is it?" Kenna asked.

"They're talking about calling you to testify."

"I think they'll find my number has been disconnected." She heard a slight intake of breath like the beginning of a laugh.

"They'll show up with a summons."

"If they can find me." Kenna squeezed his fingers.

"When they do, you'll be asked to tell them everything." He paused. "We're taking down those associated with Rushman, or confirming they aren't involved. But we need more information than what we have. I can't suddenly produce it. They know a victim was involved."

So no one was confused about Kenna's intentions.

Good.

"What's to say?" Kenna shrugged one shoulder. "I never saw Maizie. I don't know who that girl is, or where to find her." She had a thought. "Maybe we should fake her death. But we'd need a dead Jane Doe to make it convincing. Maybe Stairns knows someone who can fake DNA."

"They'll find a way to put you in prison for not talking, or they'll hold you in contempt. This is the full weight of the government we're talking about. They want answers."

"So my right to remain silent, or not say anything that would incriminate myself, isn't relevant here?" She wasn't one to champion her rights. Kenna tried to live her life, and not get involved in such a way the federal government took notice of her. She'd had enough spotlight. Why couldn't they return the favor, and live and let live with her?

"They'll dig up whatever they want from Ridgeman's life, and Maizie will have to see it splashed everywhere."

She winced. "I told her not to watch the coverage."

Jax said, "Just be careful."

"I'll make sure she's safe."

"Yourself, too. Okay?"

"What do I have to lose?" Kenna said. "I have no home. A borrowed car. No cases. I literally have a phone, a few irritating friends, and..."

You.

He probably heard the unspoken word. It wouldn't surprise her if he had. "Sounds like you have everything that's important." Jax shifted. He raised her hand and kissed the back of it.

"I need a case, or I'll start to go soft." And she didn't mean just following Ben Landry, trying to figure out who he really was.

Jax chuckled. "How terrible that sounds. A soft Kenna Banbury. What will the world even do?"

She found herself smiling. "Did you get your next assignment yet?"

"They want me in DC for the foreseeable future. After that, who knows? Probably some cotton candy assignment because they don't trust me to work a real case. Or they'll drop me in the Chicago field office where I'll be too busy to cause trouble."

Kenna's smile turned to a grin. "Don't worry. I'll show you how."

Chapter Twelve

Kenna pulled up outside the farmhouse, far enough out of Helson that it wasn't under the Helson PD jurisdiction. If anything happened here, it would be the purview of the Washington State Police.

"Ready?"

The response to her question came from her phone, on speaker. "Yep, ready."

Kenna ended the call and stowed the phone.

Maizie had dug into their database and found a number of callouts to the house by state police, a few of which had been initiated by the school. Teachers had reported to Child Protective Services both bruises and the child's statement about how he got them. Peter Underwood hadn't exactly been candid about what happened at home, but what he did say warranted a visit from CPS.

Four years ago, the family had been camping when Peter was abducted from their site in the middle of the night.

Never seen again.

She flipped the back of her jacket over the weapon holstered on her belt. If they got the impression she was a cop, she'd dispelled that notion by wearing black Converse. And by having no badge.

Kenna knocked on the front door just after nine in the evening, when the sun glowed yellow from below the horizon to paint the sky with broad strokes of orange before it went dark.

The man who opened the door had wide shoulders and a heavyset build. Whisps of dark hair on his bald head. A white T-shirt with a drop of something stained on it and gray sweatpants. "What do you want?" he grunted. Interest flared in his eyes.

From behind him, a woman said, "Who is it, Lance?"

That was Alta Underwood. They'd been married over fifteen years now, childless for the last four. The camping trailer they owned sat on the side of the house, tires cracked and broken. One window busted out and never boarded up.

"I'm Clara Shearson. I'm a private investigator. Is it possible to come in and ask you both a few questions?"

Distrust flared in Lance's eyes.

Alta appeared behind him, barely coming up to his chin.

"I've been hired by the family." If she was referring to Steve and Bianca hiring her to watch Elijah. "I'm looking into the disappearance of a teenage girl in Helson." Also true in its own way. "May I come in?"

Lance started to back up, opening the door. He bumped into Alta.

Kenna didn't give them time to object before she stepped into the space he left. Which brought her way too close to both of them.

She covered the odd awkwardness of proximity, saying, "I appreciate your time. The police in Helson are working around-the-clock trying to find Annabelle, but I'm afraid it's not as simple as that. The missing teen attempted to kidnap a young boy who lives in town. The parents are concerned it may be connected to the disappearance of your son." Kenna purposely softened her expression as she had the tone of her voice.

She'd been on duty protecting Elijah all day, running him to school. Then to music lessons and time with his occupational therapist. The glimpse into life as a mom had been as interesting as it had been realizing if she ever had children, she would likely be on the same kind of protection detail with them every day of their lives.

No way would she leave anything to chance if she could control it.

Why take the risk?

At least in this town—while Thomson was at work—Kenna could help out Elijah's parents doing the same. Ensuring he remained safe, the way she had when Annabelle dragged him out to that alley.

The whole thing made no sense. Why run off, or be taken, only to turn around and try to take someone else? She hadn't seemed like she was under duress, so what had Annabelle been up to? Kenna needed to know who the driver had been, as well.

Right now Thomson was at home, spending the evening with his family while the night shift detective worked whatever leads they had.

She would be back on protection detail tomorrow, so Kenna had to jump on the chance to work one of the cold cases. Another child who had been taken from their family and gone missing. This case had some unique elements the other cold cases didn't have.

"Is there somewhere we can sit?" She glanced between them, wondering which was the alpha—the husband or the wife.

Lance's eyes narrowed. "Not sure why you'd need to make yourself at home just to ask some questions."

The wife stayed quiet. Kenna had expected a browbeaten housewife and signs the husband had a temper. Instead, they both seemed to trade off being the one to take the reins. Not the usual kind of dynamic, but that just made it a puzzle Kenna got to solve rather than being an easy conclusion.

"I know this must be painful," Kenna said. "Hearing about the near abduction of another boy around the age Peter was when he was taken from you. I can't even imagine how hard it must be." She adjusted her stance, like settling in. "You must miss him greatly."

Lance's jaw flexed. A man who hid his grief. "It's been years."

"Of course we miss him." Alta sniffed. "And you *can't* imagine."

"What was he like?"

At Kenna's question, Lance turned and tromped away into the kitchen. The interior of the house showed as much age as the trailer outside, the one they'd been camping in when Peter went missing—or had been abducted.

"You know how boys are." Alta shook her head. "He had gorgeous blond hair. So precocious. He was about to turn thirteen when we lost him."

"And the police never found any leads about who might've taken him from you?"

She sighed. "Useless. They never got him back for us."

Kenna had seen other cases where a child went missing, and the parents had *never* stopped asking for help to find them. Offering a reward for information. Searching. Going on TV. Lance and Alta had done some of that, but when the fuss died down, they'd slunk back to their house. Once in a while the media would come by—usually on the anniversary—and reinterview them. With no new leads, there seemed to be little way to figure out the truth of where their son had gone.

Kenna heard Lance close the fridge, then the sound of a beer bottle top hitting the counter. "Given the new developments, I thought it best to hear straight from you what happened to Peter."

Alta's head jerked. "What do you mean, new developments?"

"Elijah Thomson, he's the son of a Helson PD detective, was nearly abducted a few days ago. He's around the same age your son was. A child prodigy by the sound of it—math and music. I've heard him play a little, and it was pretty amazing."

Alta said, "Well, our boy wasn't some prodigy. He was just a kid, sorry to say."

"I'm not sure it's a pattern that Elijah is so accomplished. I'm sure there were lots of things Peter was excellent at."

The mom shrugged. "Kids are pretty much the same, aren't they?"

Kenna didn't want to get into a discussion about that, though it was an interesting thing for this mom to say. Even if she no longer had her son. Instead, Kenna said, "You were camping with Peter?"

Alta nodded. "A couple of days before Memorial Day weekend. So there would be less people, and that was all the time Lance could get off. The weekend is pretty busy at the parts store."

"You're a teacher, aren't you?"

"Not anymore," Alta said. "I retired last year."

"It must've been hard to be around all those kids."

"They put me in the office after Peter..." She cleared her throat, the first sign of emotion from her. "I didn't see the kids much, except when they came in to see the nurse."

"When did you first notice he was missing?"

"Morning. I went out to check on him."

Kenna said, "Peter didn't sleep in the camper?"

"He had a little tent of his own. Liked it better that way."

"I see." Kenna tilted her head. "So you went out in the morning. About what time was that?"

"Eight, I think."

It had been closer to seven according to the police report, but the difference could just be faulty memory. Blocking things out—like the grief she felt. Seemed like Alta Underwood lived close to denial. Kenna didn't see any photos in view, or mementos of their son's short life. Then again, there could be a shrine to him somewhere she couldn't see.

Kenna then asked, "Aside from finding the tent empty, did you see anything else?"

"Was there another girl when that other boy was taken?"

Nearly taken, but Kenna wasn't going to quibble. "Yes, the teen who went missing on Friday."

"But not a ghost?"

Kenna shook her head.

"So you've come here to tell me I'm crazy, then?" Alta lifted her chin. "That a ghost didn't take Peter. When I looked out my window in the middle of the night, I didn't see her walking through the woods."

"That's not why I'm here."

"You just came to tell me still no one knows what happened to him." A hard look crossed her face.

Kenna planned to reserve judgment. She didn't assume Peter's disappearance—or his death—was connected. Nor did she assume it had been a different kind of foul play. But she wanted to find out which it was, because no one got to co-opt tragedy to hide their own actions.

"What kind of child was he?" Kenna asked.

"Well, he'd never have been president. Not like that boy

you were talking about."

"Doesn't mean he wasn't cared about. That he isn't missed by the people who knew him, and those who loved him."

"Didn't nobody love that boy 'cept me."

Was that the real reason the kid slept in a pup tent? "I would like to know what happened to Peter."

The skin around Alta's eyes flexed. She shifted her feet, and the hem of her robe swayed her longer nightgown around her ankles. "I told the police. Someone took him."

"It's time to tell the truth."

Alta pressed her lips into a thin line.

"And it's not that a ghost stole him in the night. Because if you'd cared at all about that boy, and you actually thought a malevolent spirit was out there, are you telling me you wouldn't have let him sleep in the camper?"

"Lance wouldn't let him."

Kenna frowned. "And you couldn't have persuaded him? I'm sure he cared about Peter as much as you did."

Alta huffed, a small puff of her lips on an exhale. "As if he ever cared. Now Peter's gone, so it don't matter."

"I think it does." Kenna decided to bring up the ongoing case again. "I believe something connected to the Children of the Morning is still happening here in town." She studied Alta as she said that, getting a read on how the woman felt about the cult that had been living in the compound."

It barely registered before Alta said, "That's who this is about? Makes sense. If you think about it."

"That they took Peter?"

Alta shrugged, brushing off the whole topic. "Who else would it have been? That ghost I saw is probably one of them. Taking kids. Trying to start it up all over again."

"You're right," Kenna said, even though she didn't agree in the slightest. "It would make sense that everything ties back to them." A little too conveniently, in fact. "But some of the others who were taken the way Peter was have been found since—their bodies. Peter never was."

"Maybe they kept him alive somewhere." Alta's expression indicated she didn't exactly believe that.

Still, some part of her might be holding out hope. Unless this mother had reason to believe there was zero hope of him being alive.

Their case had been thoroughly investigated by Washington State Patrol officers, as it didn't fall under the jurisdiction of Helson PD. Only part of the reason Thomson wasn't here. As far as most people were concerned there were other cases—even related ones—that had warmer leads than a ghost in the woods and the rest of Alta's statement.

For all intents and purposes, Peter Underwood had fallen through the cracks. Figuratively, and perhaps literally.

"I was wondering if you'd be able to come out to the campsite and show me around. Where the camper was, and where Peter's tent had been erected. Give me a sense of what you saw, and where."

"You're some kind of ghost hunter, aren't you?"

Kenna shook her head. "I'm definitely not that." At least, not in so many words. Or the way Alta meant it. Kenna did try to find people after their deaths, but she searched for physical bodies rather than the whisper of a life force. And she definitely didn't believe there was something in the woods floating around snatching children. "It wasn't a spirit that took Peter, was it?"

"Was or not, he deserved it."

Kenna's stomach clenched. "How is that?"

"Carryin' on." Alta huffed. "Complainin' and cryin'."

"What happened?"

"Lance cuffed him. It wasn't bad. Nothin' the kid didn't

feel a hundred times before. Like any of us get when we do something out of line." She shifted again, and Kenna spotted a bruise on her wrist like someone had grabbed her.

"Do you need help, Alta?"

She cracked a laugh. "As if. You ain't draggin' me from my home."

"But if Lance is—"

Alta burst out laughing and didn't stop until she had to take a breath. "Guess you know now, don't ya. Our dirty little secret. That snivelin' kid wouldn't quit. Cried all night about the cold, and the dark. Ungrateful, he was. So Lance got him quiet."

"And in the morning?"

"Hardly our fault he wasn't strong enough. Probably had an aneurism or somethin'."

Kenna swallowed. "He was dead in his tent?"

Alta lifted her chin. "Get out of my house."

"What did you do with him? Where is Peter?" She wasn't moving until she got an answer. The kid could be buried properly, instead of left wherever they'd put him after they realized he was dead.

Lance appeared at the end of the hall at the same time the ratchet of a shotgun sounded. He lifted it to point at her.

"Tell me where he is." She didn't reach for her gun but kept still instead. "It's over."

"For you it is." Alta chuckled.

Kenna turned and shoved the door open as a spray of buckshot hit the entryway.

Alta yelped.

Kenna dove for the front steps, and the world washed into a flood of red and blue flashing lights.

"Put it down!" Boots thundered past her. "Put the gun down!"

Chapter Thirteen

J ust after nine the next morning, with Elijah at school under the watchful eyes of his teachers, Kenna sat back in a kitchen chair.

"Seriously?"

She shrugged.

Ron Arnold, the former Helson police chief, said, "Did you know they killed him before you went there?"

Kenna grabbed the coffee mug and took a sip. "It didn't fit the other cold cases with missing children. I think she came up with the ghost after they realized he was dead and they needed a shot at convincing everyone he was kidnapped by a spirit."

Ron scratched at the gray of his stubbled jaw. "That's some work, PI. Good for you."

Since he knew her real name, she hadn't thought much of telling him the rest of who she was.

"And now you're here." He set his mug down, a glint of humor in his eyes. "Because you think I had something to do with any of those missing kids, or that cult?"

Kenna scrunched up her nose. "Not unless you did, in

which case I'll tell everyone I suspected all along."

He tipped his head back and chuckled.

"This is good coffee." She took another sip.

"My daughter sends it. Good stuff."

She nodded. "Given what you know, do you believe Elijah Thomson is in danger of someone attempting again to kidnap him?"

"You've gotta get back to protection detail soon?"

"After lunch." Not that she was planning to stay here that long, but she'd already explained about Elijah and her job to protect him. "I want to meet his teachers and the staff before he's done for the day. Get a feel for what 'normal' looks like for him."

Ron got up and moved through his cabin. It sat nestled in the hills around town on the opposite side from the compound. About as far away from it as possible without being outside city limits.

She was honestly surprised he hadn't retired somewhere away from here. When he returned with a file box, she said, "Does your family live local?"

He shook his head. "Spokane and Boise. So not too far."

"Far enough." Both places would be a whole day's drive. "Have you had this place long?"

"Belonged to my wife's family. They were the original builders, though that place burned down and they rebuilt a few times. She and I made some upgrades." He turned his face to look at the beam on the ceiling above the door to the hallway, fond memory close to the surface of his expression.

Instead of sharing the sentiment, she felt an odd kind of disassociation with her father's airstream. Maybe she *should* want to go inside it. But she found herself wanting more for Maizie to see it as her space, not somewhere Kenna might want to reclaim at some point as hers. The girl needed to be able to trust that what she had right now would be there for as long as she wanted it. The way she could trust Kenna and the others in her life.

"It's a great place."

"But..." He lifted the lid off the file box.

"I'm not sure." She put the mug down. "I've never had a home. I've never especially wanted to be locked into one location, not when I'm on the road so much."

"You'd rather drive that obnoxious car around and get people to confess to crimes no one else ever figured out."

"I'm sure you would have."

"If I'd been chief when Peter Underwood went missing," Ron pointed out. "Or it was my jurisdiction. Maybe I would have. Or, at least, it would've been one of the ones that stayed in my drawer." He tapped the side of the box. "Like these."

"The ones you never let go of?" Kenna pushed back the wooden kitchen chair and looked in the box.

He nodded. "More than what you wanted to know about."

"I'll take them all."

"Sure, you will." He chuckled. "But if you're going over them, there could be things you might not see that I can give context on."

"You want to work."

"Please give me something to do."

Kenna chuckled. "I could use a partner." But she wasn't going to ask an older man who probably had a shaky trigger finger at best to back her up.

"Doesn't sound like you do, since you had the state police on standby last night."

"My assistant." Kenna grinned. "She had instructions to call them if things looked like they were turning toward a confession. And they had a heads-up, so they were nearby."

"You still coulda been killed."

She shrugged one shoulder. "I've got a couple of grazes, but I'm fine. I left the door ajar on purpose. So I hit it, and it flung open, and I was already diving out."

"You're gonna get yourself killed." Ron tipped his head to one side. "Is that what the deal is? Solve a lot of your problems if you go out in a blaze of glory?"

She blinked. "I just found this guy I like. And a friend of mine needs friends right now, and I want to be one of them."

"Not conclusive. And doesn't mean there isn't a tiny part of you wants to go down swinging."

"If that's how it happens, it's not up to me." Saying that out loud made Kenna stop. She had to think about that for a second.

"What?"

"Tell me about the cases while I think it through first."

He frowned and rifled through the box.

Kenna didn't want to consider what she thought about her own death. Even if she wasn't at a place where she would be okay with her own life being cut short. Part of her had made peace with the fact that at some point the life she lived—or ordinary human existence—would claim her. That she'd made the statement it wasn't in her control meant it was in another's hands. God. Did she deep down believe He had her life in His hands?

However she lived it, He knew the end.

Maybe there was peace in that. Knowing whatever she did and however far she traveled, He would be there at the end. The question was, were the days between down to her, or would she give them over to God the way Ryson thought she should?

It depended on whether she wanted to give up control.

Find peace. Right now she wasn't sure she had it in her to take the risk. Not with so much riding on it.

"Here's one." The former chief handed over a thin file.

"Not much to the case."

He sighed. "Colin Maresh. Thirteen. Baseball star, so good even I knew who he was. The kid was gonna go all the way to the majors. One day, his parents get home from work and they find his backpack in the hall, dumped out. Steroid pill bottle had come open. I remember they were all across the floor."

"So you were on the force at the time?"

Ron nodded. "Found one shoe a block down. Neighbor saw a van drive away, a white one. Got a partial plate, but it didn't net us any results chasing that down. The girlfriend said he was depressed, complaining about all the pressure."

"You don't think it's possible he went somewhere and killed himself?" She flipped through written statements and reports in the file.

"One more page."

She came to a crime scene photo, dirt and vegetation all soaked with blood. "He was found?"

"Hikers discovered his body in the woods." Ron blew out a breath. "Pretty torn up, like wolves or mountain lions or something got ahold of him. Pieces were left. That's the next page."

She flipped some more. Identified an elbow, and a couple of toes. Some of the boy's scalp. "Enough to determine cause of death?"

"Ligature marks on the wrists indicate they were bound together while he was alive. But nothing that indicates if he was murdered or just left out there for the woods to consume him and the rope he was bound with." Ron shifted and sank into a chair. "Colin is the worst of them."

"They're all bad."

"When there's no way to give the parents closure. No way to figure out the truth." Ron sighed. "But you did that for Peter Underwood. You told his story, and now he gets justice."

Kenna rested her forearms on the edge of the box even though it wasn't super comfortable. "Now we can do that for Colin." Not that she thought it was the same story as Peter, whose parents had been the beginning and end of his life. "Even if justice would've been a whole lot better if it happened before their lives ended."

"Sometimes after the fact is all we've got."

"Too many people slip through the cracks, and no one cares."

Ron stared at her. "The Children of the Morning didn't. Your father and I made sure of that."

Kenna's eyes filled with tears.

"He gave that to you, which is why it tears you up so much when people are victimized and no one does anything. That's his legacy in you. That drive to save the innocent. To stop the pain."

Kenna wiped under her eye with her sleeve. "It's been a long week."

"Right." His eyebrows lifted.

She looked down at the box, wondering about common threads. She'd have to read every page and note where they correlated. If they did. But Ron had already done that. "Is there anything in here that mentions somewhere called the Gathering Place?"

Ron's head jerked like she'd slapped him. "Not in there." He pointed to the wall. "Up at the compound."

"The Children of the Morning? They have a gathering place where they meet?" She didn't want to still be awake at midnight just to see if Ben would go somewhere. She'd rather be asleep, after she'd tailed him again last night following extensive statements to the Washington State Police.

"We never found it," Ron said, an odd look on his face. "No one remembered. The kids didn't know where it was, but they said it was some kind of initiation spot." He blew out a breath. "Your dad tried to get one of them to tell him where it was."

"What did you, or he, know about it?"

"How about you tell me where you heard about it first?"

Kenna nearly smiled. This man certainly had been an authoritative cop. He still was—and even being older and seated didn't diminish his presence. "On an invitation. But I didn't have confirmation it belonged to the Children of the Morning. Or whoever is part of them these days. Until now."

"There's no group," Ron said through gritted teeth. "Your father and I shut it down."

"But there were survivors. People who might still believe and want to keep going as a faith group." As long as they weren't breaking the law, it wasn't illegal. The police would have no ability to go after them just for odd beliefs, the same way they couldn't go after other protected people.

He scoffed. "Why would they want to? There's too much stigma."

"Where do I find them? If they are operating around Helson still, the survivors or the kids, where would I track them down?"

"Now why would you want to go and do a fool thing like that?"

He didn't really need her to explain it, did he? "You might not think it's relevant, but I'm not going to let it go if it's a possibility. This could be the break in *your* cases you've been looking for all these years."

He looked away, and a muscle in his jaw flexed.

"Time to take the next case and break it wide open."

He looked back at her, something like humor curling the edges of his lips. "Is this where I tell you how much you're like your dad?"

Kenna stilled. "Would it be true?"

Ron chuckled.

She looked at the files while he worked the humor out of his system. She really did need sleep. What rest she'd had the night before had been interspersed with the sound of a shotgun blast and being slapped with buckshot on the outside of her arm. It still stung, but thankfully he'd been far away enough it hadn't had the momentum to slice through her jacket, shirt, and into her skin.

Not the first time she'd dived out the way of a bullet, and it wouldn't be the last.

"Are you looking into the survivors, trying to find them?" he asked.

"Did you keep tabs?" She closed the top file.

"I didn't want to know, I'm sorry to say." He paused. "We got them safe, and the rest was up to people whose job it is. Therapists. Social workers and foster parents. Whoever adopted them—I think the reverend and his wife might have taken in a couple. The system had to do its work and keep saving their lives."

Kenna could honestly thank God she hadn't been dumped in the system. She would've been if her dad had been killed on the job years before he was. She might not have had her life saved through intervention over the years as a child, or into adulthood, but the upbringing she'd had meant she learned to save her own life.

Maybe that was why it was so hard to give up control. It was ingrained in her to do things herself and not rely on anyone else.

"Have you ever had any indication at all where the Gathering Place might be located?"

Ron stared at her.

"Fine. My dad never found it."

"I'll get a map and mark out some options you can go look at. But not alone. Or with the staties as backup." He shook his head. "Don't do that again."

"Are you volunteering as my backup?"

"No."

They stared at each other for a second, then both chuckled.

"It's fine. I've got a lead on solid backup if I need it."

"A cop?" he asked.

Kenna shook her head. "A bounty hunter." She just needed to persuade her to come out of retirement.

"Who?"

"Can't say." She put the lid on the file box. "I should head out. I've got things to do before I grab Elijah. Thanks for your help though."

The fact she could leave a house without getting shot at settled between her shoulder blades in an odd sensation a lot like itching.

Ron watched her from the door while she walked down the front path. She caught him doing it and lifted her chin. "Take care." Which translated meant, *Don't die.*

He gave her a toothy old man grin. "You, too. And call me if you need grenades or tear gas. I know a guy at the VFW."

Kenna headed for her car, carrying a box of despair but managing to laugh despite it all.

Her phone rang.

She picked it up, still chuckling. "Hello?"

Chapter Fourteen

"Here's your visitor's badge, Ms. Shearson."

Kenna accepted the plastic and slipped the lanyard over her head. "Clara is fine."

After she'd given the state police what they needed to arrest Peter Underwood's parents as Clara Shearson, she'd gone to the former police chief as herself. Now she was back to being Clara, the fake ID private investigator who shouldn't draw too much attention to herself.

"If you'll come with me, Clara." The older woman who'd met her at the door took her to the principal's office of Helson Junior High, but the room was empty. "Let me just get my radio." She took it off the desk and clipped it onto the belt of her skirt.

"I don't think I caught your name."

"Oh." She blinked, and her white permed curls shook a fraction. "That's right. Well, I'm Rochelle Wells. I'm the principal." She gave a majorette smile, switching into some kind of preset mode. "Helson Junior High and High School are combined and have two hundred students with full enrollment."

Kenna didn't need the PR speech. "The security setup seems pretty robust."

"No one wants their school to be the one where a simple security breach cost the life of a child, or a member of staff."

"Of course." Kenna had been buzzed in the front, but at the end of the hallway a door had been propped open with a rock. The window gave her a view of the field behind the school. "As Detective Thomson no doubt explained, I work private security, and he hired me to protect his son until the case has been closed."

She'd already closed one case this week. Peter Underwood could be put to rest. But it hadn't done anything to move the open investigation—what happened to Annabelle, and what she was currently up to—forward. In fact, talking to Peter's parents only helped him. It closed a cold case, but that was all.

Sure, it was a victory on its own. But in terms of solving the mystery of what was going on in Helson, currently it did nothing.

Kenna frowned.

"Everything okay?"

She forced the frown back and smiled. "Yes, thank you for taking time to show me around."

Kenna hadn't yet heard a thing, even though she'd seen a couple of kids cross the hall. She had on her dress shoes with her gray pants suit and a white shirt. Her shoes made no noise on the carpet, though Principal Wells' shoes clipped the linoleum they crossed as they continued down the hallway.

"It's really quiet," Kenna said.

And school was in.

She glanced in a classroom and saw kids with their heads bent over textbooks—and in one case, a cell phone screen. At least that part of this situation was normal even if everything else seemed odd. But what did she know? "I didn't go to school much. I was homeschooled." Kind of. "But I got my diploma."

"A lot of kids do that. They school at home, then come here to graduate so they can walk and get the certificate." Her head jerked side to side while she talked. Principal Wells had to be pushing eighty-five at this point. It was a wonder the students didn't walk all over her.

"How long have you been working here?"

"Nearly forty years." She slowed at a door marked Guidance Counselor. "And I have to say, Elijah Thomson is the kind you don't see often. I'm on an email loop for principals. We don't give out student information, but I've been talking about my gifted kids, and they all agree he's one of a kind." She beamed like a proud grandma.

"He is special." In that way Kenna chose to believe all kids were.

One day she would meet a youth on track to be a cold-blooded psychopath with full-blown psychosis, but thankfully that hadn't happened yet. She wasn't going to be naïve. But until she saw it for herself, she planned to maintain faith that every life remained precious—especially young ones, the marginalized. People who had their freedoms and choices taken away. The disenfranchised and persecuted.

Just as people had the capacity for great evil, each one possessed the same capacity for good.

She had to continuously remind herself of that balance, so she didn't fall too far one way or the other. If she were to go too far one way, she wanted it to be the biblical direction—where good far outweighed evil in strength and power. If she fully trusted it was true in a way that changed her life, she would never be overwhelmed by the dark.

Principal Wells knocked, then opened the door and

entered right away. "This is our guidance counselor, Lila Gress. She's also the PE teacher and the basketball and volleyball coach."

The woman behind the desk came around wearing workout pants and a tank top, her red hair pulled back into a bun. She stood a couple of inches taller than Kenna's five ten and had a shelf on the wall lined with volleyball trophies. "Hey, how are you?"

Her energy was infectious enough Kenna smiled. "Good. Clara. Nice to meet you, Lila." They shook, but Kenna couldn't match her grip. Pain thrummed through Kenna's forearm by the time Lila let go, but she didn't let the other woman know. "Do you have a moment to discuss Elijah Thomson?"

Lila eyed her, suspicion in her expression. "You want me to give you personal information?"

"Of course not," Kenna said. "I wouldn't want you to break a confidence." Whether she'd spoken confidentially with him, or not—as Detective Thomson seemed to think was the case. "I'd like an impression of the intersection of Elijah and Annabelle, the girl who went missing. Since they both attend school in the same building."

"Right." Lila gave a sharp nod.

"Then I'll take Ms. Shearson to Elijah's classroom to meet his teacher," Principal Wells said.

Lila shrugged her toned shoulders. "Annabelle tried out for the girls' basketball team before school started. Couple of weeks ago. She made it, but between her homework, her job, and cheerleading, she didn't think she could fit in basketball. Last year we made state, so there's some travel involved, most likely." She seemed to want to shrug again.

"Have you ever seen them talk at school?"

Lila shook her head.

The principal said, "We keep junior high and high school classes separate as much as we can. Their start and end of day times are staggered, and so is lunch. The upperclassmen don't have much interaction with the younger students."

"So not much chance they ran into each other." Kenna shifted her stance, needing movement to think, so blood didn't pool in her feet and threaten to make her pass out.

Lila shook her head. "I only see junior highers who need counseling. Usually it's not that formal for them. They swing by if they need an ear to listen to them, or if the teacher requests they come in and see me to resolve a conflict. For high school I'm their PE teacher and 'coach.'" She made air quotes.

"Thanks," Kenna said. "Could you call the police department if you think of anything else, let Detective Thomson know what you recall?"

Lila dipped her chin.

Kenna stepped back into the hall with Principal Wells. Now she'd had face time with the counselor she had another piece in the puzzle of Elijah's world. She would better be able to spot someone out of place and hopefully see another attack coming.

The principal did that head-shake thing that seemed like a tic. Or a medical condition. "I saw on the news that Peter Underwood's parents were arrested. Do you know if it has anything to do with Annabelle or Elijah?"

"Were you working here when Peter was going to school?"

Wells nodded eagerly. "Poor child. When he went missing, I wondered if they'd done something to him. But who wants to suggest that? It's unthinkable. Until you learn that's the truth of what happened."

Kenna agreed. "It certainly should be unthinkable, and for

most folks, it is." Just not the kind of people she usually dealt with.

"But you didn't answer my question." Principal Wells stopped outside a classroom full of middle schoolers. "I'm not senile, even if I look it."

"I assure you I don't think you're senile. You hardly could be, running a school." Kenna didn't need the principal denying her access to Elijah within the confines of this building. "And to answer your question, I'm only Elijah's protective detail. I'm not working any cases in town." Officially, anyway.

The line would be precarious to walk, and eventually she figured it would get out who she was. And then the feds would come calling.

Hopefully she'd be long gone from Helson by then. Even if that meant handing everything over to Steve Thomson to wrap up. The detective could have all the credit as far as she was concerned, Kenna didn't need recognition.

Principal Wells squared her shoulders and looked down her nose. "Very well." She pushed the open door all the way to the wall. "This is Mr. Thomson's class."

Several students noticed them at the door and looked at Elijah. One girl said, "Is Eli in trouble?" She seemed concerned, but one of the others snickered.

Kenna shook her head. "No one's in trouble." Unless they knew something that would change the situation.

"Does he need a bodyguard 'cause he's famous now?"

Kenna didn't see who said that, and couldn't tell from the tone of voice if it was a girl or boy. If there was going to be forward momentum on the case, then she needed information. "If anyone knows anything about the girl, Annabelle, who went missing, we need you to tell your teacher or your parents, or another adult you trust, so they can help the police find her. We all would like Annabelle to be safe. We might need your help to do that."

"That's right, ladies and gentlemen." The teacher was soft-spoken, five-six, and slender. She wore slacks and a blouse with flat shoes and a smartwatch. On the walls were prints of the Declaration of Independence, early presidents of the US, and the Washington State flag alongside an early land map of the state.

"That's Ms. Denhill. Jolene." Principal Wells shook Kenna's hand. "I'll leave you to it."

The teacher clapped. "Let's wrap up for the day, all right? The bell is about to ring. Make sure you take the homework sheet with you."

Commotion erupted. Kids grabbing things, chatting, and dispersing. Paired off or alone, one after the other. The girl who'd asked if Eli was in trouble hung back, eyeing him. Elijah sat at his desk, writing in his notebook—or doodling.

Kenna approached the friend. "Hi, I'm Clara."

"Rachel." She slung her backpack on her shoulder, clutching a binder to her front. "Did that cheerleader really try to kidnap Eli?"

"Yes." Out of the corner of her eye, she saw Elijah flinch. "But it's my job to keep him safe now."

Rachel seemed satisfied by that. "Okay." She glanced at him. "Bye, Eli."

He didn't respond before she headed out.

Kenna looked at his notebook and the doodle he was working on, shading the corner of a fractal. She pulled out the seat in front of him and sat. "Let me know when you're ready to go, and we can head out."

He lifted his head, then flicked his eyes to the clock. "Cello at three."

"I know. Your dad told me your schedule." The kid took

three different music lessons after school on different days and was part of the chess club. Plus another group that seemed solely devoted to solving Rubik's cubes. "If you wanted to skip it this week and go get ice cream instead, that's fine, too. Whatever you want."

The kid had a traumatic past few days, so maybe he needed a break. Or maybe he found comfort in his schedule. This might be a balance between what he said he wanted, and what she could see he needed.

"Whatever I want." He closed his notebook and slid it into his backpack.

He didn't know her. She wondered if he felt some wariness spending time with her, even knowing she was protecting him. The kid had been visibly shaken when Annabelle, someone he trusted, tried to abduct him. She had no idea what he was thinking about that. It also wasn't her job to counsel him.

Just to keep him physically safe.

The Thomsons could figure out the rest, as it was their responsibility. Thankfully, they were nothing like Peter's parents.

Kenna stood when he did. They swung by his locker, and she returned her visitor badge to the front desk. At the door she put her hand out. "I go first, okay?"

He backed up half a step.

"Thanks." They'd been over this a little the other day. Kenna kept her focus on the parking lot, scanning both directions. Only ten minutes since school got out and the parking lot was practically a ghost town. A few kids. The odd car, most of which probably belonged to staff.

She walked him to her car and had him sit in the front seat.

He slid out his phone by the time she buckled up, playing what looked like a puzzle game with math questions.

"So where to? Cello or—"

"Ice cream."

She didn't know if that was his choice, or if he was restating the second option. "Or both. Cello first, then ice cream." While he thought, she said, "Do you have a cello we need to pick up?"

He shook his head. "The teacher has a practice instrument for lessons. It's too heavy."

"All right. Lesson time?"

He looked at the clock. "Seventeen minutes."

"Great." Kenna pulled out, scanning again to make sure they weren't followed. The lingering question of Annabelle's intentions gnawed at her in a way she didn't like. It meant she couldn't relax.

They were four minutes from the cello lesson—according to her phone GPS directions—when the white Toyota behind them started to make aggressive lane changes. Kenna hit the screen of her phone and dialed the detective's number.

"Detective Thomson."

"Hi, Dad!" Elijah called out but didn't look up from his phone.

Kenna said, "Possible tail." The car sped up behind them, getting close. "He's making his move."

"I'll get a squad car to you."

She gave him the location.

Elijah said, "By the Dairy Queen," which Kenna spotted coming up.

The car in pursuit revved their engine and bumped the back of her car.

Elijah yelped.

Kenna gripped the wheel, one eye on the cars in front

while she checked the rearview to see if she could make out who it was behind them. And whether they had a gun.

At the intersection up ahead, a patrol car turned the corner, lights and sirens going. The Toyota behind her took a right turn and sped off toward the west. Kenna continued south.

The patrol car passed them and turned sharply behind her, after the Toyota.

Kenna blew out a breath. "Cello?"

"Ice cream." Elijah pointed at the Dairy Queen.

That was good with Kenna. "You got it."

Chapter Fifteen

Kenna stepped out of the house as Detective Thomson shut the door of his unmarked car on the driveway. She slung her backpack over her shoulder. "Did you find the car?"

"Not me. One of our officers traced the plate from a partial. It's registered to an elderly lady in town who reported it stolen last week."

Kenna met him on the front path. "Different than the van they were using in the alley behind your house?"

He nodded. "I'm checking into all reports of stolen vehicles locally. Just in case. Are you heading out?"

"Yeah, Elijah is doing his homework. Bianca is about done making dinner."

"You're not staying?"

Kenna shook her head. "I'm meeting Ron Arnold for dinner at the diner."

"Gonna solve another cold case?" Thomson grinned. The lines around his eyes were more pronounced tonight, after a long day of working his open cases, and he had dark circles under his eyes. "That was nice work with Peter Underwood's parents, *Clara.*" He grinned. "Don't worry, I didn't give up your secret."

She didn't need to say thank you. "Arnold and I are gonna talk through the files he showed me. See what we can come up with." She wondered if he'd be up to watching over his family tonight, but didn't figure he'd want the help. This was a husband and father who could safeguard the people under his care. "Any movement on the search for Annabelle?"

He shook his head. "No sign of her. She wasn't the one driving the car, right?"

"Not that I saw, but I didn't get a good look. The officer lost them?" That was what Bianca told her that he'd said when he called.

"As long as Elijah is okay."

"We skipped cello lesson and had ice cream instead."

Thomson winced. "As long as he's okay."

She squeezed his shoulder. "He'll get through this. And you and I will make sure he doesn't have to get through worse."

He dipped his head in agreement.

"Enjoy your evening." Kenna headed for her car and made a few switchback turns on the way to the diner, just in case someone was tailing her. "Where are you, Annabelle?"

The former police chief's car was in the diner parking lot when she got there. She hadn't checked in with Stairns and Maizie, but she'd sent Jax a joke Elijah told her, and he'd responded with a laughing emoji. She figured that was good enough until he could break away and be able to talk without eyes on his every move.

Kenna found Ron at a booth in the rear of the restaurant and dumped her backpack at the window end of the seat. "Hey." She slid in. "What's good here?"

"Finger steaks." He didn't bother looking at the menu.

Kenna blinked. "Why does that sound like it involves eating phalanges?"

He chuckled. "Like chicken tenders, but bits of steak. Finger steaks."

"Why aren't they steak tenders?" She grabbed the water cup in front of her and downed the whole thing.

Ron stared at her. "You know, I've never asked that."

"Maybe you should have." She settled in, ordering a salad with her steak tenders because she needed the balance of leafy greens with her meat. Extra cheese on the salad.

Ron stared at her.

"What? Cheese is life." She pulled out a stack of four files while they waited for their food and didn't get the chance to open the first one before his attention snagged at something over her shoulder. "What is it?"

"I was worried about this." He reached over. "Don't open the top one."

"Chief Arnold." A fiftysomething woman bellied up to the edge of the table, an older man beside her. Both had an air of desperation about them despite the buttoned-up, put-together appearance. She'd guess an office manager and an accountant, respectively.

The man smoothed down his tie. "Chief."

"Mr. and Mrs. Farmington. It's good to see you both," Ron's voice softened. "How are you?"

"I'm sure you can guess." The woman glanced between Ron and Kenna. "Since it's been nine years and not one person can tell me where my boy is. Just a shoe." She zeroed her attention in on Kenna. "A shoe. Can you believe that?" The woman stuck out her hand, grasping her purse strap with the other. "I'm Irene Farmington. This is the love of my life, Bill."

Kenna shook with both of them.

"You're the one who found out what happened to Peter Underwood, aren't you?" Before Kenna could agree or disagree—or figure out which name to use—Irene continued, "Because my son went missing as well. Nine years ago. William Junior was only eleven years old." Her eyes filled with tears. "He was an artist. He could paint like you wouldn't believe."

Bill put his arm around his wife's shoulders. "We have all his work up around the house. We will treasure it always." He pinned her with a steady stare he probably used when negotiating with clients. "The way I would treasure finally knowing what happened to him."

Kenna and Ron's food was delivered by the waitress, who had to lean around Irene. She said, "Thank you," and the waitress left them to it. "I am the one who spoke to Peter's parents."

"We didn't kill our son like they did."

Ron glanced at Bill. "No one thinks you did."

"It's clear how much you love him." Kenna almost said *loved*, but that would've been a bad idea.

"That's why you need to find him." Irene sucked in a breath. "Because the police never could."

Ron frowned.

"No offense, Chief." Bill, in fact, seemed to be the peacemaker.

Irene didn't bully her way to get what she wanted, but she knew what she needed. Right now that was information about what happened to her son.

"Maybe you could join us for dinner. Talk us through the case, so I can hear what happened and what you know," Kenna suggested. Ron could fill in any gaps after they left, and she figured they'd want to talk about what kind of child they'd had in the years they were able to raise him.

They could tell her all about the art, something that made Kenna's mind click a piece into place. A baseball star. An artist. A child prodigy. Were all of the missing children ones who excelled at something?

"I'm afraid we have to be at church group. Perhaps another time." Irene lifted her chin, as though Kenna might think less of her because her life had gone on.

"I will look at your son's case and see what I can do. Can I call or visit if I need more information?"

Irene gave her a polite smile, visibly relaxing. "Yes, thank you."

"We would like that." Bill squeezed his wife's shoulders. "Come on, honey. Let's continue to church."

Irene nodded and they walked away.

Kenna watched their dynamic as they left.

"Not pegging them as the kind to bash the kid's head in and leave him buried in the woods?"

She turned back to the chief, feeling her eyebrows rise.

"The local coroner runs the funeral home on Imperial Drive," Ron said. "He called me 'cause the staties brought in the kid this afternoon. You called it. They had a cadaver dog and found Peter Underwood when no one else ever had. Because you followed up on a hunch and solved a cold case. You brought that little boy justice."

"You're gonna get nostalgic on me now?" She picked up a steak tender—she refused to call them *fingers*. "I don't need a pep talk." She bit into the meat. "Not bad." The diner version of a well-done steak, but the fried part wasn't bad. "I could get used to these. Then I'll have to run more."

She didn't subscribe to that whole "eat more and you have to work out more"—like it was some kind of punishment. She just lived her life. But it was still hard to shake off the messages that seemed to be everywhere.

"Just thought you could use some motivation. Solve another case."

"Right now?" She reached for the fry sauce. "I'm eating."

Ron chuckled. "Calm down, *extra cheese.*"

She frowned, a mouthful of lettuce she needed to chew. As she ate, she studied him. They lapsed into comfortable silence. Like two cops who shared stories of their experiences. Or a mentor imparting the wisdom of years on the job.

He ate a bowl of chili that seemed like it had chunks of beef rather than ground meat in it, and three different colors of beans. "You're eyeballing my meal. Still hungry?"

She shook her head. "Next time."

"You want a second date? I'm flattered. But what will people think?"

Kenna chuckled. "Thanks. It's been a while since I laughed about nothing that had any weight."

He eyed her. "I get that. Tell my kids to laugh, though?" He shook his head. "They don't know how. So serious about if their children are safe. Or if they have good influences. In my day, our parents kicked us out of the house until dark. Told us to *go play.*"

"It's a brave new world."

"Seems like it's a scared one. Bunch of people living in fear. Too afraid to live."

His words reminded her of Jax and how he'd told her she needed to not forget to live. As far as she was concerned, that meant solving cases so she left an impact on the world instead of hiding away for fear of what lurked just beyond the edges of what she could see or what she would face when she stepped out to take up the fight.

Kenna flipped open the right file. "How about we figure out what happened to William Farmington Junior? If it's connected, it could lead us to Annabelle and what's happening."

He sipped from a mug of coffee. "You think it's all connected."

"We won't know unless we find her." Even if that was the police's job. "Maybe when the cops catch her, she'll want to talk to me."

Ron set his mug down. "I think she might just. You have a way about you."

Kenna didn't know what that meant and didn't want to get waylaid anymore, so she read the file instead. Though, she'd read over it before. "They found his shirt?"

Ron nodded. "Craig, it was his shoe. The van, partial plate, and the girlfriend saying he was depressed."

"Maybe Craig did go somewhere and kill himself."

"We might never know. The ME that did the death certificate listed it as wild animal attack, since he was so torn up, it was a few pieces." Ron took another sip of coffee.

The waitress refilled it, and Kenna declined some for herself.

"Never did like that guy," he added.

"Who?"

"The ME. Coroner locally is a good guy. The medical examiner the county uses was nothin' but a hack. There might've been evidence or indication of cause of death in what we had of Craig. No one will ever know. He wrote it up as a tragic animal attack, and they cremated what they had."

"And William Farmington?" Kenna said.

"His shirt. DNA was run, so the detectives confirmed it was him," Ron said. "Just after I retired, so I could only call the new chief and ask for updates. He got pretty sick of that fast." Exasperation washed across his face. "That was all they ever found. One T-shirt, and a smear of blood on the front of it. No clue where he was taken, or who took him. Just like the others."

"Do you think it's connected to the Children of the Morning somehow?"

"If it is, that means your dad and that team didn't end it. They left something that festered like an infection under the surface. Hidden all these years because no one wanted to see the truth. They'd rather ignore what's right in front of their faces."

Kenna stared at him. "So we cut it out. We take the infection, and we expose it to the light. We—"

"I got it." He lifted a hand. "You don't need to convince me. Just tell me what our first move is."

Kenna sat back in her chair. "How close is the spot where William's T-shirt was found?"

"You wanna do some recon?"

"I need to get out there and get a lead." She downed the rest of her water. "Which won't happen sitting here."

"What's the rush?"

Kenna looked at her watch. "I need to be back in town at midnight."

Ben Landry might head out tonight, and she needed to be around to see if this was the night he'd meet up with the others. Or give her information on them instead. She had a theory the invitation related to the survivors of the Children of the Morning but had zero proof. The difference between circumstantial evidence and enough to get a warrant didn't factor in her job as a PI, but she still tried to follow the same principles.

When it served her purpose.

And when it didn't, she did whatever she wanted.

"Hot date?" Ron's eyebrows rose.

"I really hope not." She stuck the files into her backpack and left enough cash to cover the whole bill, and then some.

"Thanks."

"You go with me, you're risking your life." She needed him to know he might not make it. Seemed like not many others did that she met up with. "Dinner is the least I can do."

Ron chuckled. "See ya, Barn!"

An older biker-looking guy stuck his head through the pass through window. He had a chef's coat on and a tattoo on the back of his hand that held a spatula. "Later, Arnie!"

Kenna winced. "Arnie?"

"Bad memories?"

"I'll just stick to Ron if that's okay with you." She didn't want to use the name of a hacker who'd died in a house fire before she could get there.

"It's what your dad called me." He pushed out the door to the diner and left her standing there.

Kenna shook off the weight of all those missed opportunities. The way grief roiled like a wave, low one second and then bearing down to hit her with the full force of it.

Ron flipped open the back of his car and pulled out a shotgun. "Got a vest?"

"Yes." She stared at him. "I'm driving."

He grabbed his vest and slammed the trunk shut. "Good. I like your car."

Kenna headed for the Impala, wondering if getting herself another partner—this time a friend of her father's—would be a move she'd regret.

Unless she could keep Ron alive.

Chapter Sixteen

Kenna had donned a bulletproof vest since Ron mentioned it. If he thought an evening hike warranted protective gear, she'd respect that. She flattened down the Velcro tabs and had to shift her shoulders with a hiss.

"Buckshot?"

She shook her head. "I can't believe that guy just popped off a shot."

"Yeah, you can." Ron chuckled. "Friend of mine, lieutenant with the staties said you left the front door ajar so you could make a run for it."

"Pretty sure I landed funny on the porch."

"It didn't get you?"

"Nah. Not really, but I still feel it." She slammed the trunk of the Impala, which she'd parked at a trailhead Ron directed her to. She'd have missed it if it weren't for him being with her. Though, GPS worked as well—so long as phone signal existed out here.

She checked her cell. Nope. Nothing. She slid it back into her back jeans pocket anyway, just in case there was a mountaintop and she got reception. Maizie was all about being able to track her, signal or not. Kenna drew the line at satellite phones, so they'd compromised with the button-size tracker in her shoe.

They'd had to swing by her vacation rental on the way—which wasn't on the way, but out of the way, in fact—so she could wear something other than professional private security suit and sensible shoes for this. She was back in her jeans, hiking sneakers, a T-shirt, and a zippered sweater that she pulled on over the vest.

Ron pulled a ball cap on, carrying his jacket and a backpack.

Kenna left hers in the car. "How far is it to where the T-shirt was found?"

He spread out the map on the hood of the car. "Three miles, or thereabouts. Nothing up here in these parts but some old abandoned gold mines. When they ran dry, things packed up and people moved out of Helson. But back in the day, before the turn of the century—the previous one—the town boomed." He ran an arthritic finger across the map. "Trails crisscross the whole place. Campsites are too far for anyone except diehards to get this far over from that side of the ridge."

"Beautiful country."

"If it's not trying to kill you."

Kenna grinned while he folded up the map. "Does it do that often?"

He chuckled. "We might run into an animal. Most are out early hours, not so much closer to dark. Just stay out of caves that have bears in them. Got it?"

"Good advice." She followed his lead as they set off toward the trail. "Anything else, or just bears?"

"The usual. Mountain lions. Coyotes. Deer and moose will leave you alone. We get black bears and grizzlies. Bobcats."

Kenna's eyes widened.

Ron glanced over his shoulder. "Bigfoot?"

She chuckled.

"You think I'm lying?"

Kenna quit laughing.

"The legend came close to these parts once. My brother said he saw him. Early morning, we were camping with our parents. He always called it a Wendigo, like giving it some legendary name made his story more believable."

Ron trod ahead of her, up a winding path interspersed with wood beams that ran across the path left to right—there to keep the dirt from sliding. The effect created stairs on the path.

As they climbed, he continued, "I don't know about some seven-foot hairy man, probably our uncle in his birthday suit out looking for where he dropped his cigarettes. But a lot of people think they've seen it."

"Did you talk to my dad about Bigfoot?"

"You know what? I did. He was a skeptic like you."

Kenna smiled to herself. She scanned the pine trees all around, so thick not much sunlight cut through the branches. The forest floor was nearly entirely a blanket of berry bushes. She wouldn't want to run through there, except that legs cut up by thorns were preferable to a bullet if it was a matter of life or death.

She studied the older man in front of her. A retired police chief who'd spent his career fighting for justice. Managing the people who worked for him, and the town he served. He'd found some level of fame, and success, after the Children of the Morning were shut down.

Arrested. Disbanded.

The fact they might be operating again once more under

everyone's noses probably didn't sit well. He would want to do something about it, enough to follow leads.

Or this was simply about closing cases he'd never been able to while he was on the force.

There was risk in allowing someone to help her, as much as she'd have backup in case something happened. He seemed capable. He might not be part of it and suddenly turn on her, making this have a deadly end she wouldn't anticipate.

Now that she had people worrying about her, and checking on her, made her want to be more cautious than she might've been a few years ago. Life changed, and she found herself changing along with it in a way that was inevitable and intentional. Bits and pieces of things, the way she wanted to take the faith Ryson had spoken about—the peace of the Holy Spirit—and think on it.

"I'm actually the one who contacted the feds in the first place." Ron sighed but didn't seem tired of carrying all that gear and the shotgun. He had about as many weapons on him as she did. "By the time I made that call, I'd about given up trying to convince them to toe the line."

"You tried?"

"For years I warned the town to steer clear." He sighed. "Folks don't want to listen. They'd rather make whatever dumb decisions they want just so they can say they're free. Like freedom ever did anyone any favors."

Kenna didn't want to get into that, so she said, "You tried to investigate them?"

"I couldn't sit by. Not when we had some missing persons reports. I went up there a few times. They'd parade out whoever disappeared from town and get them to tell me they wanted to be there." Ron paused. "Their leader was a piece of work. Brainwashing is what it was, plain and simple. But when a young girl gets all doe-eyed, who can convince her it's not good for her?

"Tried that with one of my girls. She wound up marrying the guy. Now they're divorced and the kids don't like either of them." He snorted, what was probably supposed to have been a laugh.

It almost seemed as though Ron had been part of the group at one time, but quickly grew disillusioned. Probably from what he saw as a cop.

She wanted to ask what else he and her father had talked about. Personal questions that had nothing to do with the case. Curiosities of a little girl left behind while her father worked, in a life she'd never known him in. By the time she remembered childhood he hadn't been an agent. He'd quit the FBI and they'd gone on the road. When a posting in a city with a field office would've meant she had a stable upbringing with school and friends. A normal life.

So why had he chosen the airstream and a life on the road? Working private cases. Consulting for departments and agencies all over.

Kenna spotted a moose about a quarter mile to her left. It stared at her as they walked but didn't move.

"What made you kick it to the feds?" she asked.

"Weapons from a private collector went missing. The guy said they leaned on him to sell, but when he refused to move that volume, they beat him and stole everything he had."

"That's what got them the warrant?"

"Your dad had a guy that went in undercover. You didn't read that in the file?" Ron glanced over his shoulder.

She wondered what that look meant. "It didn't include the name."

"The guy got eyes on the weapons. Proof they had the stolen guns. That got them the search warrant."

"And the result was a whole lot of arrests and saved a group of children."

"But they killed a handful of their group anyway. Whether by their own hand, or coercion." Ron shook his head. "It was ruled poison. Choice or not, more lives were lost than the world needed lost."

"On paper it looks like a win." She'd had a few of those. "Then you see under the surface, and the cost is clear. More lives were lost than were saved."

"Unless you count all the future victims they'd have ensnared with their teaching. Persuasion. Charisma. Duress. It's hard to tell sometimes when emotion gets into it. The mind is a funny thing. I've seen a woman swear up and down her husband isn't a killer, and then she sees him murder another man. Even covered in blood, she's going, 'But he'd never hurt anyone.'"

"Because her mind can't believe what she saw."

"Exactly. She's trying to convince herself of the truth she wants to believe because reality is something she can't handle." Ron slowed to a stop.

She moved to stand beside him and checked if she had a signal. Still nothing.

He motioned toward the clearing. It was barely the size of the diner, just a manmade break in the trees, the ground cleared. "I wanted you to see this."

"What is this place?"

"No one could tell me." He waved a hand. "But someone made this. So who took the time to clear it all out, and why? There are no markers. No one has ever been seen up here. No one claims to know anything about the place."

So was this the Gathering Place?

"Is this where the shirt was found?" she asked.

"A little farther." He led her across the middle of the

clearing, where the sun could cut through the trees. It made its descent down the sky, rapidly heading toward sunset.

"If we're out here much longer, it'll go dark."

"Flashlights and headlamps. You'll find out why."

Glancing back at the clearing, Kenna figured it would be nearly pitch-black in the woods, even with the sky full of stars and the moon out. The moonlight would make a spotlight in the center.

"Definitely something, right?"

She turned back to Ron. "You're right."

When she didn't move, he said, "What are you thinking?"

"Trail cams. So we don't have to stake out the place. We can put up cameras to record what goes on when we're not here." Kenna grunted. "But no cell signal means they can't transmit. We'd have to come up regularly and check them." A time-consuming endeavor, for sure.

"Come on. It's getting dark." He tapped her shoulder, and she followed him a short way farther down the trail before he motioned to the bushes. "Over there is where the shirt was found. See that mark in the tree?"

"Looks like a penknife made that."

"I marked the tree a few months later. When things had gotten cold, I wanted to visit the site. Find it easily."

"Good idea." Kenna looked around. "We need—"

Color flashed behind him in the clearing.

"Someone's here." And they had no cell signal.

He spun. "More than one. I count four."

A gunshot cracked off from the clearing. Ron jerked and grunted. "That was close."

Kenna picked her way out of the bushes as fast as she could. "Too close."

"They're coming."

"So we fight. We're armed." She was prepared to make a

stand with both of them in protective vests with multiple weapons. Not ideal, but they could make it work.

"There are four at least. We need cover. We're too exposed." He dragged her off to the side, down the trail. "Come on."

Half a mile back she spotted them running their way. "Okay, go."

Ron started to racewalk. Probably as quick as he could go even being a spry older man. "There's a mine up ahead."

Kenna glanced back. Two had broken off to stay at the clearing, close to where the evidence was found. The other two raced after them up the trail. She needed cover if she was going to start a gunfight. "Get there. Fast."

These two men would be on them quickly if they didn't run to a defensible spot quickly enough. But if they didn't get out of this, Kenna and Ron would disappear like the rest. Eaten by the wild animals of the forest.

Never found.

Ron raced down the path, then took a sharp fork to the right. Kenna stopped behind a tree. She fired off two shots. One hit the first man, catching him in the shoulder. The other fired at her. She squeezed off another two rounds, then turned and ran after Ron.

Up ahead on the trail, he pulled back the boarded-up entrance of a mine and ducked inside.

"They'll know where we went," she said. Not a great plan if those bad guys behind them followed and saw their hiding spot. But at least a place that provided cover.

A gunshot cracked off behind her.

Kenna ducked her head and ran into the mine. She sprinted so fast she slammed into Ron's back. "Whoa. Sorry."

He didn't move. An odd sight in the dark caught her attention. "What's that?"

"Pallets. Debris. But something is under here, and they tried to cover it up."

"Those people left something?" She already knew.

"They left some*one*." Ron touched her elbow and leaned by her. "Looks like another piece of clothing. Is there something in there?"

He was going to make her look? "If I'm doing that, you're guarding the door."

If they didn't get out of here, no one would ever know that they'd found something. Whatever this was, though she figured she already knew. She spun back. "Guard the door."

Ron jerked around, his shotgun ready for duty.

I don't need to do this now. But she needed to know.

Kenna's boots laced halfway up her calves so at least she had that protection from splinters and whatever crawled in the debris. No snakes would be good. "Okay. Let's see."

She picked her way to the material. It didn't take long to see more. "There's a hand. Belongs to a female. It's a body." Before she crouched and pulled back a piece of splintered wood, Kenna knew. "It's Annabelle."

She stood up and turned to face him, the implications rolling through her like subtitles in her mind. They needed to get police up here to collect the body and evidence. Secure the scene. That meant going for help—or far enough they could get a callout and have the police meet them here.

Ron held his gun, but shadowed in the entrance to avoid being seen. "They're coming."

"I was afraid of that." She checked her phone again. No signal. *Think.* Kenna blew out a long breath. "We might be holed up in here all night."

"Or we go deeper in. Take our chances."

She moved to the entrance and looked out. More men stood outside than before. All of them with dark intensity in their expressions. Dressed for these woods. Armed with guns and knives. "Who are these people?"

"See that tattoo, back of their hands?"

Her stomach flipped. How had more appeared so quickly? "Children of the Morning."

"So we take our chances with them, or we take our chances with the mine."

Chapter Seventeen

"Recognize any of them?" Kenna pulled out her phone and thumbed up for the camera. She took a video of all of them, then a bunch of shots of each man individually, zooming in as close up as she could.

Ron said nothing.

She turned to see a determined look on his face. "We need to go deeper in the mine."

If they could defend themselves, they'd have a shot at getting out of this. There was no way to call out, or get help. No one was coming to save them. If they were going to survive, it would be up to her and Ron to make that happen.

And it's all in Your hands, so maybe You could show me how to do this.

But first, she had one more job.

Kenna had to turn on the flash. There was no other way to do this. She snapped two or three photos with her phone of the spot where Annabelle lay, then uncovered the teen. Blood coated her shirt on the front, and she had several entry wounds. With the way the shirt was slit, she figured a knife. She'd been jabbed in the abdomen with a blade over and over.

The shotgun exploded behind her.

Kenna's whole body tensed, and she heard a thump. Someone screamed. She straightened and grabbed Ron's arm. "Go."

He ran with her through the open entry to the mine, carved out like a room. This had been a working gold mine at one point, and they'd likely hung out in this entry to be out of the weather.

Ron stumbled over uneven ground.

Up ahead there looked to be a number of passages to choose from. "Which way?"

She could hear people in pursuit behind them.

Instead of turning and fighting—which would only lead to an ambush that ended their lives—she dragged Ron onward.

He motioned with the shotgun. "Left. There." Why he picked that one, she didn't know, but he was the local.

Kenna hit the mouth of the passage and spun. She fired twice at men racing into the entry.

One fell back. The other sidestepped and hit the wall.

"They're both armed!" The low-toned deadly voice called out from behind the dead gunman. The person in charge? "Pull back!"

It wouldn't be long before they were hunting every inch of this place.

Kenna spun and ran after Ron into the dark of the tunnel. Light or noise would draw attention to their position, so she dragged one hand across the side wall as she went. Dirt coated her fingers. Something sharp scratched her palm.

Kenna ignored it and kept going. She stowed her phone and tugged out a tiny pen flashlight, flicking it on for a second so she could see up ahead.

Ron wasn't there.

She sped up, trying not to go so fast she tripped or ended up slamming into something.

The tunnel turned, and she found Ron farther up. She jogged to catch up. "You're fast."

"There's no cover up here." Ron turned to her. "You should keep going. There's an underground river in here somewhere. You'll be able to hide in some of the crevices hewn out by the water eroding the walls."

"And where will you be?" She glanced back to listen at the passageway but couldn't hear anything. Who knew what those gunmen had they could bring in here. Dogs. Flame throwers. She had a few weapons, but nothing that would enable her to fight back if the threat proved too much.

"I can hold them off. Give you time to get somewhere safe." He barely paused before he kept talking. "This whole system was destroyed when the FBI raided the Children of the Morning. The tunnels used to connect back to the compound, but it all caved in thanks to some explosives."

"Doesn't look caved in to me." She grabbed his elbow and kept moving. The longer they were stationary, the greater the chance they would be found. Kenna spotted an alcove up ahead and scanned her phone light around quickly before shoving him inside and taking cover by the corner. "No one is holding them off. You and I are getting out of here, and this is a good spot to sit tight."

He would want to use that shotgun, which would only draw attention to them.

Kenna was more a fan of the stun gun in her pocket for close contact and keeping the noise to a minimum.

When a dark figure turned the corner the same way they'd come, she held herself still as the man scanned around. He clicked on a flashlight.

She palmed her stun gun. Then only moved enough to

press a hand to Ron's vest and push back. Just so he'd know she had this.

The man neared them.

Kenna waited until he was within reach, forced to step into his flashlight beam to get close enough. She touched the stun gun to his neck and heard the crackle. He let out a surprised mew, and his body jerked with the force of the electricity jolting through him.

He fell to the floor.

"Get his gun."

Kenna used the man's flashlight to show her where his weapon had fallen and grabbed it. "Good idea. We'll need it for evidence." They could run the gun's serial number—if it hadn't been filed off. Get probable cause for the current police chief to take to the judge. A search warrant. Arrests. Game over for these guys.

If they thought they could commit crimes and victimize people all over again, they were in for a rude awakening.

"I was thinking we'll need the bullets to take the rest of them out," Ron said. "I don't have many in my pockets."

"You have a backup?" She hadn't brought her second gun but had a few other weapons—like the stun gun. Thinking about her knife only made her mind revisit Annabelle's body. The manner of her death, and how close up and intentional it was to stab someone.

She'd stared her attacker in the eyes before her last breath.

The last beat of her heart.

Whether she'd been one of them, or acting under duress, didn't matter. A life was a life, and hers had been taken.

"Just the shotgun." He sighed. "I didn't think we'd meet a whole posse of them."

She patted down the guy while Ron spoke. No satphone —which would've been helpful. Not that it would work in here, but it would've gotten something outside when her phone had no bars. "Come on."

He stepped out of the alcove. "You go on. Find somewhere to hole up."

"While you face the threat coming at us?"

She couldn't see well enough to read his expression. And the tone of his whispering voice wasn't much better. Kenna needed light but couldn't risk turning one on just to see the intent in Ron's eyes. "If you're not with them, then you're with me." She didn't give him time to argue. "So let's go."

Was he really determined to take on himself the whole fight? That would only lead to his death. But maybe it was the point, and he wanted to go down in a blaze of glory.

They kept going, making slower progress in the pitch black. Once in a while she flicked on the light. Enough to see if the path ahead of them had curves. The long straight tunnels weren't going to help them if someone came up behind them.

"We need a hiding spot," he said.

What other choice did they have but to wait it out and emerge from the mine later, hopefully when the gunmen were gone?

Disquiet moved through her, like a discordant note in her mind. Worry.

"You're not taking up the fight for us," she said.

"I'm not gonna let you die."

"Whatever happens, it happens to both of us. Because we're staying together." She would live, and so would he.

If God wanted that to be the outcome, then it would happen.

Because what was the point of their tragic deaths? This was a problem that needed to be solved. A threat that needed to be eliminated. If she was put on this earth to fight injustice, then why would she be tragically killed in the middle of a case? That would only be senseless.

The problem?

Senseless tragedy happened every day in the world. Children died. The innocent were victimized. Loss and destruction ensued.

Whether hedging her bets with what she could accomplish or trusting God to secure the outcome—both were two sides of a coin. There was no guarantee either way.

"I've lived long enough, Kenna."

"You're not fighting them. You'll die."

"I'll save your life. I'll repay a debt I owe to Max Banbury."

Her skin flashed with cold, even while sweat ran down between her shoulder blades. Exertion met the chill of being underground. Cold dirt walls. Cool air. "You're not dying. You're going to tell me the story of how he saved your life."

And that was final.

She dragged him on, around a corner where they found another stretch of tunnel. "I thought you said the tunnels were caved in?"

"They've been dug out." Ron grabbed the light from her and shined it around. "Recently, by the look of it."

"And they'll lead us to the compound?"

"Eventually."

They were miles from that part of town. "I'm game, if you are. I could use a walk to burn off the adrenaline."

Someone yelled in the tunnel behind them.

"They found their friend."

"Figures." Kenna nodded. "Come on."

They rounded another corner, and she heard water. Boots pounded behind them. Kenna tugged Ron behind her and lifted her gun. She waited until the echo of people running down the tunnel toward them grew louder.

She flicked on the flashlight and shined it down the tunnel right at them. Her arms were getting tired, which made the old aches and pains wake up instead. She squeezed the trigger of her pistol, her gun hand braced on the flashlight.

She watched the first man fall, a bloom of blood on his shirt front.

A gun went off, flashing light down the hall.

White dots danced in front of her. She kept squeezing off measured shots. One of them jerked in retreat and plastered his back against the wall. She shifted her aim and killed him before he could fire at her.

Kenna's gun clicked empty.

"I got this," Ron said.

She turned and slammed a hand in his chest. "No. Go."

No way was she going to lose him as well. She let him be behind her, since he had the gun with bullets in it—he'd reloaded—but ensured he kept pace with her. She shined the flashlight up ahead, and they sprinted for safety.

"Down!" He grabbed her.

They tumbled to the dirt as gunshots erupted over their heads.

The sound rang in her ears, eclipsing everything else. She covered her head with her hands. Dirt rained down from the walls around them. The earth rumbled all around.

That discordant note grew louder.

"Run." She scrambled up and hauled him with her. "Now!"

They raced down the hallway while the earth rumbled and gunshots cracked off like fireworks. A bullet hit the wall beside her head, spraying dirt in her face.

Ron grunted. When he didn't slow, she didn't either.

Kenna's flashlight lit on a doorway, an iron gate blocking the passage.

God, this is on You.

She raced toward it with the full knowledge that she had no control over whether they could get through or not.

If the gate was locked, they would die down here.

Kenna turned at the last second and slammed her shoulder into it. The gate flung open and she stumbled through, Ron right behind her. She landed on a set of concrete steps. Hands to the cold stone.

Kenna caught herself before she got injured and started to rise. "Go."

"Yeah, with you." Ron grabbed the gate and shoved it closed again.

She released the magazine from her gun and reached around him to wedge it between the gate and the frame.

"That won't hold for long," he said.

"Neither will you." She spun him to the stairs. "Go."

"Anyone ever tell you that you're pushy?"

"Yeah, and they were alive to say it."

After climbing at least three flights of stairs, they reached the top, breathing hard. Fatigue landed on Kenna's shoulders, hard.

At the top was another door, this one solid.

"Could be anything behind there," he said. "Or anyone."

She had enough light to see the look on his face and agreed with the sentiment. This could be a worse idea than fighting back. "Let's go."

"Me first."

Before she could argue, he pulled the door open and stepped through with his shotgun—which was probably a good idea anyway, since she was out of bullets. The best she could do was throw her pistol, before she got out her knife or the stun gun, which was...

She patted her pockets. "I dropped it."

"Looks clear."

Kenna moved through the door and slammed it shut. "They're at the gate." Her phone started to vibrate in her pocket, but she ignored it and looked around. "This is the main building." It looked like the hallways she'd walked through. Maybe a lower level, as there were no windows. One open door revealed rows of cots. Bunk rooms.

He strode past her. "Let's find the exit."

Kenna pulled a knife just in case she had to defend herself, and they found the stairs up. She swung her flashlight around as they moved, making sure no one lurked in the corners. "We need a ride back to town."

The ground floor hallway looked empty.

"They'll know we came out here," she added.

Ron glanced at her. "You're getting out of this."

"And so are you." Her phone stopped vibrating, then started up again immediately. Anyone who came here to pick them up would take time to get here.

"So I guess when it comes to it—"

A man turned the corner at the end of the hall and fired at them.

Ron's body jerked and started to fall. She grabbed the shotgun from him and fired at the man, then raced over to grab his pistol and check none of his friends were lurking. She didn't want to look back and see Ron's lifeless eyes, but she had to know.

Kenna turned.

Ron leaned against the wall, one hand on his vest. Breathing hard.

"You're good."

He nodded. "Forgot how much that hurts."

"You're not dying today. Not if I have anything to say about it."

Ron said, "Fine, I yield," then lifted his other hand, palm to her. "But I don't want to walk from here, so we need reinforcements."

Red and blue lights flashed on the other side of the windows.

Kenna strode to him and got under his shoulder so she could help him walk. "Looks like you got your wish."

Whoever was here had saved their lives.

But this was far from over.

Chapter Eighteen

"I'm alive," Ron grunted, lowering his T-shirt back to his waist. "Satisfied?"

Kenna stared at him. She hadn't been amused and wasn't now, faced with his smirk. "Are you?" she asked him. "Seemed for a while down there that you were looking to die."

Kenna had wanted to say that for an hour, through the ambulance ride, where they'd knocked him out with pain meds or during his examination. One of the nurses had cleaned the graze on Kenna's cheek.

Now it was after two in the morning.

Instead of lying down, he sat on the side of the bed, chatting with the doctor on call. Like they'd been friends for years. Long enough the doctor had taken one look at Ron, tipped his head to the side, and asked, "What hit you this time?"

She blew out a long breath.

"I've gotten a new lease on life."

She folded her arms.

"Come on. This is the most alive I've felt in years."

Kenna unfolded her arms and went to the door, pretty sure someone muttered, "Party pooper" behind her. She pulled the door open and found a uniformed officer on the door. "We're ready to leave."

He shook his head. "No can do. The chief is on his way. He wants you to sit tight." He tugged the door closed, leaving her inside with Ron.

She turned. "What was that about?"

"Who knows."

Kenna didn't have time for this, but she also knew a lot of her frustration was down to how tired she was—and the fact she would be on Elijah detail all day tomorrow. She pulled out her phone again, but the low battery kept her from using it much. She had it on mega low power-saving mode, but wanted to call Maizie back.

The girl was likely as worried as she had been when Kenna finally texted her back—with three missed calls from her—and got a flurry of replies. She needed to get it plugged in and check her voicemail. Call Maizie back.

Kenna doubted the teen had gone to sleep.

The door swung open. A uniformed officer with chief bars on his collar strode in, a jacket over his shirt. Slacks and shined dress shoes. "You good, Ron?"

"Yeah, Derek." But the older former chief looked like he needed to sleep for two days and she'd seen the purple bruise on his chest. Kenna was honestly surprised it hadn't sent him barreling toward a heart attack.

The doctor who ordered a chest X-ray said there were no cracks or breaks in his ribs or damage to his sternum, which was a miracle as far as she was concerned.

Clearly, God had come through for them. Kenna didn't need to test Him to see if He would pitch in and help. She'd prayed and the gate opened, something she filed in that column in her mind.

Ron motioned to her. "This is—"

She cut him off, striding forward and holding out her hand. "Clara Shearson. I'm a private investigator."

"Chief Derek Hutton. You're the one who got the Underwood couple to confess?" The chief shook her hand, his grip soft and gentle in a way that didn't inspire confidence in her. She hoped it wasn't indicative of the rest of his style.

She gave a tight dip of her head. "I got enough for the state police to do their job. So they can find Peter. And bring charges."

"And now Annabelle as well?"

Ron didn't say anything about her assumed name, though she figured she would have to explain later—if he didn't already know.

"I didn't think we'd find her," Kenna said. "The goal was to look at the place where William Farmington's shirt was found."

"Planning on closing all my cold cases?" Chief Hutton lifted his dark brows.

"If possible...yes, that would be the goal." She studied him. Late thirties, maybe forties. His features likely had something Italian or Spanish mixed in that gave him streaks of dark hair with his silver trend.

He studied her with brown eyes, stubble on his jaw. Put together well even though it was late and she knew he'd been at the scene. "And leave me with all the paperwork, is that it?"

And all the credit. "I'm sorry, it'll be a busy couple of days for you with all the scenes that need to be processed." Kenna paused. "Between Annabelle and all the others in the tunnels."

"Shame you don't do freelance evidence collection." Chief Hutton scratched his jaw.

"I don't have the patience for it." She smiled. "Plus, I can hardly process the scenes, since I killed a number of the victims up there. In self-defense, of course."

"I can verify that," Ron said. "All of those were good kills. Justified."

"Except Annabelle." Kenna could picture the girl's body in her mind. "She was murdered by these people. But even that would mean a serious conflict of interest if I'm the one collecting evidence. I was the last person to talk to her before she disappeared, and the only one to give a statement that she tried to kidnap Elijah Thomson."

Now that they knew for sure the compound connected to the mine, through those tunnels that had been freshly dug out, she figured that was how Annabelle had disappeared. The night the teen went missing, they'd searched all over but hadn't found that door to the stairs Kenna and Ron had taken out of the mine.

The question was, how far did that maze of tunnels stretch? There could be an entire community down there for all they knew. A place the Children of the Morning could hide out for years.

She needed to find out who in town would know how far the warren of passageways stretched and pick their brain. Either that clearing had been the location mentioned in the invitation, or it was somewhere else. A place she wasn't going to find without help.

There was someone she could talk to who might have an idea what Annabelle had been involved in.

"No kidding, Ms. Shearson." Chief Hutton huffed. "It's going to be a long week."

At least he wouldn't be left with a stack of open cases. She could close those with a statement, corroborated by Ron. The physical evidence would agree.

What would there be to contest, if the chief was even so inclined? It seemed like he'd be happy with open-and-shut.

She didn't think he was a bad leader, but the fact he'd inherited this mess that had started up again was probably the last thing he wanted. And it was late. There might even be some bad blood between him and Ron, in a way this chief thought the former one was now meddling in duties he was supposed to have retired from years ago.

Kenna needed to offer him a consolation. "I can help you with some of it, at least. I took photos and video on my phone, which I can forward to your email when I have some battery life. That should help with figuring out what all went on up there, but the bottom line is clear." She glanced at Ron.

He gave her a slight nod. "The Children of the Morning are back."

"I thought you took care of that, Ron?" Chief Hutton made a face, the intention to deflect back on the former chief clear. Or her, if that would work. "Took them all down, made a name for yourself as the big hero who worked with the FBI."

Kenna realized then that the second he found out who she really was, Chief Hutton would turn her in to the FBI. He would probably arrest her like she was evading capture and keep her in a holding cell so he could present her to the FBI agents that showed up to get her—and hopefully get a medal in the process.

But if he did that, was he going to personally see the Children of the Morning taken down? She figured she could persuade him to let the secret ride until she rooted them all out. Then he'd get double credit—one for taking down the next generation of a dangerous cult, and the second for being the one who found her.

"Apparently we didn't get the root of it. They chased us through the tunnels." Ron stood, though age and injury diminished his presence. "And with the video we can identify them and start making arrests." He glanced at her. "You still have that pistol?"

"One of the officers at the compound divested me of the weapon and bagged it as evidence." She folded her arms. "Good thing, since it might provide leads." She and Ron had talked over this exact thing.

"Right. I'll get ATF on the horn, and we'll end up with a swarm of feds on our hands." Hutton shook his head. "You think I want them tromping around this town? The bad guys will go underground and we'll never find them."

Ron nodded. "Better to get Helson PD on the case."

"Except thanks to the two of you, they're going to be collecting evidence up at the mine for days. Spending hours walking back and forth to their vehicles. Then autopsies have to be done, and I've got to loop the county prosecutor in on everything."

Kenna said, "What do you propose?"

"The two of you have done a decent job of erupting trouble in select pockets around town." The chief lifted his chin. "Why not keep working it? See what else you can come up with and keep me in the loop."

She'd rather be following Ben when she wasn't protecting Elijah. If he knew who the Children of the Morning were in this decade, then Ben could provide her leads. Provided she managed to persuade him it was in his best interest to talk.

Ron looked at her, a question in his expression.

Kenna shrugged her shoulders. "I don't want them running around any more than either of you do. I just have no personal stake in the future of this town."

Hutton eyed her, like he had more questions. They were all far too tired for that.

"Ron and I need a ride back to where we parked the car so

we can get some sleep and hit this fresh tomorrow," she said. "I'll make sure you get a copy of all the photos and videos I took."

Hutton nodded. "Very good."

"I have a final question, though." When he lifted his chin, indicating she should ask, she said, "Is there the slightest possibility anyone in your department could be sympathetic to the group, or even part of it? We need to know who we can trust and who we should be wary of."

Hutton glanced at Ron.

Kenna said, "What?"

"I'd have pointed to *you*, up until you asked that question," Hutton said. "But I can vouch for every single one of them."

Kenna dipped her head. "Very well."

Ron glanced at her. "You have reason to suspect there's a leak in the department?"

"No one is infallible. I just want to gauge the threat level."

He studied her.

"Right." Hutton clapped his hands together, making her jump a little. "I'll get the officer to drive you. He'll need to know where the area is anyway."

"Tell all your people to be careful, Chief." Ron held out his hand and they shook. "Those woods were crawling with armed suspects."

Half an hour later, the uniformed officer who'd been on the door opened the back of the patrol car. Ron had ridden up front, and the two made small talk while Kenna resisted the temptation to use her phone, which would only kill it.

"Thanks." She strode toward Ron. "Come on. I'll drive

you to your car and then make sure you get to your house okay."

He glanced at the officer, then nodded.

They gave the officer and the second one, who rolled up behind them in another black-and-white car, an indication of where they'd gone. The clearing, and the mine entrance.

Ron said, "Be careful."

Kenna added, "He isn't understating the threat. Please, take care."

They dispersed to their cars, leaving the officers to it.

Kenna plugged her phone in right away and called Maizie's number before she even pulled out after Ron.

"Finally! Are you all right?"

Kenna smiled, both hands on the wheel as they headed back toward town. "I've got a tiny cut on my cheek, but a nurse cleaned it." She figured Maizie either knew already because she'd hacked the police database or the medical center one—or both—but still wanted to tell the girl herself. "The cops are taking over the scene, and I'm headed home. So I can sleep."

"Okay. There's a message on your phone from Ben Landry. I can't listen. I can just see that he called, and then a voicemail popped up after you didn't answer."

"How long ago did he call?"

"While you had no signal," Maizie said.

Kenna heard the distress in her voice. "I wasn't alone. I got out, and I'm fine." She didn't like the fear Maizie felt, but the fact someone cared enough to worry wasn't lost on Kenna. It was nice to be worried over by someone with a good heart. "I'll listen to the message when I'm home."

"I've catalogued everything I can get from the video and the photos you took. They uploaded as soon as you got signal, and you popped up in the compound."

Kenna frowned. "It was you who sent the police?" She'd figured as much but didn't know how the teen could've ascertained they would show up there.

"I got into a website that is all about those gold mines. They had a plan for the one closest to your car. I figured it was fifty-fifty between the mountain and the compound, so I asked state police to respond there while I had the locals go to the compound."

"Did they?"

"The state police had a crash up the freeway, so I think they didn't have the personnel to respond, but the Helson PD sent a car to the compound just in case."

"You probably saved my life and Ron Arnold's."

"That's who you were with?" Maizie asked.

Kenna slowed as Ron pulled into his driveway. He got out and waved at her, so Kenna waved back and continued on to the vacation rental. "The former chief, yeah. Why?"

"The undercover agent the PD sent in?" Maizie paused. "It was a local cop, an officer at the time. He was one of them. A member. Ron Arnold was one of the Children of the Morning."

Chapter Nineteen

Kenna knocked on the door to Jordan's hospital room. It might be a long shot, but she needed information about Annabelle. Her mind had spun all morning while she drank coffee in the car on the way to pick up Elijah for school, and all the way here.

Ron had been the undercover sent into the Children of the Morning because the former chief—an officer at the time—had been one of them. A registered member of the church. Apparently, they'd persuaded him to turn on his brethren. That, or he never had. He'd simply facilitated the feds in their work and never given up his beliefs.

Which meant he remained one of them.

But would they really have shot at him if he was? As far as she could see, there were three options. One, he'd told the truth about wanting answers. Two and three involved a double cross and a triple cross.

"Come in."

Kenna sighed and opened the door.

Jordan, the kid she and Thomson had recovered from the basement of the barn, sat up in his hospital bed.

"You look well." She smiled. "Lot better than the last time I saw you."

He studied her for a second, then it clicked. "You. From the compound."

"That's right." She left the door open since there wasn't a parent or guardian here, and she didn't exactly have permission to talk to him. Most seventeen-year-olds she met didn't need mom's permission to talk to someone—nor did they want to have to ask for it. "If it's all right with you, I'd like to ask you about Annabelle. I'm a private investigator."

Jordan scrunched up his nose for a second, his gaze on the blanket up to his waist. "I heard they found her body."

Kenna explained about the mine, and the gunmen, but didn't give too much graphic detail. "You might be able to help me fill in some of the gaps. Even if you don't think it means anything, it could help."

This young man was a far cry from the football captain she'd met in the compound, but she figured he'd bounce back in front of his friends. He'd have to prove his strength, and that meant saving face even if what happened put a crimp in the fall season.

She glanced at the window, covered with tall sheer drapes. The curtains hung either side of the window so light streamed in. Elijah would be all right at school, and the police had a detail in the building just in case. No one was prepared to take any chances even if the chief wasn't convinced the near kidnapping had anything to do with it.

Jordan shrugged one shoulder. "What do you wanna know?"

"You and Annabelle were friends, right?" Enough they'd gone together to the compound. "What did she tell you that she wouldn't have told her parents?"

"You want me to spill all her secrets? She's dead." He

looked up, tears in his eyes until he sniffed and blinked them away.

"You were close?" She'd pegged him as a self-absorbed teen football star, but evidently there was a heart in there. "I'm sorry for your loss. Since I didn't say that before."

He did that nose-scrunch thing again. Like he didn't think he needed pity—as if that's what condolences were.

"I know she didn't like being in a small town all that much." Kenna had spoken with Annabelle a little about being new here.

"I don't think joining that group helped."

Kenna frowned. "The cheerleading squad?"

He shook his head. "Her friends met at night. She snuck out. Apparently, they found her because she's one of them? She told me she was adopted and they were her real family." He sniffed. "She's the whole reason her family moved here. Not because of her dad's job or anything else. She wanted to be near the group."

"Do you know who they are, her family?"

He shook his head. "She wanted me to join, I think. Like we could be together if we were part of the group." He lifted one hand and waved. "I have enough going on in my life, between school, football, and work. I don't need religion or whatever it is."

"Good call." Kenna wasn't sure "religion" was what the group was about. At least, not in any good way that made its members better. "Do you know who any of the other people in the group were? Did you ever meet anyone?"

"She was new. It didn't get that far." He sighed. "But she said they had something big going on. Some plan."

"Any idea what it was?"

He shook his head.

"You've lived in this town your whole life, right?" When

he nodded, Kenna said, "What can you tell me about the Children of the Morning?"

"That's who they are?" Jordan gaped.

"I'm not sure yet. But it's looking likely." And people in town seemed disinclined to even mention them. But was that a trauma reaction type of avoidance or ignoring the elephant on Main Street?

Jordan blew out a breath. "Everyone knows someone who was part of them. My dad was a kid, but his best friend at school lived at the compound. He told my dad all kind of crazy stories, and my dad told me. Those people were sick and twisted."

"Sometimes when the government comes in and shuts down a group, folks don't think that's a good thing. That the authorities should leave people be."

Jordan shook his head. "No one could do anything about them. My dad says if they hadn't been shut down, they'd have taken over the whole town eventually. Killed everyone, or made them a member."

"Then it was a good thing."

"They should've burned down that compound with everyone in it." Jordan's jaw flexed.

"Sometimes it feels like that's the answer, but if there's even one innocent person inside, then—"

He cut her off. "None of them were innocent."

"Did they do something to you...or your family?" Kenna asked gently. "You don't have to tell me if you don't want to talk about it."

He shrugged one shoulder, a hard look on his face. "My dad told me what they did to my mom. He said we don't treat women like that. *Ever.*"

Kenna figured that said enough. "I'm glad she's safe with you and your dad."

"She is."

"Did you try and rescue Annabelle the same way?" she asked. Maybe their friendship—or relationship—had been more like dating someone with the intent of fixing their worldview.

"She wouldn't listen. She wanted me to believe like she did."

"What did she believe in?"

Jordan huffed out a breath through his nose. "All that New Earth crap. Like the true believers will inherit the lands, or whatever. I need a football scholarship so I can get out of this crazy town. Religion isn't gonna get me that."

Kenna wanted to smile. She had to rub her thumb on the corner of her mouth to cover what crept through. "Jordan, I hope you feel better real soon. I'll be rooting for your senior season." She held her hand out.

He shook like the almost adult he was. "Thanks."

She headed out, then called Maizie on her phone as she walked to her car, putting her earbuds in as she went.

"Hi." Maizie didn't say more than that.

"Do you need me to translate teenage boy?"

The girl only sighed, loud enough it was audible through the phone line. "You're probably sick of explaining what's normal and what isn't."

"A lot of body language comes into it." Kenna checked both ways and crossed the lane between the curb in front of the hospital and the parking lot. "So if you can't see that or his facial expression, then you aren't going to get a good read on what he wasn't saying."

"Even if I see that, I won't know what it means." The girl had been sheltered for years—and not in any good ways. She'd grown up with a captor and a warped world full of pain and terror. Whatever instincts she had were honed through that.

"It's like learning a new language. It takes time even immersed in the culture you're trying to get to know."

"Ugh."

Kenna chuckled. "Seems like you're learning just fine."

"It's annoying. I'm frustrated. I want to understand, but it's taking too long."

Kenna slid into the driver's seat of her car, smiling to herself. "Now you know how I feel about people who *choose* to live in a suburb. All that manicured grass and HOA fees. *Why?* It baffles me that anyone would actually want that for their lives when instead they could have open spaces and the freedom to go wherever they want."

She heard Maizie chuckle a little. "Fine. I'm not a freak."

"Or you are and so am I, but we should just own it."

"And if I don't want to be a freak?"

Kenna drove toward the school. "Maybe everyone is in their own way, and people just hide it better than we do." She didn't want the girl to feel bad, though, so she added, "You'll get there."

"I'll get there faster out with you, seeing what you do and learning on the job."

Kenna winced. "Maybe when the heat dies down."

"The sitcom I'm watching, the girl says her mom only says maybe when she means no."

She didn't need to point out that she wasn't Maizie's mother. "Maybe just means maybe. Like 'not right now.' Or 'perhaps.'"

"So, no."

"You know why it isn't a good idea." Even if Maizie felt trapped the way she'd been living with her captor. They gave her freedom in healthy ways, and it would take years to work through everything. "Whatever we do decide isn't going to be perfect—because things never are."

"They could be not perfect with you, instead of here."

"I would be distracted making sure you're okay. It would split my focus." Kenna paused. "What's wrong with Colorado?"

Quiet filled the line.

Finally, Maizie said, "Nothing. I'm doing the work."

"It's always easier to do nothing than it is to do the work." Inertia crept in. Excuses were formed. Avoiding change altogether certainly proved easier—but if Kenna was going to figure out what she believed, then she had to tackle the problem of whether to hand over everything to a God who didn't seem all that involved.

She needed to find Him. See for herself what He was up to.

Otherwise she would always wish she had. And Kenna didn't like regret.

"When you wrap up that case, are you going to come back here?" Maizie asked.

"If you want me to." Kenna figured she could swing that drive, on the way to her next case. Then again, she also wanted to head for DC so she could see Jax and they could talk more than just over text. In a couple of weeks, the investigation into Michael Rushman would be over. Until then she had plenty to do.

"I gotta go," Maizie said. "Elizabeth is waiting for me."

"Call me later."

The teen hung up. Kenna stowed her earbuds since Maizie would be in a session with Elizabeth. Kenna found a space in the back corner of the school parking lot. The pickup lane was filled with idling cars and SUVs, alongside the line packed with school buses. The quiet before the eruption at the end of the school day.

She remembered that mad scramble to get out, even if

she'd only been to school for a short time. In a way, she'd felt a lot like Maizie did now when she'd gone to high school senior year. Like she'd stepped into a place where she didn't know the language. Customs were foreign to her. People assumed she knew what things were, but she had no frame of reference.

Kenna had winged it until she assimilated. Maizie needed a more measured approach, given her history and the tenuous grip on safety she had.

Maybe You could help with that. Keep her mind safe.

They could all do everything they could to ensure Maizie remained physically safe, but the real battle would be in her mind.

The bell rang as she walked to the front doors, so Kenna hung back as kids poured out headed for buses lined up at the curb. In a few days, or a week, Jordan would be back here. Then he'd be back to football. Life would move on, but the infection that was the Children of the Morning would continue to fester beneath the surface. Like a hidden illness, or a disease with few visible symptoms.

"Hi."

Kenna looked down and found the girl from Elijah's class in front of her. "Hi back."

"I heard you killed Annabelle." She gripped her binder to her front, her chin set and one hip cocked.

"Rachel, get to your bus." The teacher from Elijah's class shook her head. "I'm sorry about that."

"No worries." She stuck her hand out and remembered to say, "Clara Shearson" at the last second. She and the principal had hung back by the door in the classroom, but she wanted to meet the teacher.

"Jolene Denhill." The woman had a marshmallow hand-shake. Soft-spoken like the church choir member who hid in the back row and didn't talk to anyone. "Elijah should be right out. The officer was walking him to his locker."

"Thank you, Ms. Denhill. I appreciate the help keeping him safe."

Jolene brushed back some flat hair that was a lifeless brown color. "I can't believe he's a target. Such a sweet boy, in his way, and so brilliant. He leaves me behind sometimes."

"Yeah, he's pretty great." Kenna had no idea what to say. Like Maizie and other teens, Kenna had no frame of reference for kids except Ryson and Valentina's baby. And she didn't see Luci much. "I'll make sure he's safe. Then one day he'll be leaving his college professors in the dust and making waves on campus with his brilliance."

"I'm sure he will." Jolene smiled before her attention zeroed on something. "Excuse me." She strode away, calling out, "Eleanor, put that down!"

Kenna watched the doors and the crowd, noting the moment when Elijah emerged from the building followed by a uniformed officer. She lifted her fingers, and the kid walked to her.

"Dairy Queen."

"Not today, buddy. Sorry to say we're just headed home this afternoon. No stops." She glanced at the officer. "All good?"

"Yep." He nodded.

"I appreciate it, thanks." She noted his name pinned to his chest, then waved Elijah toward the car. "Let's go."

Kenna kept her hand close to her weapon as she walked, refusing to allow anyone to kidnap this kid. Whatever big plan Annabelle had told Jordan was in the works, it wasn't going to involve Elijah Thomson.

Not if she could do anything about it.

She might not be able to rid Maizie of her frustration, or

tell what Ron wasn't saying and why he might be keeping things to himself, but this? She could do this. She could continue working cold cases and hopefully find William Farmington Junior, make sure no one else got hurt because of the Children of the Morning.

Work the case.

Let the rest take care of itself.

Chapter Twenty

Kenna banged her fist on the door of Ron Arnold's home. Eventually, it swung open, and she saw him rear back realizing it was her on his doorstep. Kenna pushed the door wide and stepped in. "I have a question."

He touched the front of his T-shirt. Sweatpants. Slippers. This was an older man dressed for a night at home in front of the TV. Not a guy in deep with a religious group that only victimized people. "I did a web search on you," he said, his slippers whispering on the floor into the living room, where he eased down into a recliner. "I know why you're Clara, not Kenna."

So he planned to flip this around on her and not let her ask her question? She leaned against the wall at the entry to his living room. She'd been in the kitchen the other day but not in here.

The couch had seen better days, but it was clean. On the wall he'd hung a framed painting of mountains and horses. Pictures of his kids and grandkids on the end table by a lamp with tassels reflected the outline of a horse on the far wall. The TV was on a news program but with the sound turned down and the remote on the arm of his chair beside a dry whiskey glass.

She could admit she wanted to sit by him and fall asleep on the couch, but she wanted to have this conversation before she went home to do that. Thomson had come home to relieve her with no news about the search for the people whose images she'd taken. They'd ID'd a couple but hadn't located them, and the ME hadn't determined cause of death for Annabelle yet.

Instead of updating him on that or the investigation into who Annabelle really was, she said, "The current chief will find out soon enough who I really am. There's no need to extort me."

His chest jerked with a laugh, which made him groan and touch the front of his shirt.

"But you do need to tell me why you neglected to mention *you* were the undercover my dad sent in."

His laughing quit. "He didn't send me. I volunteered."

"And it wasn't worth mentioning?" She shot him a look. "It's not even in the FBI case file. The name of the undercover isn't Ron Arnold, local police officer."

Whichever way she looked at it, the whole thing smelled like some kind of cover-up. But why would it be necessary to keep the information under wraps? Taking down the Children of the Morning had been a success—a good thing for the community.

"They used my member name for the official record. I didn't want Ron Arnold in the file, or it would link back to my personnel file at the PD. When I rose up the ranks, I didn't want that to be a help, or a something that held me back." He leaned his head back against the cushion. "I don't owe you an explanation for my choices, or why I didn't tell you."

"But you're going to give me one anyway."

"I took a week of vacation time, met with your dad, and went in. No one I worked with was aware of my assignment except my chief." His fingers flexed on the arm of the chair, shifting the tendons in his arm. "I knew what you would think, even if I explained it to you."

"Because it's suspect. Unless you tell me why it was so important that it was you who did the job and no one else."

"It made sense," he said, "and I wanted it done."

And he'd considered it to be over. "You were already embedded in the Children of the Morning as a member. I get why it made sense it was you since they already trusted you. Didn't you tell me before that you were the one who called the feds?"

"I didn't like where it was going." He said it like his ice cream place discontinued his favorite flavor. "So I put a stop to it."

"And you think I'll believe you're sympathetic to them?"

"I don't know," he said. "Do you?"

"I haven't been part of it since I turned on them. Do you know how many death threats I got from guys in prison? They knew it was me, and they weren't going to let it rest." He sighed. "But we managed to keep it from the media."

"Which is a small miracle given your involvement, and your career."

He shrugged his shoulder. "My brother-in-law was the chief at the paper. We came to an arrangement."

"So it was a cover-up."

"Your father understood the risk I took. He didn't want me to destroy my career just for the sake of doing the right thing."

She tried not to feel the pang of grief over never getting to know her father as an adult—or a fed. Even if it was good for her to remember that he'd been a good man. A solid agent.

Someone she wouldn't be able to talk to, or see, for the rest of her life.

Anything new for her to learn about her father would come from men like Ron Arnold who had known him before his death.

"The chief cut me out." He looked in his empty glass and sighed. "Any updates?"

"How is your chest?"

He waved his hand.

"Annabelle's cause of death hasn't been determined." Even though Kenna had clearly seen she'd suffered multiple stab wounds. "And none of the Children of the Morning's current members have been brought in. Yet. But I spoke with Annabelle's friend earlier, the one who got injured at the compound. They're planning something big."

She wanted to go back up to that clearing and plant some trail cams. Except with the police all over the mountain now, going back and forth to the mine, the Children of the Morning weren't likely to use that spot.

"Big like what?" he said.

She shook her head. "He didn't know."

"So who does?"

Ben Landry was a solid possibility if she could convince him to be their "in" with the group. He'd come up here, and it might not be just because he was packing up his parents' house. As one of the survivors, the invitation had called him to assemble for something.

Would tonight be the night he went out at midnight, or had they missed the event because he was determined to avoid it?

She tugged out her phone and saw a couple of missed calls. She thumbed a return call and put the phone to her ear.

"Hey," Maizie said. Her voice sounded hoarse. Before

Kenna could ask her about it, the teen said, "Movement on the camera you have on Ben's house."

She turned to the hallway. "Where is he going?"

"He didn't leave. Four guys showed up."

"Got it. I'll head over there." She strode to the front door. Ron said, "What is it?"

Kenna glanced back. "Could be trouble."

He kicked off his shoes and grabbed a duffel from his hall closet. "I packed for another adventure. Just in case."

She didn't figure he meant a change of clothes. "Did you get a new vest?"

"No, but I charged my stun guns." His eyebrows rose.

Kenna shook her head, not sure what to say all the way to the car. Ron rode in her passenger seat. "So who is this guy?"

"Ben Landry."

"Never heard of him."

"Con man. Multiple IDs. Ties to the Children of the Morning, but he said he wanted nothing to do with them. He's just here to pack up and sell his parents' house." She pulled outside the single level, not stopping a few doors down or wasting time with recon. These people might've already killed one person, and Ben could be in real danger now. "Could be multiple assailants."

"Let's try and grab one. Ask some questions." Ron pushed out the passenger door, they both geared up because she kept an extra vest, and then they headed for the house.

Kenna jogged past the older man and reached the front door first.

She heard a cry from inside, from someone—likely male—in pain and distress. Kenna adjusted her stance, then she kicked the door in.

Gun first. Stun gun in her other hand.

A man stuck his head into view down the hall. Not Ben.

Kenna got within range and fired the stun gun.

He collapsed to the floor, jerking.

"What the...," she said. "Go. Go."

A thunder of feet moved away from her through the house. She reached the guy twitching on the floor and stepped over him.

Ben had been tied to a kitchen chair, hands behind his back. Blood dripped from his mouth, his shirt smeared with it. Sweat dampening everything.

She crouched beside him and checked for a pulse. The back door stood open.

"They ran?"

She glanced at Ron, standing over the twitching guy. "Yes."

"Darn."

She felt the side of Ben's neck for his pulse. "He's alive, but he needs a hospital."

"Take him." Ron motioned to the downed man. "I'm gonna talk to this guy. See what he can tell me."

Something about his tone had her straightening. "I'm not leaving you to that."

"Aww, sweet of you." They both knew her not leaving him was more about not leaving the guy alone with a man determined to get answers than over concern for him. But it could be both.

"I'll get a pickup." She tugged out her phone as Ben started to moan. Kenna cut him free with a steak knife, and the plastic ties fell to the floor. She caught his shoulder as the phone connected.

"Detective Thomson."

She hoped this was the right call, but Maizie would draw more attention to herself with an anonymous tip. "I've got an injured man here. I need a pickup, someone who can deliver him to the hospital."

"Did you hurt him?" he asked amid shuffling on his end, then some muffled talking.

Kenna explained finding him, and the man on the floor, now unconscious, who they needed to talk to.

"I get the questioning."

"No can do." Kenna shook her head even though Thomson couldn't see her. "You need to be above reproach on this. Ron and I don't have careers to protect, just innocent people."

And if the case her dad had thought closed was still open, she wasn't sitting around trying to figure it out.

Now was the time to turn the tables on these people.

"Fine." Detective Thomson hung up, and Kenna texted the address to him, as he asked, so he'd know where to be.

Ron motioned. "Wanna help me get this guy up?"

Kenna was still keeping Ben from sliding over onto the floor. She also couldn't lift a man with the strength of her arms. Just as Ron probably couldn't with the massive bruise on his sternum. Ben had clearly been punched a few times, but as long as there was nothing internal going on, he would likely be just mad but fine in the end.

Kenna shrugged like there was nothing she could do to leave Ben and come help him. "You're on your own."

Ron stowed whatever weapon had been in his hand, then flipped the man to his front. He grabbed plastic ties from the table, probably discarded after they weren't needed for Ben, and secured the man's hands. Then he rolled him to his side and splashed a cup of sink water on his face.

Ben lifted his hand and grabbed her elbow.

"Easy. It's me." She touched his other shoulder and waited while he blinked awake. "Easy. Help is coming."

He eased out a breath between his lips, now split and swollen.

Ron had to do the cup-of-sink-water thing again. The second time the man came awake, sputtering and yelling. Ron stepped one foot on his chest and held him down. "Don't even think about it. My friend and I aren't cops."

Ben shifted in the seat, and she let go of bracing him.

Kenna said, "Good?"

He managed to nod.

"There's someone coming to get you to the hospital," she said. He eyed her, but she continued, "Are they Children of the Morning?"

"Yes." He touched a hand gingerly to his cheek. "They don't like my lack of commitment." His gaze glared daggers at the man on the ground. "I don't know any of them, so don't ask me who this guy is."

"Easy enough to find out." Ron knelt by the man and patted his pockets. "No wallet, but I've got a phone."

"Good," Kenna said. "Hang on to it."

Ron pocketed the phone.

Down the hall someone called out, "Just me!" Then Detective Thomson strode into view.

"I figured you'd call in a favor," she told him.

"The favor is at the house watching Bianca and Elijah," Thomson said. "There's a veteran lives next door, but he can't get off work when I'm on shift."

"You had another option?" She raised an eyebrow. "I'm insulted I was your backup plan."

"At this rate, you might be the entire plan." Thomson moved around Ron and the man on the floor, muttering, "Not gonna ask." He helped Ben to his feet. "Let's get you looked at and take a statement about how you fought off your attacker."

"There were four," Kenna called after him.

Thomson waved a hand.

Ron grinned. "I always liked that kid. Friend of yours?"

"It's complicated."

"Like my being an undercover?"

Kenna pressed her lips together. She heard the front door close. "Go check the backyard is clear and shut that door, will you?"

Ron moved away and she crouched.

The man on the floor stared up at her. Late twenties, maybe early thirties. Younger than her at least. Smooth hands, so he didn't work with them. Little muscle tone under the T-shirt. Clean jeans and sneakers.

"How'd you get mixed up in all this?" she asked.

"I'm not talking." His jaw hardened.

"Your buddies ditched you at the first sign of trouble." She studied him. "Think they'll come rescue you?"

"Doesn't matter. We are one."

"You're one. There's no group, or club, or whatever. Not when I'm done."

Ron shifted into view out of the corner of her eye. "Tell us why you beat that man, Son. Then tell us what the Children of the Morning have planned. Then we'll let you go."

Kenna picked it up immediately. "You can tell your friends we roughed you up a little bit, but you refused to talk so we had no choice but to cut you loose."

The guy eyed her, then the older man beside her. He huffed. "What are the two of you gonna do?"

Ron stepped over and set the toe of his boot on the man's fingers. He applied pressure. "You'd be surprised."

Chapter Twenty-One

Kenna pushed open the door to the Helson Police Department. The clock on the wall behind the reception desk indicated it wasn't quite two in the morning. A radio played somewhere in the corner, classic rock with the volume on low.

"Mark, right?" Ron held one elbow, and she held the other as they walked the guy between them to the desk.

The uniformed officer set down his coffee mug. "Chief?" He glanced at Kenna. "And you are…?"

Thankfully, Ron didn't answer for her, which meant Kenna was able to say, "Clara Shearson."

"The one Detective Thomson hired to be protection for Elijah?"

She nodded. "And right now we're working other angles. Unofficially, of course."

He eyed her, then the chief. "So this is a citizen's arrest?"

Kenna turned sideways. The guy she'd hit with her stun gun knew what to say. They'd had a long conversation about what he knew and how he could be helpful to the police. To say they'd been persuasive would be a good explanation.

The guy lifted his chin. "I'd like to make a statement."

The officer blinked at the three of them.

He'd likely be asking the guy if he was under coercion, but they hadn't threatened him. Much. They certainly hadn't beaten him or used threats of physical harm. Even though old-school policing methods could be effective, this was a new century. Guys like Ron Arnold, who had run his department the way he wanted to in his day, had to accept that this was a new era of policing.

However, she didn't know all that much about how this department was run, so she couldn't be sure there had been much of a culture change.

Ron lifted his chin. "You have somewhere we can park him so you can take down what he has to say?"

Officer blinked. "Right." He looked around. "We can do it out here since I'm the only one in right now."

Small department, light on personnel after midnight. Had Ron known they might get to listen in on what the guy had to say? Probably why he hadn't wanted to wait until morning. And Kenna disliked the idea of holding a man for hours.

The officer lifted a divider in the counter and swung the low door out.

"He's one of the Children of the Morning, and he tried to beat a man to death earlier this evening," Ron said. "So it should be good."

Kenna kept her composure, as thought there was nothing significant in that—at least, no more than the average day of policing in Helson.

"They don't exist anymore." The officer shook his head. "There are no Children of the Morning, Chief." He probably thought Ron was senile.

Ron didn't show any signs of losing his mind. "That's why he needs to make a statement, Son. So it can be on record."

Kenna gave her most diplomatic smile.

Her phone started to ring in her pocket. Regardless of who it was, she said, "I need to take this." Then slid the phone out, stepping away so the current officer and the former chief could deal with their suspect without outside interference.

Maizie's name flashed on the screen. Kenna put it to her ear. "Hey, kid." Anyone listening would believe she had a family, a façade that presented a woman as less of a threat because she had something to lose.

"So you're somewhere you can't talk freely?" Maizie caught on pretty quickly, but she was crazy smart.

"Maybe," Kenna said, as though she had been asked for her permission over something. "We can talk about it." Kenna walked to a message board covered in flyers and posters that seemed to be all about department barbeques. Not too dissimilar to the one at the church. Something small towns like this would probably never get rid of, even with the internet and online social groups.

"Good, you don't have to get off the phone," Maizie said. "Because I need to send you photos to see if you can ID the other guys, the ones who ran out of the house."

"Sure." Kenna wanted to ask why Maizie hadn't simply sent them, rather than call to tell her she was. But at this time of night, she might want to connect over the phone so she didn't feel quite so alone tonight. "How are you sleeping?"

"How are you?" Maizie fired back, over the sound of a keyboard clicking.

Kenna smiled, reading off a flyer for a counseling group for people who had lost a loved one. Did the town have another for survivors of the Children of the Morning? "Touché. But I'll get home soon enough."

Maybe.

"I'll send you the pictures," Maizie said. "You can tell me who they were."

"Anything else I should know?"

"I can call in a bit, right? If I need to?"

"If I don't answer, it's because I'm tied up." If the phone ringing woke her up, she always answered Maizie's call. She knew firsthand how it felt to have to survive those lonely night hours when the memories crept in like the cold, and there was no way to get warm.

"Sending now."

Kenna looked at her screen. She had a text from Thomson that he'd dropped Ben off to get seen by a doctor and was hanging around to take his statement. The download came through. "Got it."

Kenna hung up with her and went to where Ron sat at a desk across from the officer taking the statement.

"You understand you're entitled to have a lawyer present at any time during this conversation?"

The guy nodded.

"Please state your name."

"Joshua."

Ron reacted, just a tiny inhale of breath. Because of the name? He'd made mention of having a name within the Children of the Morning, different from his real name.

Kenna glanced over at the guy. "Is that the name on your driver's license, or your birth certificate?"

"Fine." The guy shifted his shoulders. "Lance Reardon."

"Thank you." The officer made a note in his pad, then started in with questions.

Kenna glanced at Ron, half listening. "You okay?" she whispered.

"Because I'm old? Or because I don't like how this department is run?"

Kenna shrugged one shoulder.

He made a face, nothing more. If he wanted to keep his own counsel, he was entitled to do so. However, like the fact he'd been part of the group and a bigger part of the FBI investigation than she'd realized, she did need all pertinent facts.

Kenna scrolled through the IDs on her phone, recognized a couple, and let Maizie know.

Ron pointed at one she'd never seen before. "That's the mayor's boy. Go figure."

"Was the mayor part of the Children of the Morning?" Kenna asked. "Because this guy was outside the cave the other night." Even if he hadn't been at the house earlier.

Ron lifted his gray brows. "Wonder if Chief Hutton knows that?"

She didn't want to believe in a vast conspiracy. However, the facts would be what they were. The truth would come out one way or another, and the fallout was up to the people of this town. But like they had swept the past under the rug and tried to forget it, she hoped this new evidence wouldn't lead to yet another festering wound.

She tuned back in on what the officer was saying, even though her mind wanted to mull over Chief Hutton and what he'd done with the photo and video she'd taken.

The officer said, "How long have you been part of the group?"

"Forever," Lance said.

"So they never quit operating?"

"I was born part of the group." Lance lifted his chin. "It's who I am."

The question Kenna wanted an answer to was why. Given who they were, and what they stood for, what person would want to belong to a legacy like that?

"You're telling me," the officer said, "that the Children of the Morning never disbanded? The group remained an entity since the FBI came in and broke it up?"

Lance smirked. "You can't destroy what is eternal."

Right. "Maybe not," Kenna said, "but what is illegal can be prosecuted. And that includes attempted kidnapping, murder, and attempted murder."

Her father had done his duty. The way she had as an FBI agent. What Kenna wanted an answer to was why he left the Bureau. He'd retired not a year after the search warrant was served in Helson. Maybe Ron had a clue as to what her dad's mindset had been in the months before he quit and opted for a life on the road.

Ron said, "She's right. We spared no one. Those that weren't killed faced jail sentences most are still serving. We saved the innocent who were their victims. People like you."

Lance leaned forward in his chair. "If they are all either dead or in jail, then why aren't you?" He barely paused. "Because people in authority think they can do whatever they want. Like make exceptions for their friends, those who betray the truth."

If they were going to talk about how the powerful often victimized those under them, Kenna could relate.

Was that a way in?

She might need to talk to Ben.

"We aren't talking about me," Ron said. "We're talking about you assaulting a man. A brother even."

"Judas isn't one of us."

Ah, so they'd given Ben Landry the name of the disciple who betrayed Jesus.

Lance continued, "I don't recognize him as a human being."

"The law does." The officer made another note on his pad. "And also recognizes you've committed a crime, but you can help yourself. You can tell me what you know about the Children of the Morning. Right now. Tell me everything about what's happening with them today."

Kenna liked that way of putting it. Lance wouldn't be able to talk around the answer and end up exhuming the past.

"I have no idea." Lance crossed his arms.

Kenna shot Lance a look.

Ron said, "What did we talk about, Son?"

The officer didn't ask what that meant—which was a wise choice. "Tell me how many members there are?"

"We are limitless."

Kenna nearly rolled her eyes.

The officer said, "Why was Annabelle killed?"

"Who is that?" Lance said. "I've never heard of her."

"Why assault a former member?" The officer leaned back in his chair, getting into it now.

"Because he deserved it."

"And what are the Children of the Morning planning?"

"Something big." Lance grinned. "We will be reborn, and all men shall be witness to the glory."

Ron pushed his chair back.

Kenna said, "Don't leave." Then she turned back to Lance. "How is the group reborn?" They could plan to reclaim their compound. Or maybe they were instituting new leadership.

Lance stared at them. "And in the last days—"

"Cut the crap, Lance." The officer blew out a breath.

Kenna shrugged. "The FBI took down your group before, they can do it again."

"This time we are ready."

"How many members are there?"

He only stared at her.

"Who is your leader?" Kenna pressed. "Give me his name."

Lance had refused to tell them at Ben's house. Ron had been emphatic that he could get the information out of their suspect. She hadn't wanted to witness how he planned to do that. Even walking away with knowledge of a crime about to be committed made her an accessory.

She didn't kid herself that he thought being in a police department, making an official statement, carried the weight to convince him to tell the truth.

"Whoever it is," she said, "they screwed up. You've drawn too much attention to yourselves. The cops have a dead body, which means an open murder case on file. The FBI gets wind of the name, and they'll be crawling over this town like ants. You think they were determined to put a stop to it before? This time it's a vendetta. They're going to roll in here, determined to finish what the Bureau started."

Kenna heard movement behind her. The door opening and closing, followed by the presence of a person standing there. Not that Ron had left, but that someone had shown up.

Still, she said, "You will all lose. Like you lost last time."

Lance only grinned. "Guess it's kismet that it's you then, Kenna Banbury. It was your dad, right? The one who pulled us out of the cistern. Tore us away from our family and everything we knew."

"You remember."

He nodded. "How could I ever forget?"

"Tell me the name of whoever is in charge now."

"We will be reborn."

The person behind her shifted. "Okay, that's enough." Chief Hutton was here.

The officer jumped up so fast his chair wobbled and nearly fell over.

Kenna turned and looked up at the chief.

Hutton said, "You're Kenna Banbury?"

Uh-oh. He knew who she was, either from police briefings from the Washington FBI field office, or from her father's case files. Or both.

Kenna stood. "I know what the Children of the Morning are up to."

"Is that right?"

"So do I." Ron had a pained expression on his face that she didn't think was only about the bruise on his sternum.

"Well, as it turns out, I don't require the help of either of you." The chief lifted his chin. "This is my town to police, and a washed-up old retiree and a private investigator wanted by the FBI for questioning aren't who I'd call even if I needed help. Got it?" Before they could respond, he turned to the officer. "Get this man processed and take him to holding."

"Yes, sir." The officer sprang into action.

Chief Hutton turned back to Kenna. "Both of you will also be making statements. Then I'll call the FBI and have them pick you up." He just about grinned.

"As long as I get my phone call." Kenna stuck her fingers in her pockets like she didn't care, even though this quickly turned into a royal disaster.

"So you can get someone to come and break you out?"

"No." Kenna shook her head. "So I can warn Detective Thomson that his son has been chosen as the next leader of the Children of the Morning."

The chief flinched.

Kenna turned to Ron, but he was nowhere to be seen. The one person who might be able to corroborate the theory she'd come up with had left.

She was on her own.

But then the door opened, and Ron came back in, followed closely by Detective Thomson.

"Let's figure this out, shall we?" Thomson said, not letting Ron do anything but walk with him over to Kenna and the chief. "Sit." He pointed to an empty chair, then folded his arms. "We're gonna figure this out."

Chapter Twenty-Two

Ron sighed into the chair, looking wrung out and exhausted.

Kenna wanted to suggest they let him go home and get some sleep, but the fact he'd tried to walk out without talking to anyone just a second ago couldn't be ignored. She needed to know why he wasn't being forthcoming. Since she could only tackle one thing at a time, she twisted around to Thomson.

"Can you check on the officer watching your house and make sure all is good?"

The last thing she wanted was for Elijah to be hurt—or taken. Even if her theory was correct, and they needed to hash things out here, that short delay could cost them far too much. Arresting bad guys was one thing. Saving a child's life meant more to her, and she figured the same was true for the cop in front of her that was the child's father.

Even Dixie would agree with her, whatever name she was using now.

The detective frowned. "And why would I do that?"

Chief Hutton answered before she could. "They think the

Children of the Morning are back, and that they want your son... I'm not clear on what for."

"They *are* back." Thomson turned to Ron. "What do they want Elijah for?"

Hutton shifted. Hadn't expected his detective to be up to speed about what was happening in town? It was clear the chief didn't like any of this, but burying his head in the sand hadn't done him any favors. Now it was all hitting him in an unmistakable way.

He couldn't walk away from this—or ignore it.

Ron barely looked up from the desktop in front of him. "They have chosen their new leader."

"Elijah?" Thomson gaped.

"It makes sense," Kenna said. "Lance said they were going to be *reborn.*"

"Except in all the ways it doesn't make sense *at all.*" The chief spun around and strode off to a door marked CHIEF. He called back over his shoulder, "Figure this out, Detective. I'll assign more officers to watch your house."

"Thanks, Chief." Thomson turned back to her and Ron. "Both of you had better explain this."

When Ron didn't offer anything, Kenna settled on the edge of the closest desk. She felt as wrung out as Ron looked. "Something Lance said about them being 'reborn' when the officer interviewed him. I'm guessing Ron knows what that means."

"The guy you took down at that house?" Thomson said. His face remained passive, but she could see in his eyes this father was riding the edge of his composure. "I took the vic to the hospital. He said his name was Robert Jones."

Since Ben Landry was a con man, Kenna wasn't sure she believed that Robert Jones was his real name. Maybe just what he went by when he was in Helson.

"Did Robert say anything to you?" Kenna figured they needed to compare notes.

Thomson sighed. "He stressed to me it was his real name, like it was significant he told me instead of you?"

She had to concede it was a power struggle, even when the man was hurt. He would continue playing the game to the end.

Given Thomson's connection to all this, the chief needed to remove the detective from any investigation where he went after the people trying to take his child from him. He couldn't be conducting any more interviews. Which meant Kenna had to stop asking him for help.

"He's a con man as best I can tell." Kenna shrugged. "But there are a lot of question marks about the guy." Until she got him to talk, at length, about everything including Intellectus and Michael Rushman, she would have too many blanks where Ben Landry aka Robert Jones was concerned.

Thomson said, "The bottom line is, he's one of the surviving children."

That made him older than Kenna had initially believed him to be.

She nodded. "I figured."

"And he told me about an invitation he received. Some big event."

Kenna had no other ideas for the Gathering Place than that clearing. "Did he say when?"

Thomson frowned. "You know about it?"

She wasn't going to tell him that she had broken into Ben's motel room and read his mail. Kenna shrugged. "Did he give you any detail?"

"The date came in an email. Three days from now."

Kenna winced. "That doesn't give us much time to figure out who the rest of them are."

"You think they're all just the kids that were rescued?"

That didn't account for Annabelle. Kenna pulled out her phone and texted Maizie, asking for the "how" of Annabelle's connection back to them. Then she said, "I think they've branched out. Added some new blood. But still, they recruit from those who have reason to be sympathetic."

Thomson looked at Ron. "Anything to add? I'm trying to keep my son safe here."

"And I worked for years making sure every son remained safe." Ron lifted his gaze. "Keeping them leashed so this never happened. And now it's here."

"You know their teachings." Kenna wasn't going to let him skate out from under this. At least, not without finishing what he started first. "What do they do with him?"

Thomson flinched. "I'll go call Bianca. She'll want to know more cops are on their way." His attention snagged on her for a second. "Kenna, will she be able to take care of them if push comes to shove?"

"Does she have a gun?"

He shook his head.

"Then get her one," Kenna said. "She knows how to use it."

Before he could ask why his wife hadn't told him that, she said, "Is the chief going to rat me out to the feds?"

"I'll make sure it's not before we finish this." He strode off to the chief's office.

She supposed that was meant to make her feel better. But the town of Helson wasn't her only concern.

She had to know where the threats to Maizie were before they cropped up. That way she could eliminate them before the teen took another hit she didn't have the strength to withstand.

Kenna dragged over a chair and sat knee-to-knee with Ron. "Talk."

"It's been too long." He started to shake his head. "I didn't remember until Lance said what he said about being reborn."

"What about the limitless thing? How many are there?" Kenna needed to know if he knew of a way to find out.

"Could be anything. It sounded like bluster." He paused long enough, then finally said, "They want eighty-eight."

She nodded. "Tell me how the group is reborn."

Tears filled his eyes.

"I know you thought it was over. I'm sorry it isn't, but maybe that's the real reason you're still here. Because now you get to finish what you started. End this for good." She understood well enough believing something was over and trusting that the work had been done. That the worst part of the pain had passed. Now he had to face the fact it had been hiding all this time.

"You really care about that when the chief in there is going to call the feds?" Ron said. "He'll tell them you're here."

"One problem at a time." Kenna shrugged. "That's all any of us can do if we want to do anything well."

Truth was, until he confirmed what she believed, all she had was a crazy theory.

Ron's shoulders sagged. "I was nine during the first rebirth. Too young to be chosen. They want a boy who would be considered on the brink of manhood in most cultures, or other countries."

"They find one to be their leader?" She didn't like the sound of that no matter what it meant.

Ron gave her a clipped nod. "There's a ceremony. I watched them perform it on my friend Charles, and then he became Peter."

"'On this rock I will build my church?' That Peter?"

He winced. "Except even that is debated in the church—outside the Children of the Morning. They just choose a Bible-sounding name."

"What did they do?" Kenna wanted to know about the ceremony, about as much as she *didn't*.

"Is it enough to say you don't want to know?" Ron's eyes had darkened.

"For now, yeah," Kenna said. "What happened to him? Did he die, or was he arrested?"

"He was killed. But the Children of the Morning don't view him the same way the followers of David Koresh viewed their leader. He's not the be-all and end-all of their faith. He's just a figurehead put there by the caretaker. Someone who stands for what they believe in, and what they follow. But he's more of an everyman type."

Kenna frowned. "Isn't the whole point of groups like that they flock to the leader? That he's so charismatic they'll do anything to follow him?"

"In a way that's what it's like with the Children of the Morning," Ron said. "Except that he is entirely replaceable."

"So they pick whoever?"

"It has to be the right type of son. Someone with promise."

She thought about the cold case files. "Like a baseball star. Or a child prodigy."

Ron dipped his head.

"So you've known all along that they were looking for their replacement?" She stared at him. "You knew why those boys were taken, what would be done to them, and who the perpetrators were."

"You think I sat on information that would've ended it?" He gaped. "I had no idea who they are. How could I?"

"You know them."

"Not anymore."

"Because you decided you were done?"

"I told the chief what was happening," Ron said. "He didn't listen. You're the first person to care about the truth in thirty years."

Kenna studied him.

"We all make mistakes. We do things we wish we could go back and change."

"Agreed," Kenna said. "So let's do the right thing now."

"None of them are going to talk. With Lance in cuffs and too many cops in the hills around the mine, they're going to close ranks. We'll never find them."

"How do we find out who the caretaker is?" Kenna motioned to the door through which the suspect had been taken to holding. "Will Lance tell us?"

"He may not even know." Ron frowned. "The identity of the person is kept tightly under wraps."

They were still going to ask. Even if the guy didn't know. "Seems to me like you keep trickling out information bit by bit. Why not tell me all this up front, rather than when it came up?"

"You'd have believed the ramblings of a crazy old man?" Ron stared at her. "Really?"

"I'm sorry people view you that way."

"I'm only sorry it cost lives." Ron swiped at his papery cheek. "Because no one believed me."

"Both of you. In here with me."

Kenna twisted in her chair.

The chief stood in his office door. When neither of them moved, Hutton said, "Please?"

"I believe we've been summoned." Kenna stood and held her elbow out to Ron. "Shall we?"

He gave her an odd look but wound his arm in hers. Kenna didn't want to warm up to him, not even on the off chance he would end up meeting his demise the way Joe Don Hunter had, then the Father she'd met in Albuquerque, and lately Anthony Santino. All three had known her father. She didn't want to bury another of her dad's old friends or colleagues.

Part of her wanted to distance herself just so it would be less painful, regardless of how things worked out. But the part of her that missed her father in a way that was palpable wanted to keep this man close.

They entered the chief's office, where Thomson sat on the edge of a pleather brown couch, on the phone. "I will." He paused. "I love you too, Bee."

Kenna didn't want to be around when he found out his wife had changed her identity just a short time ago. There had been enough disaster in his life—and she hoped for his sake it wouldn't all come crashing down more than it already had.

He stood and pointed at the wall. "As you can see from this, we've been working on the case since Annabelle was found."

Kenna scanned the evidence board. "Whoa."

"Agreed." Ron pulled his arm from hers and wandered to the collection of pictures, ID photos, and arrest records. Along with phone records, licenses for liquor sales, and gun permits.

"Bottom line?" Thomson said. "We're gonna take these people down."

Ron made a noise in his throat.

Chief Hutton said, "I was in the army when the Children of the Morning were either killed, rescued, or arrested. By the time I came back to town, it was two years later."

Kenna took a wild guess. "And the whole town was pretending they never existed. Deep in forgetting it ever happened."

Hutton said, "Just because Annabelle tried to abduct Elijah Thomson doesn't mean—"

"They need to be taken down." Ron turned from the wall of papers to the room. "Trust me on that."

"We can stand here all night and debate who they are and who the caretaker might be," Kenna said. "But it won't lead to any arrests."

"I'm done with the murder investigation," Thomson said. "It's being passed to the other detective. Which leaves me free to head home and protect my son."

Kenna glanced at him. "Because you think they'll come to you either way, and you'll get a face-to-face?"

He only stared at her. Then he said, "You think I would put my child in harm's way just to close a case?"

"I think you would leverage my desire not to be caught by the FBI in order to get me to protect Elijah."

"I protect my son." He slapped his chest.

"Then go home and do that."

Thomson glared.

"But all that sitting around waiting for something to happen leaves you with one option."

"And what's that?" the chief asked.

Kenna stared at him. "Drawing them out."

"You want to use my son as bait." Thomson didn't even flinch.

Kenna let him process what he'd just said aloud. "We can keep him safe."

"You can't possibly control all the variables." Thomson shook his head.

"I get that it's risky. It's not ideal, but the reality is, if we want to find out who they are, then we need to turn the tables. Get them to show themselves." He might not believe they could control all the variables, but now that she knew the chief had military training, she was more convinced than before it was a good idea. "We can make this work."

Ron had opened up. He was peeling back layers, showing her the truth underneath.

The chief could help them keep the plan under wraps.

It was a risk, but one they could absorb. Even Dixie—Bianca—wouldn't let anything happen to Elijah. The kid would be safe.

Thomson stared at her. "You're fired. You don't come near my family. I don't need your help to protect my son, and we won't be using him as bait."

He strode to the door, hauled it open, and stepped out.

Chapter Twenty-Three

"Just like that, he fired you?" Stairns sounded like he wanted to hang up the phone and drive to the Pacific Northwest just to give Thomson a piece of his mind.

"He only wants to keep his son safe." Kenna flicked the vent away from her face and stared out the windshield at the hospital. "Can you really blame him for that? Can I? Neither of us would do any different in the same situation."

Stairns grunted. "At least it frees you up to focus on the case. Taking down these dirtbags."

Kenna chuckled to herself. "Now you're getting it."

"I still can't believe Dixie Cabrera is living there. What's he going to do when he finds out his wife used to be a bounty hunter? Or that you and she are on the same side?"

The ambulance pulled out from a lane on the right side of the building and onto the street, where they turned on lights and sirens.

"I don't think she is right now. *Bianca* is all-in with her husband."

"Sure, why not?" Stairns said. "That's a safe place to be. Not that a woman needs a big strong man to protect her, but whatever was shaken in her by Peter Conklin needs to be safe."

"Can't say I really blame her."

"Because you have a boyfriend now?"

Instead of answering that ridiculous non-question, Kenna said, "Any progress figuring out who in town is part of the group?"

"Working on it," Stairns said. "You?"

"Same." Speaking of, she rolled the back of her head across the headrest. After a few hours of sleep, she'd called the hospital and pretended to be Robert Jones' next of kin. Ben was about to be released from the hospital, and she wanted to catch him. After all, he could possibly help her find these people. Coordinate a way to have them come to her. Elijah wasn't the only one who could be bait.

But did they listen when she tried to explain that? No. They just kicked her and Ron out. Apparently, the chief didn't need help from anyone who wasn't his subordinate, and Thomson was going to protect his son.

Even Bianca thought it was better that way. Maybe she just wanted her husband at home. Or she thought Kenna wasn't best utilized on protection detail. She'd sent a text, and Kenna hadn't replied.

If everyone wanted her working the case, that was what she would do—her way.

"Earth to Kenna," Stairns said.

"I should go." She shifted in her seat.

"So you can spiral alone?"

"I'd rather have my meltdown in private." She grinned. "With a milkshake and a large order of fries."

"Maizie caught me with the nacho cheese dip. She told me we're not supposed to eat our feelings."

Kenna laughed.

Just then, Ben rounded the corner of the building, heading for the ambulance bay.

"I do have to go, though. Bye." She hit the button and pocketed her phone as she strode from the car. Later that day, she'd have to swing by a mechanic shop and get them to look at her spongy breaks. Given the age of the car, she didn't want to mess around with an issue that could be dangerous.

Ben walked the sidewalk to the corner of the building on the right.

Kenna picked up her pace to a jog and caught up. Just around the corner, Ben spun. She grabbed his shirt and slammed him against the brick.

"What is your problem?" He grunted the question, and she got a look at his face. One eye nearly swollen shut, a cut on his lip.

"Broken ribs?" She eased off his chest a fraction but didn't let him go. When he didn't answer the question, she said, "I need your help."

"Funny way of asking. I thought I was the bad guy. But I guess now I'm the victim." He lifted his chin. "That's what cops do, right? Get the victim to go in with a wire, have the bad guy confess on tape. Then the cops roll in and arrest them. Everyone knows the victim snitched even though they said nothing."

"I feel like you might have some unaddressed issues." She remembered that community board. "Maybe there's a therapy group you can join. Someone might care enough to want to listen to your sob story." A guy with this many hard edges wasn't going to respond to empathy. She needed a different tactic than that.

Skin around his eyes flexed. "Whatever it is, I'm not helping you."

"Then give me enough I don't need you." Kenna would

prefer a different route, but that would happen if he didn't respond to this. "Tell me what I need to know."

"I've been gone. How do I know who's part of the group and who isn't right now?" Ben lifted his hands. "I can't help you."

She wanted to know if he was simply scared of them and that was why he wanted to avoid everything. "Why did they come into your home to attack you if you have nothing to do with them? Wouldn't they just leave you alone?"

He glanced aside.

"Do you need a ride home?"

"You think that's going to get me to tell you what they wanted?"

"You should tell me anyway. It'll help me take them down."

He snorted.

"My chance of success is greater if you tell me what you know. We can at least agree on that, right?" He couldn't debate her much, though she figured he might try. "But still. You live miles from here. It's too far to walk."

"Fine." He pushed off the wall and walked past her. "I'll nap on the way."

Kenna kept pace, walking beside him. "I'll need directions. I don't remember exactly where you live."

"Sure."

Kenna motioned to her car.

"You think I'm gonna believe that?"

She slid in, and they buckled up while the air-conditioning struggled to beat back the warmth. "I think if you consider it, you'll realize we both want the same thing. For the Children of the Morning to be gone out of your life. Otherwise will they ever leave you alone?"

"I didn't come here for this."

Kenna twisted in her seat to face him. "Neither did I. I came here to see if you know anything about some missing pages in my father's journal. And to find out if you're connected to Michael Rushman."

Ben flinched. "I had nothing to do with that freak."

"Good," she said. "Why did you join Intellectus?"

"Can you just drive?"

Kenna left the parking space and turned toward the street. "Talk."

Ben let out a long sigh.

She could've been sympathetic to his injuries, or the fact he had to now lie in the bed he'd made. However, she had trouble dredging up much empathy since he refused to be forthcoming. Kind of like Ron and most of the other people in this town.

Finally, he said, "I joined Intellectus because I was bored. I just got off a job with this heiress in Palm Springs. I figured they might have info on some treasure, or a lead on a new mark."

"And if I sent your information and a photo to the FBI, I'd get multiple hits back on warrants for your arrest all over the country, right?"

"Well, I can't just stay in one place, can I?" Ben's tone oozed with sarcasm. "Except for that social media group. Women I stiffed out of cash or jewelry. Like I care they want to hunt me down."

Kenna pulled up to a red light and glanced over.

"Yeah, fine. I probably didn't need to tell you about the group." He lifted both hands. "The doctor gave me good pain meds."

"Why keep going if things are getting hot?" Kenna had done the same, though. She'd carried on working with an assumed name, not really giving up any of her life or what she wanted to do.

He did it by committing crimes, and he didn't seem to want to quit.

As far as she could see, there wasn't too much of a difference between them on that front.

Kenna drove across town toward his house, avoiding the part of town where the police department was. As she did, the brakes still acted sloppy. She had to drive slower than she wanted and let off the gas early to reduce her speed. Meaning she ran at least one red light.

"I know you don't like them." Kenna gripped the wheel and kept an eye out for the cops. "I know you only came home to hide out and clean out your house." Assuming he'd told the truth about that. "All I'm asking for is information. And missing pages."

"You think that invitation is some kind of in?" Ben stared out the window. "They would've killed me. After they found out how much I told you about them."

A note of worry flickered in her mind. "Will they come back and try again?"

"Why?" He huffed what might have been a laugh. "Are you volunteering for protection detail?"

"You'd rather suddenly come face-to-face with one of them in some unsuspecting moment and then in the next, you're dead?"

He shifted in his seat. "Is that how you think you'll die?"

"This isn't about me." Kenna hit a patch of traffic by Walmart. She ducked through the parking lot and headed east instead. No sense going to Ben's house if they would only be walking into an ambush.

"Who cares how I get it?" That was how he spoke about dying? "I won't care." Ben scoffed. "I'll be dead."

"Then you have no reason not to tell me about them. Everything you know, before you die." She shrugged a shoulder, as though she felt the way he did about death. "Then at least it won't have been a waste."

Ben snorted.

"Do you know who the caretaker is?"

"She changes in every generation."

"Knowing at least that it's a woman helps me narrow it down," Kenna said. "Information like that could save my life or the life of an innocent person."

"But you're not innocent."

She shrugged and found the speed limit on this road, and the flow of traffic meant she had to go faster than she would've liked.

Should've pulled over.

Kenna could handle a risk—she'd faced worse than a finicky car before. It was probably because of the age. Something had worn out.

She kept to the edge of the lane and drove slower so other vehicles could pull around her.

Ben had his head back on the chair and didn't seem to notice her driving.

"Neither of us is innocent." Kenna spotted a cop and eased up to the same speed as the flow of traffic for a second before she let off the gas. "But unlike you, I'm going to see this through to the end because it's the right thing to do."

"Great. You're a do-gooder. We already know I'm not. Why bother arguing?"

Kenna sighed. "How hard is it for you to just give me the information I need? I'm the one taking the risk."

"For people you don't know or care about?"

"That's not why I do it." Kenna didn't feel the need to

explain her "why" to a guy who would only dismiss what drove her. "And that's all you need to know."

"You're right. They're gonna kill me."

"If you leave, and they carry on operating, will they hunt you down?" She gripped the wheel, looking for a break in traffic so she could ease off the gas more. She tapped the brake just as a test and felt the usual resistance. *Good.* "Well? Will they?"

"Yes." Ben sniffed. "I know too much."

And the Children of the Morning would tie up that loose end. They would want to finish what they started.

"For a second there, outside the hospital, I thought they'd sent you to kill me."

"That's not what this is."

"No, turns out it's you that wants to die," Ben said. "Because that's what will happen if you do this."

"That's my choice to make." Kenna checked her rearview and spotted a car changing lanes aggressively behind her. She needed to check on Ron Arnold this morning. "I need to know who these people are, and where to find them."

She spotted a gap up ahead and ducked between two cars in the left lane.

The car behind sped up, trying to find a space.

A truck up ahead turned off the road. The car in front increased speed. Kenna ducked back into the right-hand lane, watching for a turnoff up ahead.

"What's going on?" Ben twisted in his seat to look out the back window. He grunted and faced forward again, hissing out a breath.

"Where is the Gathering Place?"

"You want to do this now?"

"Tell me."

Ben groaned. "I only remember it was dark. I was a little kid. I don't know where it is."

"But if you asked, because you want to go to the ceremony or whatever is happening, they would tell you. Right?"

"They'll know it's a front." Ben rubbed his hands down over his knees. "As far as they're concerned, I already betrayed them. They'll know you're coming."

Good. "Who is the caretaker?" She would end this. Not just for Steve and Bianca and the safety of their son.

"I just know there is one. They never refer to her by name, and I've never met her. I haven't been back in years. So same answer." He shot the words at her like that buckshot.

She didn't want to go any faster, or it would be too dangerous. Kenna was already risking too much with the speed she'd gained so far, even though she wasn't going much above the speed limit on this highway.

Up ahead she spotted a corner.

The guy behind her was gaining. Another car had joined it. Now both vehicles advanced behind her, making untrained aggressive maneuvers that could get them all killed.

"You're gonna want to hold on."

Ben looked in the side mirror. Kenna checked the rearview.

She counted seconds to the corner, braced to make the turn. When the curb neared, she turned the wheel to the right. Hard. The back end flung out. Kenna tapped the brake to get a little control, but nothing happened.

She pushed down harder.

Nothing.

They careened around the corner at full speed. One of the cars behind bumped them. Someone honked their horn, but she could only think enough to wonder what they expected her to do.

The car started to spin out.

Kenna gripped the wheel, and everything rotated around them. She lost her grip on her equilibrium and heard Ben start to scream.

The car flung left into something hard.

Her head slammed the window, and everything went black.

Chapter Twenty-Four

Kenna gasped awake, then right away had to cough. She sucked in a breath and tried to figure out what was happening. Red and blue lights flashed across the hood. No glass.

"He's gone." A male voice. Helmet and turnout coat. A firefighter.

"What about her?" The second male sounded familiar.

"Conscious now. No visible injuries. Let's get her out, guys." The firefighter slid across the hood in a seated position, then ducked his head to look at her where the windshield should've been. "Hey, there."

Kenna looked down and took her own assessment. "I'm fine."

"Right. Let's keep it that way." He seemed to have found her comment amusing. She didn't know why he would.

She stabbed at the button to release her seatbelt. It snapped back and hit the window, which she realized was a concrete wall. The whole left side of the car had been hammered into a straight line. She managed to let out a noise, not even sure what she was trying to say.

She brushed at her lap, but pricks of broken glass poked at her palms.

"Easy. Let me." The firefighter reached in with an ungloved hand and felt her pulse.

"I'm not dead."

He grinned. "That's good to know."

"Don't laugh at me."

"I wouldn't dare." He slid his coat off. "Hold tight. We're going to cut off the roof so you can get out. All right?"

Her world descended into darkness. She used the few minutes of whirring machines and creaking metal to find her phone. The screen lit up the underside of the coat, which had the name SAMSON written in permanent marker on the size label. Several missed calls and texts. She called Maizie.

As soon as the teen picked up, Kenna said, "I'm fine, but the car is toast."

"Did you lose consciousness?" the girl asked. "Because the internet says that puts you at greater risk of a concussion."

"I did, but I'll keep you posted on the long-term ramifications."

The coat whipped off her, the roof of the car now an opening that let the full force of the morning sun in. "Did you just—are you on the phone?"

Maizie said, "I'll let you go." And it almost sounded like she was laughing.

Kenna hung up and lowered the phone. "I'm ready now."

"Great." He checked her extremities and head, then ended up just picking her up by her armpits and hauling her out. Someone grabbed her legs, and they put her on a stretcher.

"I don't need medical attention." She held up her hands, one still holding the phone.

The EMT moved to stand in front of her. "That is still to be determined."

The whole street was chaos. Pedestrians. Cars. Emergency vehicles. Uniformed first responders.

"Did anyone give the police a description of the car that clipped me?" Kenna asked.

The EMT shined a light in her left eye, then the right. "Maybe."

"I'm in one piece."

"You still need to be checked out by an actual doctor. Not something I'm trained to do, much to my mother's despair."

Kenna studied her. Late twenties. Too young to be one of the survivors of the Children of the Morning. But she could still be the caretaker. "Regardless of whether you feel all right —or if you don't, but you just want to pretend you do—it's worth being treated."

Kenna looked around for an out. "I don't have a great history with hospitals." She spotted the police chief, of all people, and shouted, "Hutton!" louder than she should have with a bump on her head.

Thankfully, he heard it and came over. "Ms. Banbury?"

She frowned. "What? I was run off the road."

"That's not my biggest problem right now."

She should be happy she wasn't at the top of that chart. "What is?"

"Your passenger? Robert Jones?" The chief frowned. "His throat was slit. Which I'd be arresting you for if I didn't have a witness who states a man ran off seconds after the crash holding a bloody knife."

"So whoever slammed into the back of us came over and finished him off?" She frowned, having to think for longer than it should've taken her. Why not kill her, too?

"You're probably only alive because you were hard to reach pinned against the wall."

"Any idea who it was that did the deed?" Had the witness ID'd the perpetrator?

"The mayor's nephew." More frowning.

"So the Children of the Morning came after us to finish what they started." Kenna motioned the EMT back and slid off the gurney. "Let me see him."

"Is that wise?"

"You think I'll flip out about a bloody dead guy, just because you've read what the internet has to say about my history?" Kenna sized him up. "Anyway, did you call the FBI or not?" She couldn't move forward with this case without the question hanging over her head if he didn't answer.

"Not yet." Chief of frowning studied her.

"One wrong move, is that it?"

"With your history—according to the internet anyway— I'd do much better with you in my corner than getting rid of you," he said. "Although, there's a sheriff in Colorado who seems to want your head on a platter about an assassination attempt and the death of his brother. I'm not sure if he's clear on whether you're the suspect."

"The brother was holding undocumented people as workers. They were living in a cellar under the barn, denied medical treatment. Forced to work his land."

"There usually are two sides."

She motioned to the wreckage of her car. "And you're going to ask the mayor's nephew for his? The guy is a murderer."

"Don't tell me how to do my job, Kenna."

She wouldn't have to if he was any good. Except that wasn't fair for her to say. Passing judgment when she didn't have all the details was how people had destroyed her life.

"I have two uniformed officers looking for him now. We will find him."

Kenna glanced around and had to wince at the bright sun. "He won't talk. Has the guy in lockup said anything?"

Hutton shook his head. "What about Ron? Should I be worried about him?"

"Don't tell me how to do my job."

He barked a laugh that made more than one firefighter turn to see.

Kenna watched them go back to work extracting Ben's body from the car. The gurney was being put to better use now. "You have to see that working together is better than not. Combining resources."

"I'm not going to like how you do things. And I don't take orders," he said, studying her. "Do you?"

Kenna pressed her lips together.

"Yeah, that's what I thought."

She sighed.

Before she could figure out a compromise, the EMT shoved a clipboard in front of her. "Just sign." The woman didn't look impressed, but it was for the best. "I'm not going to persuade you, and if anything happens later, I'm not going to be responsible."

Chief Hutton glanced at the uniformed woman. "If only we could all wash our hands so easily."

Kenna shot him a glance. "I'm an asset and you know it." Just in case he wanted to argue, she said, "And right now I'm a woman in need of a ride home."

It took an hour to wrap things up at the scene and get her belongings transferred from the car to his. Long enough Hutton took pity on her and sent one of his officers for coffee.

She signed all the forms, provided a full statement, and felt relieved when they finally got in the car.

She gave him the street name. "The blue house." Then promptly closed her eyes.

Hutton sighed. "You really think that just because it's the mayor's son I'm going to let it slide. That I'll look the other way and work the case from any other angle just to avoid a scandal."

She didn't open her eyes. "I think Annabelle was stabbed, and you've got a guy with a knife killing a second person."

"So I find him, and this is over?" His tone held no hopefulness, just irritation.

"You know as well as I do this is bigger than one person. It's about destroying an ideology that has threatened this town for years."

"Can't put handcuffs on an ideology."

Kenna nearly snorted.

"So either I work this case, as the chief of police in this town, or I call the FBI and pass this over to the feds." He paused. "Your call."

"Your job," she said. "Your career and your town."

"I'm aware."

The car stopped. Kenna opened her eyes. "Thanks."

"I'll help with your belongings. If you want."

"It's fine." She waved him off, hoping he didn't get out of the car and push it. That would be awkward. "I've got it."

She hauled the duffel out of the back, grateful she'd taken more of her things into the rental house than maybe she'd needed to. But right now it meant one trip, and he didn't argue. She waved at him, but he didn't pull away from the curb.

Great.

Kenna twisted the door handle. "Please don't be locked." It gave way under her grasp. "Thank you."

Now wasn't the time for deep theological questions of Who might be listening. Or working in her life right now. She just dumped her bag in the entryway of Ben's parents' house and shut the door.

Her phone buzzed with a text.

> Where are you?

Kenna replied to Dixie—Bianca—with the street address. What was the point in lying? If Bianca wanted to come over, then she could help by giving Kenna a ride to the vacation rental on the lake when she was done looking around.

Soon enough the cops would come here and wanted to look through everything. She planned to have gone through it all already.

She took the kitchen first, where she found ibuprofen in a corner cupboard and downed a couple by sticking her mouth under the tap at the sink to get a drink. The place mostly remained as she and Ron had left it. Kenna got through the mail, along with a couple of boxes Ben had packed and stacked where the dining table had been pushed aside.

Someone knocked on the door, closely followed by it opening and a yoo-hoo ringing out down the hall. "Kenna?"

She shifted to sit on the floor beside the box. "Did you bring everyone, or is it just you?"

Bianca stepped into view, the full effect somewhat muted by the gray skirt. But not enough to cancel out the pink cowgirl boots and the denim shirt. Big gold-hooped jewelry. Blond curls at max volume. "Just me." She frowned. "Are you all right after—" Bianca looked around. "Is whoever lives here moving?"

Ms. Realtor was on duty. "He was gonna sell it. Now he's dead."

Bianca cocked her hip. "Did you kill him?"

"Surprisingly, no."

Bianca laughed. "What's goin' on?"

"You tell me. Your husband must have filled you in."

"And now you're sitting on the floor of a dead man's house instead of taking down a murderous group of religious fanatics?"

Kenna leaned her head back against the wall and closed her eyes. "Waiting for the meds to kick in so my head will stop pounding."

"And what are we lookin' for in here?"

Kenna opened her eyes but didn't move. "You're gonna help me look?"

"It'll give me time to assess if this place has good bones." Bianca set her hand on her hip. "Are we going through the dead man's things first, or his parents?"

Kenna didn't have the energy to ask how Bianca knew that just from assessing what she could see. "Ben. Robert. Whatever he was calling himself."

"Who does the blood belong to?" Bianca motioned to the mess over by a chair.

"The dead guy. He wasn't done here, though."

"I know about the car accident," Bianca said. "I told Steve I had a showing, which is true, but it's not until later. So let's figure this out."

"Thought you were done crime fighting."

Bianca laughed. "It's a sickness, what can I say?"

"So you wanna help now?"

"I want to do what it takes to keep my son safe. Steve and I might have different methods, but that's fine. He has his skills and I have mine."

Kenna made herself get up off the floor. Bianca took the main living areas while Kenna searched in the bedroom. Ben's childhood bedroom still had the same furnishings, cartoon bed sheets folded on the bare mattress, and aged curtains. The dresser drawers were empty. She checked the closet and found a few shoe boxes and storage totes, which she hauled down and spilled open. An old paper envelope contained a stack of photos.

Kenna sat on the end of the mattress beside the folded sheet set and flicked through the developed images. Friends together, side by side at a lake. A few blurry photos that seemed to be of a frog. Sunlight filtered through trees. The next four were only black, like the inside of a lens cover. Then lights, orange and strung up high on the walls of somewhere. Maybe a basement, or a cave like the ones she'd run through in that mine. It could be outside, and the lights were strung on trees.

She kept going and found an image of a group, one figure in the center in white robes. "The Gathering Place."

She checked the rest but found no more, then went back through just in case. All she could tell was that at some point in his life, Ben—or whoever took the photos—had visited the Gathering Place. It seemed to be underground. A mine would be the most logical, or a part of the compound that had remained undiscovered since the raid.

How she could find it within three days would be the biggest issue. And she would much rather work on identifying the caretaker first.

Kenna's phone rang in her pocket. She lifted her hip and dug it out, swiping the screen as she lifted it to her ear. "Yep?" She needed to show the photo to Bianca, so she started out of the room.

"Kenna?" the voice croaked.

"Ron? What is it?" She picked up her pace, and the hallway spun a little around her.

Bianca straightened with a flip of her hair. "What's goin' on?"

Ron hadn't answered.

"Chief Arnold?" She figured that might jog him into gear.

"They're here. They came for me." He cleared his throat, his voice almost a whisper. "They're going to kill me."

Kenna said, "You're at home?"

"Yes." His voice sounded thin.

"We'll be right there." She hung up and asked Bianca, "You wanna work this case?"

"If it makes Elijah safe." Mama bear was out in full force.

"Then let's go." Kenna grabbed her duffel, and they stepped outside. "I might need backup."

"So I'm gonna need my gun?" Bianca closed the door behind her.

They hadn't finished looking through the house, and the police might come by before they got back, but Kenna had the photo. She knew more now than she had before Ben was killed. She checked she had all her own weapons and jogged to the car. "What do *you* think?"

The other woman grinned across the hood. "Good."

Chapter Twenty-Five

Kenna pulled her gun, already racing up the front walk. No vehicles within view. Not even Ron's, though it could be parked out of sight. Maybe so it didn't look like he was here.

She used her free hand to ease the door open. The former chief was the kind of guy to keep it clicked shut, but a lot of small-town mentality still hung on such that he might not necessarily lock his doors.

She listened.

"I'm goin' 'round back." Bianca trotted to the front corner going as fast as she could in her boots and that skirt.

Kenna stepped inside and right away started clearing rooms.

A gunshot cracked on the other end of the house. Bianca, or someone else?

Kenna heard thundering boots moving away from her. She raced to the kitchen, nearly skidded, and came face-to-face with Ron. The older man's face paled, his eyes wide. He lowered his gun. "Out back."

Kenna heard a yelp. Then two shots.

She hit the back step. "Don't shoot!" Just in case Bianca had some latent Dixie instincts in there and was inclined to shoot first and ask questions after.

She hopped off the back step and saw Bianca on her butt on the grass, looking perturbed. Kenna switched her gun hand, held her hand out, and let Bianca use it to lever herself to her feet.

Bianca used her own momentum, not relying on Kenna to lift her to her feet nearly as much as she could have. Which would hurt Kenna—a lot. "Go. I'll see to Ron."

Kenna raced after the man fleeing across the backyard of Ron's farmhouse. Past empty raised beds, nothing but dirt and dry brown weeds. She settled into a rhythm of running with far less to weigh her down.

The hair color was wrong for the mayor's nephew. Far too light. Jeans and boots not made for running, unlike the Converse she'd broken in months ago. Heavy jacket, also not helpful right now.

She caught up in time to slam him against the side of a pickup truck. His forehead bounced off the top of the door frame.

A group of bicycle riders with tight clothes and helmets pedaled past. One gasped and nearly fell off.

Another said, "She's got a gun."

They all sped up down the one lane road through this rural part of the county.

The shooter slammed into Kenna, catching her off guard. She hadn't been paying attention.

Her behind landed on the ground, and she grunted.

He raced for the front end of the truck.

Kenna lifted her gun and shot at the tire. It popped, and the truck started to lower on that corner.

"Are you kidding me?" He spun around.

"New?"

"New to me." He sounded exasperated. That was too bad. "You're unbelievable." He pulled out a gun. "She said not to kill you. Yet. But this is justified."

"Put it down!" Bianca's voice rang out.

Kenna didn't lower her weapon. "Two against one now."

"Maybe that's how I like it."

Bianca made a gagging sound.

Kenna said, "There's no need to be disgusting."

"Only way a guy like me knows how to be."

"Then be it with your weapon on the ground." Kenna got her feet under her and shifted her weight so she could stand without moving her aim from him.

The man's jaw flexed. After a second of indecision, he set his gun down on the ground.

Bianca said, "Kick it to me."

He complied.

She picked it up.

The guy glanced at her. "Aren't you that Realtor?"

"Sure," Bianca said. "You lookin' to buy a house...or sell one?"

He blinked. "Neither."

"Then shut up about it."

"She's right," Kenna said. "If you're gonna talk, then talk about the caretaker." She wanted to ask about Ron but figured Bianca wouldn't have left him if he was anything but all right.

"What about her?" He smirked.

"Who is she?" Someone who didn't play dumb? How refreshing.

"The caretaker."

"What's her name?" Kenna took a step toward him. "Who is she?"

"I have no idea. We all have family names. She's Lydia."

"So that's not her real name?"

The guy shrugged.

They stayed in the stand-off like three corners of a triangle, beside his truck. Thankfully, no one else rode past. "And you came here for what?"

His expression pinched.

"You were ordered to?"

"How'd you know that?" He frowned.

"Call it instinct," Kenna said. She knew what being under duress looked like. "What did they want you to do?"

"Kill the old man. But he shot at me first."

"No kidding." She nodded. "Hands above your head, turn around." She tugged plastic zip ties from her pocket—the kind with two hand holes.

Bianca said, "You carry those just in case?"

"After the last time I had to apprehend a suspect, yeah. Figured they might come in handy."

The guy looked at Bianca. Kenna told him to turn his head away and let Bianca cover her. He didn't exactly comply willingly, but she got his hands secured behind his back, then took hold of his elbow.

"I still have my gun pointed at you." Kenna pulled it out and held the muzzle pressed against his side. "Don't make me take your future. Right now you still have one."

Ron and Chief Hutton were both on the back porch when they returned to the house. If Kenna needed a ride, this guy's pickup wasn't going to be used while he sat in a jail cell.

"Another for your holding cells, Chief."

His eyebrows rose. "Mrs. Thomson."

Bianca nodded. "Chief."

He glanced at Kenna. "Friend of yours?"

"Turns out, it's none of your business," Kenna said. "Did you find the mayor's nephew?"

"I keep getting called out to your stuff. It's hindering my ability to find a murderer."

She motioned to the guy and realized she was still training the gun on him. "No knife. So he's not the suspect." And the wrong hair color. She stowed her gun in its holster, her head swimming. She managed to say, "All yours."

"Thanks." The chief stepped off the porch and took the guy's elbow, turning to Ron so she couldn't see his face. "I'd like you to come, also, Chief Arnold."

She spun around and nearly toppled over. "Hold up a second—"

"This doesn't concern you, Kenna," the chief said over his shoulder. "I'd rather have Chief Arnold where we can protect him, and he can lend his expertise to the case. Until he's no longer in danger."

When he put it like that, it made sense. She wanted to talk to the older man, but Ron didn't give her a chance where Hutton wasn't watching. He even had her go to stand with Hutton while he locked up.

"Don't worry," the current chief said, "we aren't going to let anything happen to one of our own."

Kenna had seen plenty of people die anyway even with all the good intentions in the world. "I hope so."

She was even tempted to give that to God, asking for His help. But it would only be because she wouldn't be directly involved. For some reason, there was a difference in how she viewed her own capabilities and others' actions. Go figure. She was as prideful as anyone else in the world. Not that the truth made it better.

Ron got in the chief's car.

Bianca moved to stand beside her. "Where to now?"

"Let's check out his truck."

They jumped in Bianca's car, and she drove to the street

behind the defunct farm. "Not a bad location. I should scout out some sellers around here."

"Not sure I'd want to put down roots where you can hear gunshots go off in the morning and drink your coffee staring at the Canadian border."

Bianca snorted. "You just can't handle change. You think things should be the way you want them to be and—"

Kenna cut her off. "How about just the way they are. That's realistic."

"Fine. But you don't want them to change."

Kenna pressed her lips together. "I know things will change. I'm okay with it."

"So long as it slow rolls and you can get used to it on the way."

She didn't want to think about Jax in that context, but thoughts about him were always inevitable. Especially when it had been a while since they talked. "Pull over."

The gunman's truck was unlocked. She found a phone in the glove box and took it with her, since she hadn't found the keys. Kenna gave Bianca the address for the vacation rental, unlike what she'd done with the chief.

"I love those houses," Bianca gushed. "They're all so cute, and the lake is gorgeous."

Kenna said, "I just hope it doesn't get wrecked like everything else."

Cars. Homes. She didn't have a great track record lately. And maybe that was the real reason she hadn't wanted to lay claim to her father's airstream. Not only did she want it to be a safe space for Maizie, but it would have increased the risk of it catching fire or being breached and destroyed.

As soon as they walked in, Kenna put on a pot of coffee.

"Yes, girl." Bianca slid onto a stool at the kitchen counter.

Kenna eyed her. "You good?"

"Are you? You were in a car accident this morning, then you chased that guy."

"He shoved you."

Bianca rolled her eyes. "I get it. We're both 'fine.'" She made air quotes with her fingers.

Kenna's laptop started to make a ringing sound. She opened the lid and turned it away from Bianca. "Hey, Sunshine." A code they had which meant Kenna wasn't alone. She sent Maizie a direct message to turn off her camera.

When the girl had done that, Maizie said, "How are things?"

Kenna nearly said she was fine. "I'm ignoring the worst of it, which will catch up with me sooner or later." She turned the laptop. "This is Bianca Wynn."

"Nice to meet you," Maizie said through the speakers. "I'm the assistant."

Bianca glanced at Kenna. "You have more staff?"

Kenna shrugged. "Business is good." To Maizie she said, "Did you ID the Children of the Morning?"

"Yeah, but you should know Stairns is reading the case file, and he got copies of the witness interviews. He wants to come out there and be your backup. Elizabeth is trying to talk him off the ledge."

"If I need rescuing with every case when things get hot, then why would I go out on my own all the time?"

"Besides," Bianca said, "she's got backup. Me."

Kenna raised her eyebrows at the screen, where she could see herself but not Maizie. "She's right."

Which meant Kenna trusted Bianca, so Maizie should also.

She asked Maizie, "Can you show me what you've got? Maybe Bianca can fill in some gaps."

"I'll share my screen." Maizie went quiet for a second.

"Here. I have four men in town who were rescued from that cistern, all outside the cave."

Four images popped up on the screen.

Bianca immediately said, "Two of them are the preacher's sons. Adopted. Which I figure you could've guessed, but I had no idea where they came from. They have failed marriages and estranged relationships with their kids. Even Mom and Dad don't talk to them these days."

Kenna said, "Okay, that sounds promising."

Maizie hovered her mouse over two of the images. "These two live in town. One is a registered accountant."

"I'd put money down he's not part of it," Bianca said. "He doesn't have it in him to hurt a fly."

Kenna turned to her. "But does that mean he has a hit out on him?"

Bianca shrugged. "Maybe they only do that with troublemakers."

"Maybe." Kenna poured two coffees. "Who is the fourth?"

"I don't know him," Bianca said.

"He works remote for an information security company in New York." Maizie didn't waste a second before asking, "Can I hack his computer? It could be fun, and I can find out if he's still with the group."

"And come across all the trash he's got buried on his hard drive?"

"I can be careful. And Stairns can help."

Bianca glanced at Kenna but didn't ask questions now. Kenna would have to figure out what to tell her about the teen when she inevitably asked later.

"Be. Careful." Kenna didn't want her even to let go of that for one second. "I mean it."

"I know." She sounded every bit the teen.

Bianca smiled into her coffee.

"Anything else?" Kenna asked. "Did you manage to ID any of the girls?"

Another set of photos showed up. All were teen girls or younger. "Two are deceased. One worked outside of Tacoma, to the south. The other was closer to Portland. Both died in the last eighteen months. Then we have the one who dropped off the radar at seventeen. She lived in town, and one day her parents reported her missing. Junior year, a month from summer, suddenly she doesn't come home from work. Doesn't call. Cops found her phone on the side of the road."

Two dead, one missing.

"She escaped," Kenna said. "Got herself out of this life. Who is the last one?"

"I'm having trouble figuring that out. From what I can see, it might be Jolene Denhill."

Kenna blinked. "Elijah's teacher? *She's* the caretaker?"

Bianca flinched. "That's a stretch. It could just as easily be the missing one. Jolene is sweet. She wouldn't hurt a fly."

Kenna glanced at her. "Because every skip you ever took down looked like a bad guy. None of them ever look like unsuspecting innocents who can fool you with one bat of their eyelashes. Or a hot guy who doesn't come across like a serial killer."

They'd both been fooled by Peter Conklin.

"It's not her." Bianca set her mug down so hard it clanked on the counter. "I'm telling you."

"I'm still coming with you."

"Well, then it's good I'll be there so I can tell you I told you so." Bianca shot her a look.

Maizie made a sound across the conference call connection that might've been a laugh.

"I'm happy to be proven wrong." Kenna shrugged. "That means we can scratch one name off the list."

Bianca said, "She's teaching today."

Assuming the woman hadn't called in sick, they at least knew she wasn't up to no good at the school.

"Call Steve," Kenna said. "Tell him to keep an eye out."

"He's volunteering in the classroom all day."

Kenna said, "In the meantime, can you find the other girl, Sunshine?"

It took Maizie a second, then she said, "I'm looking. I'll let you know."

"Great. We'll go chat with the preacher. See what he can tell us about his sons."

"I only have two hours," Bianca said. "Then I have a showing I told Steve I'd be at."

Kenna nodded. "Let's get to it then. Time's a wastin'." She upended her mug in the sink and went to the computer. "You need anything, Sunshine?"

"I'm good."

"And I'm trusting that's true." She stared into the camera so Maize could see all the things she wasn't saying in her expression. "See you soon."

Chapter Twenty-Six

"Thank you for your time. We appreciate it." Kenna stepped into the entryway of the "rectory" as Bianca had referred to it—the tiny house behind the church where the reverend and his wife lived. Then Bianca came in behind her.

The pastor shut the door. "It's what I'm here for." He'd already said to call him "Jim." The man she'd met at the church in his robes now wore jeans and a T-shirt that showed off the frame of a man not a stranger to physical labor.

Kenna stopped at the edge of the living room, in the hall. If she stretched out her arms she could simultaneously touch the stair rail and the back of the couch. She would get claustrophobic in here pretty fast. "I'm afraid this isn't about us needing a listening ear, Reverend. It's about your sons, Daniel and Mark."

Both men were in their forties. They'd been found in the cistern by her father and adopted by the reverend and his wife, who appeared from the kitchen. Kenna had expected a mousy woman in a flowery dress with no shape to it. Instead, the wife strode down the hall on bare feet wearing skinny jeans and a shirt that hung off one shoulder. Maybe it was '80s day at ladies' Bible study.

Kenna introduced herself. "And you probably know Bianca."

The wife smiled wide. "Of course, girl." Then to Kenna, she said, "I'm Clarissa," and wound her arm through the reverend's elbow.

Jim spoke softly to her. "This is about the boys."

She frowned, and the smile dropped from her face. "We should sit. I only have a few cookies, but I can make tea as well."

Bianca gave them both her full-dazzle smile. "That sounds great."

Reverend Jim led them to a living room of light gray couches that invited a person to sink down and rest, and the theme appeared to be Hobby Lobby *Be Still* signage, even though the nearest store was miles away.

"We really do appreciate your time." Kenna sat on the edge of the couch, and Bianca sat beside her while the reverend took the armchair. "Like I mentioned, it's about your boys." She tried for a sympathetic smile. "Which I understand might be difficult. But we need all the information we can get."

Jim nodded, deep enough to reveal thinning on the top of his head. "It is difficult. But if we can further the cause of truth and justice, it will be for good."

Clarissa came in, opting to settle on the arm of her husband's chair so she could lean against his side.

He laid his hand on hers. "They came to us at eleven and nine, though even that was a guess at best. The Children of the Morning kept no birth or death records, so we had to use their height and weight as a measure. Even that may not have been entirely accurate, given the treatment they received from those who were supposed to raise them may have stunted their growth. Certainly both of them were malnourished."

"They were part of the group rescued from the cistern, were they not?"

"That was Kenna's father." Bianca tapped Kenna's shoulder with the back of her hand. "He was the FBI agent that found and rescued them. Max Banbury."

Jim and Clarissa's eyes widened. "I didn't know that," he said. "Wow. What a legacy."

Kenna felt her cheeks get warm. She wanted to finish reading her dad's journals so she could get to know that part of his life better. "What were your sons like, growing up with you?"

Jim shifted in his seat. "They had good days, and bad. We had to reteach all the indoctrination they'd received and show them the truth. The state provided weekly sessions with a counselor who gave them tools to deal with trauma and help process their emotions. We showed them the Bible and walked that road with them as a family."

Clarissa patted his forearm. "It was hard, but it was also beautiful to watch them realize they didn't have to do anything to earn the love of Jesus. For some people, grace is a hard thing to accept. They hold on to bitterness and unforgiveness and build walls to avoid looking inward where they would see all their own pride."

Kenna had heard some things about grace. She knew basically it meant Christians didn't need to do anything but believe in God. It also set them apart from other religions that required believers to do certain things in order to earn their reward. If she was going to adhere to a religion, it would be the one where the yoke put on her was light rather than heavy.

Jim said, "As the boys grew into high schoolers, they shed

a lot of the things they'd been taught but chose to embrace the world rather than the Bible. They began getting into fights at school. Daniel was expelled more than once."

"A few times," Clarissa said, "Mark was arrested, and we'd have to pick him up."

"After they left home, they managed to settle a little, as far as we could tell. Even got married and did the domestic thing for a while."

"Had our adorable grandbabies." Clarissa motioned to a photo frame on the mantel, then stood. "I'll pour the tea."

Jim picked up the story. "There were periods where their wives would seem upset dropping the kids off. Sarah kept attending our church, even after the divorce. We made it clear we fully support her since Mark took all their money and left her high and dry."

Bianca said, "Do the boys work?"

"Daniel had a construction job. The boss let him go, so he started a lawncare company this summer. He did our land-scaping for free so he could take pictures for his website, but I haven't seen it go live yet. Mark works at a body shop where they repair and repaint cars."

Kenna had never worked in a field like that. It had been far too long since she worked a shift or anything like a regular job.

Jim continued, "They're good boys. They followed the ways of the world, and they are certainly selfish. But who isn't? As long as they don't hurt anyone else, then there will still be time for them to hear the truth of the Gospel and turn their lives around."

Bianca said, "I'll keep them on my prayer list." The local Realtor talked the talk. She fit in here—whether because she'd learned to assimilate, or she genuinely liked this life.

Kenna needed to move the conversation along. "Do you

have any idea specifically who they spend time with, maybe outside of work?"

Jim blinked. "I'm not sure I know their friends. Not since youth group."

The reverend motioned to the wall, and rows of framed group photos. Each one had a year at the bottom. Annual trips.

"Do you have reason to believe the Children of the Morning continue to operate?"

"No." Jim's head jerked as though he had been slapped. "How could they? Didn't your father take them all down?"

"It appears there's some form of the group still in operation now." Kenna needed to explain how his sons had been outside a mine with a dead woman inside. That they'd chased her and Ron through the dark. "And we believe it may be connected to Annabelle's death, and the attempted kidnapping of Bianca's son, Elijah."

"That's why you're here?" Jim asked. "Because you believe my sons are involved?"

"Would it surprise you?" Kenna kept a measured tone. "If they were?"

"I suppose not."

"Do you think what they learned might've been strong enough to have stayed with them?"

Jim frowned. "I suppose."

They weren't going to get far if he kept to that answer. Was he done talking?

Clarissa trailed back in carrying a tray containing a plate of cookies alongside a teapot, mugs, and a little pitcher of milk or cream. "You suppose what, dear?" She set it on the table. When she straightened, every bit of the years on her face seemed more pronounced than before.

Jim only sighed.

Bianca shifted in her seat. "I'm sorry, ma'am, but it sounds like the Children of the Morning are still around. And they're targeting people in town."

"B-but not my boys," Clarissa blustered. "They would never harm a woman or...or...kill someone."

Sure, the preacher's wife didn't *want* to think that might be true. However, most people whose loved ones chose a path other than the straight and narrow never wanted that for them, or believed they were capable of it.

"Honey—" Jim turned in his seat.

Just then, the front window shattered. At the same time, a series of gunshots erupted into the living room like every firework in a display being set off at once.

Kenna pulled Bianca down, between the coffee table and the couch, and covered both their heads. The reverend slumped off his chair to land awkwardly in front of the footrest. His mouth moved, but his words proved inaudible over the steady three-round bursts. She squeezed her way in a crawl over to him, keeping her head low.

Bullets hit the wall. The TV.

Kenna moved far enough to see what he was looking at, then swallowed back a cry of her own. The reverend covered his ears, despair on his face. Clarissa lay on her back, blood pumping from her neck to dampen her blond curls with bright red.

Kenna shoved the coffee table on its side. The wood wasn't going to provide much cover, but she crawled over to the preacher's wife and pressed down on the wound with both hands. Hot red blood seeped between her fingers. "Stay with me."

The words were swallowed up in the noise of rifle fire.

The shooter shifted aim, just a brief pause, then howled in low-toned laughter.

"Yes, the rectory," Bianca said into her phone. "That's what—"

Gunfire started up all over again.

Clarissa blinked up at Kenna.

"Help is coming." Kenna leaned closer so their noses almost touched, in the hope Clarissa could hear her. But there was no time. Whoever had fired that shot hit her artery. "Hang on. Just hang on."

It was already too late.

Clarissa's eyes filled. A tear rolled down her face. "I'm sorry."

"Don't be," Kenna whispered. It's okay."

"I"—the dying woman swallowed—"called them."

Kenna's stomach clenched. Clarissa had called her boys, from the kitchen? "It's—"

The spark of life left Clarissa's eyes, and her head lowered to one side. In her last breath, she stared at her husband. A second later, her chest deflated for the last time, and she passed on to the life that came next.

Kenna's awareness came back into focus.

The reverend shoved her back. "Let me."

"Stay down." The gunshots had stopped, but Kenna wasn't going to sit here and wait for help. She stuck to a crouch but wound her way to the back of the house, stepping out the patio with her gun drawn.

She raced around the outside of the house, flipped the latch on the gate, and cleared the space beyond it before she stepped out.

Two men stood by the side door of a rusty pickup truck. She knew who they were from the photos Maizie had shown them.

Daniel took the last swig of a beer bottle and threw the empty in the truck bed. He lifted his rifle again, laughing at something his brother said.

Kenna took cover at the left front corner of the house. "Drop it!"

He swung the rifle toward her. His brother dropped his beer so that it shattered on the asphalt. He reached for the rifle he'd set on the hood.

Kenna squeezed off a shot. With the distance, and the fact that she'd no longer qualify as an FBI agent in shooting accuracy, the shot clipped his shoulder—the outside of his arm.

He yelped.

The brother swung his rifle around.

Kenna squeezed off another shot and hit the front quarter panel of the pickup.

The injured brother yelled, "Go!"

They jumped in and took off before the doors were even closed.

Kenna darted across the grass, squeezing off shots into the back of the truck and its tires.

A blood red haze washed over her vision. All she could see in her mind's eye was their mother, her lifeblood seeping through Kenna's fingers. The way another woman's blood had just weeks ago.

A victim. Senseless death. And for what?

Her gun clicked empty, and she realized she'd expended all her bullets.

"Put it down!"

"Put the gun down!"

Kenna still held it raised. The fleeing truck had gone out of sight. Her mind flashed back to Justine, lying on the floor. Then Clarissa. Blood.

She heard a screen door snap back on its hinges.

Someone yelled, "It's okay!"

"Stay back, Mrs. Thomson," the officer said. "Put the weapon down, ma'am."

Kenna stared at her hands still holding the empty gun raised. Blood coated her fingers. Her palms.

"Kenna."

"Stay back, Dix." She didn't want her friend to get hurt because of her. Not again.

Dixie stepped in front of her. Close, so her outside arm touched Kenna's elbow. She laid a hand on Kenna's shoulder. "It's Bianca, remember?" One of her eyebrows rose.

Kenna stared into her friend's eyes.

"She needs to put that gun down," one of the cops said.

Kenna sucked in a breath.

Bianca said, "How about you give it to me for safekeeping?"

Did she think that would disarm Kenna? She lowered it slowly, holstering it at the small of her back, and sucked in a long breath. Instinct had her wanting to close her eyes, but that would always be a bad idea. "Mrs.... The reverend's wife is dead."

Bianca glanced at the cops. "There's a victim inside."

"Who killed her?"

Bianca turned back to Kenna. "Did you see who was out here?"

Kenna faced the cops. "It was their sons. Daniel and Mark." She would never forget the laughter. The drinking, and that cavalier way they fired at their home. Their parents.

One of the cops headed inside.

The other stayed where he was. "I'll need statements from both of you."

Kenna looked down at the blood on her hands.

"Come on." Bianca tugged on her arm. "Let's clean up in the church."

"Then you need to get to work, right? You have that showing."

"I think I need to activate the prayer chain first." Bianca hauled open the rear door to the church.

"Is that going to do anything?"

"It will make everyone aware, and they can help take care of the reverend."

Kenna frowned.

Out of the corner of her eye, she spotted someone in the sanctuary. A flash of dark hair. White clothes.

She hurried to the heavy door and looked in. "Is someone in there?" Then turned back. "I just thought I saw a woman."

"Come on." Bianca winced. "You need to wash up."

The officer stood at the end of the hall, watching them.

Right. Kenna needed to look like a stable person, not a wildcard. That meant keeping it together long enough to solve this case.

The trip here had cost Clarissa her life, but they knew more now about the threat than they had before.

She was one step closer.

Chapter Twenty-Seven

Kenna sipped the last of her smoothie and stared at the Thomson house from the front seat of Bianca's luxury SUV. Apparently, being a Realtor paid well.

After the day they'd had, she'd stuck close to Bianca through her work. When Bianca had gone home to dinner with her husband and son, Kenna borrowed her vehicle to go shower and change. Then blended a drink to go.

She had also snuck to the back via the alley and hooked a camera on the fence to see if anyone approached that way. It didn't give her a great angle, but anyone passing by that route to the back door would pass her camera and her phone would send her notifications. So far the only movement alerts she'd received were local cats traversing the alley.

She texted Maizie that the camera she'd delivered to the house by same-day delivery seemed to be working fine. They'd only connected by message since the reverend's wife died. Kenna didn't want to talk to anyone unless they pushed it. Right now she needed her space. And why not? She'd literally held a woman's life in her hands and watched the light go out.

Kenna sighed into the dark and quiet of the SUV, while the engine clicked as it cooled. A breeze drifted in the cracked windows. The trees rustled.

Control isn't the same as peace.

That was what Ryson had said. And now it turned out she didn't have peace at all. Not even a semblance of it.

All she had was what she could control. It was the only thing holding her together, and that grasp was tenuous at best.

The phone buzzed in her hand, against her leg. She didn't recognize the number, but the area code was New York. Maybe a new case?

"Hello?"

He chuckled, soft but not like he was laughing at her. "I shouldn't have waited so long."

"Jax."

"In my defense, it took this long for me to get a day off. I took the train to New York. I'm calling from a hotel room phone I booked under a fake name Maizie gave me."

Her eyes burned. She scrunched up her nose.

"Kenna, you good?"

She cleared her throat.

"You're not okay. What's happening? Is it Maizie?"

A stupid tear escaped. Kenna swiped it away. *I'm fine.* The words sat on the tip of her tongue. But she didn't want to brush it off, and it wasn't nothing. "Rough day. Maizie is fine."

"Okay." His voice softened. That was the worst part. That she would need sympathy, and he would give it. Because he cared.

"You know, my father would just tell me to quit crying. Suck it up."

Jax huffed a laugh. "Of course. Because you being a girl was too much to handle. Max Banbury, renowned international investigator, and he's felled by a teenage girl with feelings."

Kenna found a chuckle. "He really was. He thought guacamole and chips solved everything."

"He was wrong," Jax said. "It's cheese dip that solves everything."

"Mister health foods and yoga? You're telling me you medicate with cheese dip?"

He laughed. "Don't tell the FBI. They already think I should spill all my secrets."

Kenna groaned. "Are they putting pressure on you to tell them where I am?"

"They do want to know where you are. They want to know where the teen girl is that they know is connected to this case. As much as it sucks, it helps that I have no contact with you, of course."

She smiled. "Of course."

He sighed. The sound of it allowed her to do the same.

After a few seconds of comfortable silence, she said, "A woman died today."

He let that be, then said, "Like Justine."

Of course he would make the connection. Her mind certainly had in the moment because of the blood on her hands at the dedication ceremony in Vegas months ago where they'd honored her deceased partner.

"Yes." She had to swallow against the lump in her throat. "I winged one of the shooters, one of her sons. The cops are chasing down that lead. Chief Hutton is complaining I'm outside his purview, but he can't deny I'm handing him leads." The chief was probably getting all the information he could from Ron since he'd taken the older man to the station. "What do you know about the Children of the Morning?"

"Never heard of them." His voice worked better than the

dark and being alone. Working to keep someone safe. "Should I have?"

"It was in the weeks before Waco. The coverage got lost in all that. You probably would have no reason to hear about them." She paused. "My dad worked the case."

"I'll look it up." Jax hissed. "Except any search outside case bounds goes on record. So anyone watching me would get a clue where you are, and what you're doing."

"Are they watching you?"

"Close enough I should've already been released to my next posting, and yet I'm still in DC. Using a fake name to travel on my weekend off just to call you." He paused. "But I'm pretty sure they just have a detail watching. Making sure I don't meet up with you."

"Good thing I don't like New York."

He chuckled. "Shame."

"Yeah, it is." Kenna let out a long sigh.

"Complicated case?"

"Just a lot of moving pieces. And ideology that wrapped people up in something it's going to take more than one conversation to clear up their misconception." That made for a powerful enemy. She thought about Daniel and Mark today and explained the adoption. "They were given every opportunity to see the truth. To leave the toxic mess they were raised in and have a good life. But something in them never quite let go of it. They had to have wanted the belonging, or the power. I don't even know. Have you ever been in a club?"

He chuckled. "I don't think the football team—before I got hurt—is a good example. But it was a powerful sense of belonging, especially in high school. We got to strut around like hot stuff."

She chuckled just thinking about it. "And now you do it with a badge."

"But what you're dealing with is a whole lot more pervasive than a sports team, or being a fed."

"Maybe not that farfetched." Kenna saw a car pull into a nearby driveway. "Doesn't everyone want something to belong to? At least I've heard."

"Like a group, or a label. Some kind of association." Jax paused. "Everyone wants to feel like they belong. It makes us less alone."

"I like being alone."

"You call it that, but you have people who care a lot about you. And they're not far."

Kenna smiled to herself and watched the neighbor—a gray-haired man in slacks, shined shoes, and a buttoned shirt —get a backpack from his back seat and head inside.

"You know that, right?" Jax added.

"A lot of people would tell me I need to land somewhere. Let people in." Kenna wasn't sure she was wired for more than a close, very small support group—and plenty of personal space.

"You have," Jax said. "Don't you think?"

"More than I ever planned or wanted to."

He chuckled, then sighed. "I want to make a plan so we can meet up somewhere. But at this point, it would be easier if I quit the Bureau and went freelance like you."

"And have you breathing down my neck?" She didn't want him giving up his career—the life he wanted—for her. "You can get your own cases."

He barked a laugh. "Calm down, honey."

"I know that's a Golden Girls GIF. I send it to Maizie when she's being a dramatic teenager."

"I'll figure out what I'm doing." He sighed. "But I get what you said in Colorado about needing a new case or you'll go soft."

"You can't have any of mine." She knew full well she was being deliberately antagonistic about this, but she didn't need him ruining his future for her. At least not until they'd talked it through when they were both in a better frame of mind than this.

"Do you need anything?"

Kenna wasn't going to lie to him. "Yeah, but I'm okay with what I have."

"See you soon."

"I hope so."

He was quiet for a second. "I won't let you get into trouble over this. You did the right thing."

"I won't answer questions about Maizie. I'll plead the Fifth or something." Kenna bit her lip. "But I will consider coming in. After this case is done. But only if it's necessary."

"Thought you were going after a loose end?"

Ben Landry. "He's dead now."

Jax didn't say anything.

"I'm not the one who killed him." She had to say that? Really? She was off her game if she thought he needed her to defend herself. Still... "I crashed my car trying to keep him alive."

"The Impala?"

She winced. "It's toast. I had to borrow one." And she'd had to get another magazine for her weapon. Plus a backup, just in case. "I guess I need a new car. And a home."

"Might be a good time to start fresh." Which he'd tried to do by buying the airstream she'd passed on to Maizie.

"I might get another RV. But for right now, I'd settle for four wheels."

"Not a motorcycle?"

Kenna frowned. "You think I should?"

"I think you'd be unstoppable. Super cool."

"The kids don't say that anymore."

"Turns out I'm old." He chuckled. "Which my nephews have great fun informing me. My sister just rolls her eyes. Her husband hands me a beer even though I've never finished one. I don't like it."

She had noticed he only drank soda water at the Fourth of July celebration in Colorado. But she'd been more concerned about whether the others would know how much she noticed things about him. "Thanks for calling."

He made a *hmm* sound. "I'm falling asleep. It was a long train ride."

"Don't get into trouble in New York."

"I promise."

She smiled, calculating the three-hour time difference that put him at past midnight. Nearly one in the morning. On a Friday night? He had to be exhausted. "Get some sleep."

"'Kay."

"Bye." For some reason, she said, "See you soon."

"Hope so." He grunted, and the line went dead.

Kenna pictured him on the second bed in that Vegas motel room, when he'd been all unassuming, sleeping on the other queen bed in her room. Apparently, he'd thought she needed someone to watch out for her. As if protection had anything to do with falling asleep. Like he wanted to be her backup, no matter what threat came at her.

She supposed he was her boyfriend. If they were going to put a label on it. Hardly seeing each other definitely put a damper on it. Even though at the same time it made it easier to keep doing what she was supposed to do. If he were here, she would be worrying about their "relationship" rather than focused on the case. She'd be distracted.

Having their whole thing on this simmering slow burn

made it easier to make each small adjustment she inevitably had to make for this to ever become a permanent thing.

Kenna didn't plan on changing her life.

If Jax wanted to be a regular part of it, she would. Relationships meant sacrifice. If she didn't give up something, then it hadn't cost her anything to make it work. Which meant she'd have no skin in the game.

She fought constantly against what people would always think her life "should" be. Who she was would never align with people's expectations, and she'd accepted that a long time ago. Being with Jax would be hard work in all the right ways—making it worth doing. Like choosing a faith-based relationship with God, rather than just what she could understand with her intellect but never allowing it to change her heart.

She was pondering those verses in the Bible that said God was mysteries, and His ways unsearchable, when a light flashed inside. An odd shadow against the window.

She checked her camera feed. No notifications. That meant someone hadn't approached via the alley.

The back of her neck pricked with awareness.

She watched, but nothing else happened. Then the front window exploded and a person landed on the grass, rolling to a stop.

Kenna flung the door open and ran across the street. She palmed her phone and her gun, then called 911.

"Helson Emergency Dispatch—"

"Detective Steve Thomson's house," Kenna said, cutting off the dispatcher. "He's on the front lawn. Injured. We need police. An ambulance, for sure. Tell the chief Kenna is on scene." She dropped her phone on the grass and knelt.

Shards of window glass pricked her knees.

She rolled Thomson to his back and winced. She yelled

toward the phone, "We need that ambulance! *Now.* Detective Thomson is hurt bad."

Given the state of that head injury leaking blood, he might not last long enough to be helped. Kenna had to leave him, though. She had to check on the others.

She lifted her chin and screamed, "Dixie!" through the open window.

No answer.

She ran to the front door and kicked it in. Who had entered the house, and how had they done it when she'd had the front and back covered? Unless they'd climbed over the fence from the neighbor's—and planned to leave the same way.

Kenna cleared rooms with her pistol ready.

Bianca stood at the bottom of the stairs in her robe, her hair twisted up in towel. "What happened? I heard a noise."

"Steve is on the lawn, hurt. Where's Elijah?"

Bianca turned to the stairs. "I'll check his room."

Kenna moved through the house while she did that, systematically checking each one. The door Annabelle had taken Elijah out last time stood open.

The backyard was quiet. No one around.

She checked the alley, but no one was parked there.

A scream ripped through the quiet evening.

A van passed the alley at the end, driving on the street. The door slid shut as it went. Closing Elijah in the back.

Kenna raced to the end of the alley but missed it. By the time she barreled onto the road—with her gun up, even though shooting at a fleeing vehicle was a bad idea—they were gone. Shooting at a fleeing vehicle twice in one day would be even worse.

She raced back to the house and found Bianca out front with her husband.

Kenna crouched by her friend. "How is he doing?"

Tears rolled down Bianca's face. "He won't wake up."

Right now Kenna was just glad he was breathing. She didn't look too closely at the blood given the day she'd had.

An ambulance rolled to a stop at the curb.

Bianca said, "Where's Elijah?"

Kenna tugged Bianca out of the way of the paramedics.

Bianca grasped Kenna's elbow. "Where is my son?"

Two uniformed officers raced up. "What happened?"

Kenna glanced at each of them in turn. "Steve was attacked, and Elijah has been taken."

Bianca gasped. "He's gone?"

Chapter Twenty-Eight

"Bring him home." Bianca gripped Kenna's arm. "Or don't bother coming back." She climbed into the rear of the ambulance, and the EMT shut the door.

The vehicle sped away.

Kenna looked at the front of the house, with the smashed-out living room window. Then she turned to the car.

"Excuse me, ma'am." One of the uniformed officers stepped in front of her. "The chief is on his way."

Kenna waited for it.

"He'd like you to wait until he gets here."

She let out a long sigh. "Of course he does."

She went back to the spot where Thomson had been lying and retrieved her phone. She sent a couple of *I'm fine* messages, then stowed it in her back pocket. She tried not to pace, but with a child in jeopardy and no way to race after them and track the suspects down, she had to get rid of her pent-up energy somehow.

The chief's car pulled up. She strode down to meet him at the hood of his vehicle. "We need to find Elijah."

He nodded. "So what's the plan?"

He really wanted to team up? Maybe she didn't need his help, despite what he seemed to be offering. Kenna folded her arms. "Did you find the mayor's nephew yet?"

One of the other officers coughed. She and the chief both ignored him.

Hutton said, "Not yet."

"What about the reverend's boys? I winged one of them. He'll need medical treatment."

Hutton shook his head. "Nothing. They're in the wind."

"And some of your officers are checking the woods where that clearing is, and the mine. The area around that?"

He frowned. "Angling for my job?"

"My friend's son was just kidnapped, and her husband is probably going to be labeled as in critical condition as soon as he gets to the hospital."

"Okay, fine. You're on this." Hutton lifted his chin. "It would go faster if we work together."

"That usually doesn't go so well for the cop in the mix." He had to understand the risk inherent in working with her.

"The common denominator in that is you." He enjoyed pointing that out, she could see it in his expression. "But don't worry. I can handle myself."

"That's what they all say." She sighed. "Has Ron told you anything?"

"He's been pouring over maps, trying to figure out where the Gathering Place might be. But it's been so long since he was there that he doesn't remember much except that they walked for hours, and it was a stormy night."

That didn't give her much to go on. "We need one of the suspects you've got in custody to tell us where to find them."

"They aren't talking." Hutton shrugged. "It's like a silence pact."

"Whatever it is, it's been going on under everyone's noses."

"But they messed up," he pointed out. "We know what they're doing now. We know what their plan is."

They knew who the group wanted to get their hands on, but did that stop Elijah from getting kidnapped? "All that's left is who the members are and where they're going to be."

Like those would be easy to figure out. She could think of one more survivor. Elijah's teacher. Perhaps Jolene Denhill had information she could give them.

Kenna pulled out her phone and asked Maizie for the woman's address.

"Go home," Hutton said. "We'll take your statement and follow up with any leads. Try to find the van, and where they took Elijah."

"Right. Will do." She could use sleep, but it still felt wrong to do that when Elijah could be hurt. Or killed. But if she didn't know where to look…

They also had two days still until the big event.

Kenna slid into the front seat. All she had was a photo, and that symbol written on the wall under the barn. Why didn't she know more about these people?

The call to her assistant connected before she pulled away from her parking spot.

"I feel like I have to ask if you're okay every time we talk." Maizie sighed. "Is every case like this?"

Kenna gripped the wheel. "Can't you just text me the address?"

"You'll have no backup going there tonight on your own."

"Too many people have died already."

"So going alone is the answer?"

Kenna blew out a breath. "Don't tell me Stairns is already on a plane on his way here. I don't need help every single time

I work a case, and he nearly got killed last time." The guy needed to let go of the glory days of the past and think about his wife and children, his grandchildren.

Maizie chuckled. "I think he would be if it wasn't the middle of the night."

"Good." Maybe this would be over before he heard.

"The address is in your messages." Maizie paused. "Call me when you're done."

"Will do." She could handle regular check-ins for both their sakes.

Elijah's teacher, Jolene Denhill, lived across town in a cute yellow cottage with flowerpots on the front steps. Not exactly the residence of a psycho, but then again it was often hard to tell.

The woman had a camera doorbell, so a chime would've rung through the house when it spotted Kenna. Still, she hit the button to add the buzzer just in case that was the extra alert Jolene needed to wake up. Being at home and asleep in bed probably indicated she wasn't involved. However, like the flowers on the porch, it could mean she was a diabolical woman.

The exterior light flicked on. Kenna blinked at the glow and heard, "Who is it?" in a crackly voice through the camera doorbell like a bad phone connection.

Kenna gave her fake name. "We met at the school. I was watching Elijah?"

"Why are you here?"

"He's been kidnapped." She needed to say more than that if she was going to explain the severity of the problem, but before she could the door handle clicked, Jolene was visible in the few inches she opened it. "Elijah is gone?" The teacher's expression seemed genuinely concerned. "I'm sorry to hear that."

Kenna indicated the door. "I'd like to come in and ask you a few questions, if that's okay."

"I don't know anything about it." She started to step back, so Kenna grabbed the chance to put one foot inside. Which forced Jolene to open the door all the way.

If she asked Kenna to leave or called the police for the same result, Kenna wouldn't push it. But she had to ask questions. She needed answers. "You were one of the children found in that cistern, weren't you?"

Jolene wrapped her robe tighter around her. "I was a baby. The youngest. I don't remember a single thing about that place, and I've never been back to the compound."

Kenna leaned against the wall because she would come across as less imposing to the five-five woman with the slight build. "You were adopted like the others?"

Jolene nodded. "I suppose I could tell you who some of them are. But we aren't friends. I don't associate with them. I wasn't even raised in this country. My adoptive mother and I lived across the border in a town on the Canadian side. She's a college professor. We both have dual citizenship."

"So why come back here?"

Jolene glanced aside at her entryway table and the dish of assorted keys and lip balm. "I suppose I wanted to see the town where I was born. Hear about it from the people who live here. Maybe even help the other survivors, or their children."

"How did that go?"

"No one talks about it." Jolene shook her head. "It's bizarre. Almost like collective selective amnesia."

Kenna had experienced the same thing. She dug out the photo of the cave she'd discovered. "Have you ever seen this place before?"

Jolene took the picture and studied it. "Not from

anywhere I've been, but it looks like..." She trailed away through the house to a dining room she'd made into a formal sitting room with fancy couches and shelves spilling over with books. If Kenna ever got a house, this would be the reason to do it.

Jolene crouched in front of one of the shelves and slid out a thick photo album. She laid it on the floor and creaked pages as she leafed through it. "This." She lifted the book and stood, showing Kenna the page. "Doesn't that look similar?"

The image was a yellowed vacation photo. Jolene and an older woman with dissimilar coloring stood side by side in a cavernous space whether carved out of rock or naturally occurring.

"There are even sconces on the wall." Kenna frowned. "But how do we know if it's the same space? Maybe there are miles and miles of these all over this part of the US and Western Canada."

"My mom dragged me all over British Columbia looking at historical sites. She was a college professor and an amateur geologist. Unless she got her PhD in that as well. Last time I saw her it was only a doctorate in early North American studies."

"Only?"

They shared a smile.

"I honestly think it was her way of humanizing the cult for me. When most people elevate groups like that to some great evil. She looked at the historical angle. Tracking their path down to Helson through the generations so I could see that there was nothing I could've done, and I should live the life I wanted to." Jolena took the album back and closed it. "I don't think she figured that meant me becoming an elementary school teacher in one of the smallest districts in the country. Though I do love history. There's just more of it than simply what involves the Children of the Morning."

The caves had been about following the cult? "What do you mean 'tracking their path'?" Kenna asked. Did Jolene know how to find where they were located now?

"Have you ever seen this?" Jolene grabbed a notepad and pencil from the counter and swirled a symbol under a list that included milk and yogurt. She showed it to Kenna.

"That's..." Kenna's brows rose. "I've seen that." On Annabeth's wrist, and the wall in the room under the barn.

"It'll be on the wall in that cavern or carved into a tree. Though your picture is too dark to tell."

"What does it mean?"

Jolene sighed. "Sometimes I think the only reason she adopted me is so she could have inside access to the information available if I wanted to know more about where I came from. Plus, it softened her in the eyes of her colleagues."

"She knew what that symbol means?"

Jolene nodded. "She'll explain it much better than I ever could, but it's a rune. It goes back to medieval times, as far as she could tell. She found it on the walls of caves in Wales and Scotland. Then Nova Scotia. Upper Ontario. They traveled west every time things got hot. Over the generations people have suspected they are places where hidden treasure is buried, but no one ever found anything there. Instead, they only found bones."

"So they made their way to Helson." Kenna couldn't believe the group had been a thing for so long. Centuries even.

"By the time they planted roots here, it was easier to assimilate as a cult. People understand those. Not the way they treat legends like Bigfoot. A cult is a known enemy you stay away from, not something you go looking for."

"Your mom found all this out about the Children of the Morning?" Kenna needed to get Maizie to look into the symbol and the history behind it.

"It was her life's work." Jolene's expression turned wistful. "Maybe I was her life's work. Getting to raise one of them."

Kenna had been raised by a fanatic, in a way, so she could empathize to an extent. Although, who didn't get a little into the job they loved sometimes? "Did they ever approach you and ask you to join their group, as it is currently?"

Jolene shook her head. "Maybe they don't know I was that baby in the cistern."

Or they had a caretaker already and therefore had no use for Jolene. "That's a really good thing, as far as I can tell." Assuming Jolene was telling the truth. "Where was that place you went with your mom?"

"It's in Canada. Not far from the border. It would only take you an hour or so to drive from here. My mom lives in Calgary now."

Kenna nodded. "Is there anyone you know who might be in the middle of this? Part of them?" Even if she had asked already, Kenna had to sometimes restate a question just to jog an answer loose. Or catch someone in a lie.

Jolene shivered. "Even if I walk past one of them in the grocery store, I don't want to know."

"Have you ever spoken with Ron Arnold?"

"Wasn't he the former police chief?" When Kenna confirmed, Jolene said, "I don't know that I've ever met him. Maybe I've seen him at church, though."

"Thanks for helping." Kenna needed to follow up on all this symbol—or rune—stuff. Usually the fights she had were in the here and now. She wasn't sure how she was going to fight an organization that had gone back generations and crossed continents. If that's who these people were, the ones in

Helson were flesh and blood. Contemporary Helson residents. Friends. Siblings. Children.

People she could track. Catch.

Someone knocked on the door.

Kenna turned to Jolene. "Are you expecting a cop?"

Jolene frowned at Kenna's question. "How do you know it's a cop?"

"Only one type of person knocks like that." She strode to the door, her hand behind her back close to her gun. She flung the door open. "What do you—Chief?"

He did the same move to enter that she'd done with Jolene, and Kenna allowed it. "Jolene?" His gaze found her behind Kenna. "Are you okay? Is this woman bothering you?" It wasn't his usual "chief" tone, but one far softer.

Kenna's eyes widened, and she stared at the chief's back. Someone was sweet on the local elementary teacher.

Jolene blushed. "We were just talking, Chief."

"You know you can call me Derek."

"Oh." She blushed even more.

Kenna coughed so it didn't come out as a laugh. She didn't want them to think she was laughing at them, but this was about the most adorably awkward thing she'd ever seen.

"Thank you, Derek." Jolene laid a hand on his arm. "I'm perfectly safe."

Kenna wanted to say, *See?* but didn't want to spoil their moment.

"Good." He shot her a dirty look.

Kenna said, "Jolene was extremely helpful. But it's late, so I should be going."

She stepped out of the house so they could talk more, and Chief Hutton could ask her out—something Kenna was relatively sure he hadn't worked up the courage to do yet, even if Jolene was giving him all the right signals.

The whole thing made her want to call Jax just to say hi—if that wouldn't wake him up. But she wasn't a teenage girl, or a sweet woman. Maybe she never had been. Now wasn't the time to start acting like a middle schooler.

Kenna strode to her car trying to wrap her head around the scope of this case. She needed a location, and a suspect to point her gun at.

Case closed.

God willing, she would bring Elijah home to his parents. Two living parents.

Please, God.

She started the car, swallowing against the lump in her throat.

Every case had a moment where she had nothing—right before something broke. This might be that moment, or there was another to come.

Had that breakthrough been God working all along, with each case she worked?

Whether that would prove true or not, Kenna was going to do her part to bring an innocent boy home.

Chapter Twenty-Nine

In the end, Kenna got some sleep. Whatever was going to happen, she would need to be well rested. Even so, she set her alarm for six, put her phone on silent, and got a solid four hours, waking up to a notification for a new voicemail for a call that came in while she slept.

She laid back in bed and hit the button to play it.

"Hey, it's Jax. You're probably sleeping still. Resting, I hope." His tone deepened. "I looked up the group you mentioned? Be careful. I'm not flying over there to identify a Jane Doe. I'll make Stairns do it."

He chuckled, but there was nothing humorous about what he'd just said.

"Anyway, I'll call again later. I'm having breakfast with the ASAC for the FBI office here in New York. We went to Quantico together. I'm going to ask for that favor he owes me. See if he can request me specially for a taskforce or something. Get me out of DC."

She heard the frustration bleed into his tone.

"Like I said. Be careful."

The message ended.

Kenna let out a long sigh. She could stay here in a bed, in a house, all comfy, but was this her life? Right now it was only a temptation to ignore the world. To do what she wanted, rather than what she should. Instead, she got up, poured a cup of coffee from the pot she'd set up the night before, and took a shower.

By the time she was dressed, she had another notification on her phone. A number.

Kenna took her coffee to the couch while the phone rang.

The woman who answered said, "Professor Amara Denhill."

Kenna explained who she was, and how she'd spoken with Jolene the night before. That she was looking into cold cases connected to the Children of the Morning. "If you're available, I'd like to speak with you about the group and anything you might be able to tell me about where to find them."

"I'm out on a historical survey this semester, on a sabbatical until school starts up again in the spring."

"Anywhere near Helson?" Kenna said.

"What are you thinking? You probably don't want to drive all the way out here."

"There's a symbol Jolene showed me. I saw it in a room under the barn at the compound. Maybe you'd like to see it?" And in the process, Jolene's mom could give Kenna some more context about the group and where they might have taken Elijah.

"We can do that." Amara rustled across the phone line. "I'd like to see it. The whole thing has been something of a lifelong study, even if the university would rather I look at the plight of indigenous peoples. Shaming the government is far more fashionable these days." She suggested a time.

Kenna said, "I'll meet you at the compound front gate."

Two in the afternoon would give her plenty of time to run down more leads in town.

She filled a hot cup with coffee, packed up her duffel, and drove to the police station.

Once inside, she approached the front desk. "Chief Hutton, please. But I'd actually like to speak to Chief Arnold."

The officer eyed her. "Are you who I think you are?"

"Probably." She spotted the former chief in the break room and waved to get his attention.

Ron came to the door. "Let her in, Nicky."

The officer muttered something about Sunday school and let her in. To Kenna he said, "It's Officer Walden." The guy was maybe twenty-three.

She said, "Good for you, Nicky."

He sighed.

Kenna took her hot cup to the break room and faced down Ron, who had settled into a chair. "You told me you were part of the group as a kid. Not just that, but long enough that when the FBI needed to get involved, you—a cop at the time—went in undercover. You betrayed them."

"They deserved it."

"Because they didn't choose you as their leader?" Kenna leaned against the door frame. "They chose your friend instead."

"He treated me like trash."

"Yeah, kids will do that. Especially if suddenly they're the top dog." She took a sip of her drink and pulled the paper from her pocket. She unfolded it and showed him. "Do you know what this symbol is?"

"Their emblem. They put it up all over, and on the letter-head." Ron moved to the coffee and poured a cup. He had on jeans and a lumberjack shirt, his hair mussed. There was a pillow and blanket on the couch. The chief hadn't been kidding about Ron staying here.

"Since the Middle Ages."

Ron turned, nearly spilling his drink. "What now?"

"I'm going to meet with a history professor at the compound so she can look around and maybe help me understand."

"Is that a good idea? They could be there."

"I'm pretty sure the compound is the one place they're not." Kenna hadn't seen anyone there. It might be connected to the mines through tunnels in the basement, but the only place she'd seen these people was up in the hills and in town. "The chief has officers up in the mountains, right?"

Ron leaned against the counter and drank his morning brew. "Probably. He's stretched pretty thin, and now Thomson..."

"Any update?"

"He's in a medically induced coma. They need the swelling in his brain to come down before they'll think about waking him up."

Kenna blew out a long breath. She wanted to go see Bianca, but with no information that would give her hope it would only be an exercise in futility.

"Yeah." Ron sighed.

They stood in silence for a minute or so, as though the moment demanded a little reverence.

Then Kenna pushed off the wall. "I'm getting Elijah back."

"Before tomorrow night?"

"You don't think I'll find him?"

Ron winced. "Might be best if you don't. Going up against them is suicide."

"You survived." Kenna paused. "They didn't know it was you that ratted them out?"

"Your dad made sure I was arrested alongside them, but then officially cleared of wrongdoing, which of course everyone only saw as preferential treatment because I was a cop." He made a face. "I clawed my way back to being a respected officer in this town."

"And you never ran into anyone who gave you the impression they were still part of the group? Not one single time on the job did you ever wonder if the Children of the Morning might be back?"

Ron stared into his coffee.

"Because as far as history is concerned, this group doesn't die. They set up shop in a new spot."

"They know how to go unnoticed."

"But there's no leader until a child is found?" Kenna shook her head. "What about some kind of holy book, or a manual I can read that will explain all this to me?"

"The FBI burned them all. As though doing that would get them to stop believing," he said. "I thought breaking up the band with different prisons would do it. Sending them all over the country. We worked hard to make it so that none of them ever saw each other again."

"Now we have a new generation."

His eyes darkened. "I'm going with you to the compound."

She tried to argue against it, but the concept of taking backup should override the desire to fly solo—and it did.

Kenna had to remind the old cop to put on his seatbelt. They reached the compound with enough time for Ron to produce a cigar from somewhere and light up. The smoke drifted over.

Memories sparked to life in her mind, like a match to accelerant.

"My dad used to smoke those," she mused. "On the chair by the fire pit. I'd leave my window cracked and fall asleep reading, smelling the smoke." She smiled to herself. "Or I'd listen to him on the phone. Sometimes he would mutter about the case he was working."

She'd forgotten all about his fire pit cigars.

"He told me about you." Ron grinned around the cigar. "Said his wife was killed right after you were born. He worked out of the Seattle office when we met, and he used to leave you with a neighbor who watched you while he was at work, an older lady from church. Said you were the most precocious thing."

"I don't remember back then." Kenna might have to look up the older lady though, after she figured out who it was. Still, with the time that had passed, a woman like that had probably moved on from this life.

"He didn't like it. He missed you, so he'd show pictures." Ron smirked. "You were a funny-looking kid."

She smiled.

"He wanted a way to stay with you more and not be gone for long days, or sometimes weeks on end, when he worked a case."

"So he quit the Bureau and took me with him?"

Ron stared at her for a second. "If you're looking for a perfect father, you're talking to the wrong guy."

"I know I had it better than most." Kenna stared at the desolate compound. "He loved me. I was healthy, and as safe as anyone ever is."

Given all she'd seen and done, safety was a fluid concept. Anyone who thought they were safe had to realize it was tenuous at best.

She shifted her hands, patting a couple of pockets. The gun on the back of her belt was only the beginning of the ways she had to protect herself.

Her phone rang. Kenna didn't recognize the number, but it was local.

"Yep?"

"It's Chief Hutton. Where'd you go? And with Ron?"

"We're getting information on the group. As soon as we're done, we'll be back at the station." She had just been thinking about how tenuous safety was, so she continued, "If anything happens, call this number." She gave him Stairns' digits. Safety wasn't as important as making sure Maizie stayed so far below the radar that anyone even aware of her existence should only think she might be an AI-generated image at best.

"Got it. What's that for?"

"My people can track me." Given the button-size device in her shoe. "Just in case."

"Copy that." Chief Hutton hung up before she could ask him if he'd actually asked out Jolene the night before, or if he was still being a chicken about it.

Kenna nodded. "She's here." She pushed off the hood of her car and turned to see a small SUV make its way up the dirt road.

Jolene's adoptive mother got out wearing a brown suede jacket with fringe under the arms. Several strands of her straight dark hair had been woven into tight braids with a bead at the end that clacked with the others as she walked. She looked like a pottery artist from Phoenix.

She stuck her hand out, and they shook. "Amara Denhill."

"Kenna Banbury." She motioned to Ron. "Former Chief of Helson Police, Ron Arnold." Then said, "Jolene tells me you're a history professor?"

"University of Calgary." Amara had to have indigenous heritage in her background and was maybe five four tops. "As I said, I've been studying the Children of the Morning for years."

They started walking toward the main building, but Kenna wanted to start with the barn where Jordan had fallen through the floor. That was where she'd seen the symbol. "Jolene mentioned they've been in existence for generations. How is that possible?"

"At first I just chalked it up to being some defunct secret society."

Ron piped up from behind them. "Like the Knights Templar?"

Amara glanced over her shoulder at him. "In a way, yes, Chief."

Ron snorted, and Kenna wasn't sure she disagreed with them. The idea the Children of the Morning weren't just a modern-day cult, but something that had been going on for much longer, didn't sit well. Not just because it was a fantastical idea—but because it would be so much harder to disband.

Which was why her father hadn't cured the disease. He'd only eradicated the symptoms of infection.

"But they're not?" Kenna asked.

"In the sense they are still operating today, no." Amara motioned to the main building as they headed around the side of it. "That's the difference with this group. It seems they pass down the lore and their beliefs to the next generation each time."

"You mean like with their version of a Bible?" Kenna wanted to see it if there was one. It would provide a lot of information people seemed disinclined to give her.

"I suppose there is one, but I've never found it. The FBI

burned what they found." Amara's expression darkened. Maybe she didn't like to see books destroyed.

As far as Kenna could tell, most of the surviving children had been brought back into the fold. But who had carried the torch after the FBI raid? There had been nothing in her father's reports or the rest of the case file about a caretaker. No one even mentioned it—not even Ron, who should have known and shared that information.

And if he had hidden that from everyone, what else had he kept to himself?

She kept him close today for backup, but that didn't mean she was prepared to trust him. Even if she put her own life in his hands, she wasn't going to make that mistake with Elijah's.

They entered the barn and headed for the back.

"Keep to the edge," Kenna said. "See that hole?" She led them to the corner and the ladder down into the basement below. "Watch your step. The whole place is precarious."

The basement still smelled like it had been shut up for years, no airflow coming through the opening at the far end.

"This place is fascinating." Amara wandered through the room, passing breeze blocks stacked like walls to divide what would be animal stalls if Kenna didn't think they'd been used for two-legged beings rather than four.

"The symbol is on the wall at the end." Not bigger than four inches in diameter, it had been carved into the dirt wall above the doorway. Kenna turned back to Ron and saw a pinched expression on his face. "Ever been down here?"

"Maybe." He frowned. "It seems familiar, but like déjà vu. You know?"

She still wanted to know what he *wasn't* saying, but shelved that for the sake of asking Amara, "Have you seen this symbol anywhere locally, in mines or caves? I'm looking for the place where the Children of the Morning may have gone with Elijah Thomson."

"That's the boy who was taken?" Amara wandered away from her to get a closer look at the doorway.

"Yes. I need to find him before he's hurt or killed."

Amara nodded with her face lifted to look at the carved marking. "Fascinating."

Kenna understood then what Jolene had said about her mother adopting her just for research purposes. So she could raise someone who belonged to the group she had been studying for so long. She shivered against the chill in the air. "Amara?"

"What?" The professor started to turn around. "Oh yes—" Her body jerked. Her eyes rolled back in her head, and she fell to the ground.

Kenna reached back for her gun. A sharp prick hit the skin of her stomach. She looked down to see a dart sticking out of her abdomen.

Darkness started to suck her under. She turned as she fell and saw Ron already on the ground, out cold.

Kenna was out before she hit the dirt.

Chapter Thirty

Kenna's whole body convulsed, and air expelled along with a good amount of dust and dirt. She coughed again. Her chest crackled. She rolled to her back and stared at a dirt ceiling.

A room carved out of the earth.

Pallets stood vertical on either side of her. Stacked up, nailed together. About four feet wide. She rolled again to see the last side of this enclosure. Bars.

What energy she'd had on waking dissipated into the dirt under her.

Kenna managed to shift her hands. She looked at her fore-arms. No blood, just scars.

You're okay.

Those old memories of the night she'd woken up at the mercy of a deadly killer—with no way out, covered in blood—rose up in her mind.

But this wasn't that.

Reality consisted of what she could see. Feel. Touch. Smell—though, that was generally a bad idea in some situations.

She listened.

Her fingers curled in the dirt under her. She was alive. That meant they didn't want her dead. Yet, at least.

Ron must've given them up to the Children of the Morning. There weren't many other plausible explanations aside from someone following her. But why not take her from the vacation rental if that was the case—why wait until she was with two other people? Unless it had only been about where they were, not *who* they were.

This wasn't the lower level under the barn. Given the chilly temperature, she figured this was a room in a mine. Maybe in the network of hallways between the compound and the mine.

Kenna patted her pockets. Though, she knew from the fact her lower back was flat on the ground that she had been disarmed of at least her pistol.

Most bad guys or cops searching for a weapon would find the first couple and then figure that was all. It gave her a shot at never being unarmed.

She bent her knees and felt for what she stashed at her ankles. Nothing. It had all been removed. She didn't even have the pocketknife she kept tucked in her bra at the front, sewn on the front. She sighed. They had been thorough, leaving her completely weaponless.

Which meant no way to get herself out of this cell.

You're okay.

Kenna pushed up to a sitting position. They'd left a bucket in the corner.

Through the bars of the gate was another gate on the other side of this room. Inside that cell a young preteen boy—Elijah Thomson—lay still on his back on the floor. His face pale. Eyes closed. If he woke up, the predicament he was in would only become all too real. Unconsciousness was sometimes a mercy of its own.

Once she had looked at everything there was to see, she focused on hearing past the blurred rush in her ears. The same fog that clouded her mind also seemed to have plugged her ears. Kenna held her nose and swallowed.

When her ears popped, she realized...

She was underground. Far enough her ears had reacted to the pressure change. Great. If she'd thought getting out would be difficult if she could get free, it would prove much harder if they were a significant distance from the surface.

She tried manufacturing a yawn a couple of times. Her ears cleared a little more.

She could hear something. High-pitched, like a whimpering.

"Hello?" Kenna shifted toward the pallets closer to the sound. "Is someone there?"

"Kenna?" A woman gasped. "Is that you?"

"Amara?"

"Y-yes. I thought you would never wake up. I was all alone, with no idea where I was. No way to escape."

"Now you're not alone. Okay? Whatever happens, it happens to both of us." Kenna couldn't offer her much. She glanced at the gate enclosing her in this cell. "Is your door padlocked?"

"I think so." Amara whimpered. "Can you pick the lock?"

Not without the tools to do that. "We will figure a way out of this. Can you see Ron Arnold from where you are?"

"The old police guy?"

"Yes." Kenna glanced at Elijah. She could see a slight rise and fall of his chest. Was Amara able to see Ron from her cell? "Is he locked up nearby you?"

"I don't see him." Amara sniffed. "Didn't you say he was part of their group?"

"That was a long time ago. He helped the police take them down. He's the reason you got Jolene."

Amara whimpered again. "He probably told them where to find us."

Kenna wasn't sure the simplest explanation was always the right one, even if it was the easiest to believe sometimes. Ron might be in the same predicament as them. Shut up in one of the cells, like on the other side where she couldn't see him. Unconscious. He could also be dead.

Until she knew for sure, any explanation was a possibility.

The same way that until she was able to rule out a method of escape, any of them were possible.

"How are we going to get out of here?" Amara asked.

"I've been wondering the same thing," Kenna replied. "Trying to figure it out."

"Why did they tranq us and bring us here?"

"I don't know." Kenna also didn't want to think about why this group needed them alive for now. Just so they could torment them further. That sounded just peachy.

"They have to want something." Amara's voice notched up in tone and volume.

"It's going to be okay. We're in this together, remember?"

"Okay."

Kenna said, "What do you fall back on when you don't know what to do?" Maybe Amara had a belief system that could give her comfort right now.

Kenna understood God existed, but had she ever asked Him for help? Or asked Him for the peace He could give her? Ryson thought she relied too much on what she could do—and control—on her own. He was probably right, but who wanted to be told they were doing things wrong with their life? If she submitted to another way, she would only be doing it to get out of this situation, and it couldn't be about that.

Amara said, "I believe in what I know. The land, my knowledge. The things I've learned. What else is there?"

"Where do you draw strength from when you have none?"

"My will. My determination."

"And when you have none of that and you're just empty?" Kenna said.

"Life goes on."

But she had no power. The earth, or whatever Mother Nature thing she believed in, couldn't give her anything. The same way Kenna's knowledge couldn't give her more than a knowledge of comfort—what her mind could discern.

"We need what we don't have," Kenna whispered.

A prayer, or something else. Prayer seemed like a strange thing. Kenna just wanted someone to talk to who knew everything, so she could just be honest.

"I don't know how to get us out of here," she whispered again, reaching out beyond what she understood or could control.

Would God be there?

"What did you say? I didn't hear you." Amara had caught the whisper.

"Nothing." Kenna shifted around and tried to peer left or right in this room.

"Who are you talking to?"

"It doesn't matter." Kenna scooted as close to the gate as she could.

The rows of cells matched the basement under the barn. Elijah was the only visible occupant. The cell beside his, the gate was open.

She sighed out all her frustration. The only thing that

hung in the air was desperation, and it seemed to seep into her skin.

"Amara." Kenna gripped the bars of the gate and waited.

She heard a shuffle. "Yes?"

"Talk to me. Tell me what you know about the Children of the Morning. It might help us figure out what this is about."

Amara whimpered. "We probably just made them mad going into their sacred space. They'll leave us here until we die."

"They'll have to come and get Elijah." She had no idea what time it was right now, but the ceremony was at midnight tomorrow, or tonight. If it hadn't already happened. "We can try and get them to talk to us."

"They aren't going to tell prisoners anything!"

Kenna said, "Tell me what you know about how the group got started. You said it was back in medieval times?"

More whimpering.

Kenna was just about to prompt her into answering when she cleared her throat.

"It was." Amara took a breath, her voice stronger now. "The symbol was first found in a castle. The site of a massacre in the late thirteenth century. No one is really sure what happened, but over fifty were found dead. Men, women, and children. The castle was home to all of them, and they had little contact with outsiders. At least according to church records. There were some accounts that talked about them all bearing the same mark and never mingling with the village other than to trade."

Kenna wondered if it was the four-petaled flower. "And after the massacre?"

"I managed to find where they cropped up again, hundreds of miles away. Looking at tragedies that occurred not related to sickness or war. Plus communities on the fringe who kept to themselves. Most were believed to be a religious order of some kind."

"What does the symbol mean? Did you ever find out?" At worst, Amara could be distracted enough to pass some time.

"It always looked to me like two eights, one vertical and one horizontal."

"I see what you mean." She'd thought it looked a bit like a flower. Or a four-leaf clover. "Is there a significance to that number?"

"Eighty-eight seems to crop up often," Amara said. "They always appear to have eighty-eight members. Wherever they go, and whenever they pop up, it's always that many."

"We can't fight off that many."

"If they haven't chosen a new leader, they might not have that many here. Yet." Amara paused. "They will rely on the leader to recruit new members."

"So then it is about a charismatic male figurehead."

Amara said nothing.

"At least to an extent."

"I suppose that's true enough." Amara huffed. "They may realize the world is changing and have a woman leader this time. In order to embrace the future."

There could be some in the group who would support that, but if it was happening that way, why would they want Elijah Thomson? He would be unnecessary if they were going to continue with a female in charge. And after they'd gone to the trouble of kidnapping him and everything?

Perhaps it was only Amara's frustration at having to succeed in a largely male-dominated profession. Things in the world were beginning to change. Kenna didn't tend to worry unless it affected her directly. She hadn't been sidelined or disparaged in the FBI for her gender—though female agents in decades past certainly were. She'd enjoyed the results of their struggle, kind of like her ability to vote.

She had her own struggle. Mostly with herself, or with whoever the perpetrator was for the case she was working.

Maybe she should care more because it would affect Maizie. But the truth was, there was far too much evil in the world. She couldn't possibly take a stand against all of it. Who had time to fight every battle?

Instead, she fought the one in front of her and wondered why anyone would ask more than that of her.

Maybe it was a symptom of her need to control the world she lived in—making it narrower than most people would be comfortable with. But would life, or God if that was what this was, really ask more of her than she was capable of giving?

She didn't want to champion causes.

She only wanted to save kids like Elijah and return them to their families. To see the relief on Bianca's face when he came home.

It was enough for her.

Or it had been for a long time. Lately, she wanted to add a phone or video call with Jax at the end of the day. Something that would eventually become more.

Kenna had no weapons and no way out, but she realized then that she was okay. Instead of falling apart in despair, she still had her resolve. The situation might be dire, but she had a fighting chance.

"Why did they choose Helson?" she asked.

"How would I know?" Amara replied.

"You aren't aware of some kind of rhyme or reason to the direction they migrate?" Kenna leaned against the gate, saving her strength. The fogginess from being tranqed was almost gone.

"I guess they just keep going," Amara said. "Progress

doesn't move in a straight line. They crop up somewhere else eventually."

"But they stuck here, even after the compound was raided."

Amara huffed. "They probably hid in the caves. Or used them to escape. How should I know?"

"Okay. Sorry I keep asking so many questions." Kenna winced. "I'm just trying to get as much information as I can." She needed to talk about something positive. "You've done an amazing job raising Jolene. She's a wonderful teacher by all accounts and welcomed me into her home."

"She's a beautiful girl."

"And she cares about the kids." Kenna had seen it in the school parking lot. "She helped me, too."

"Great, she's amazing." Amara huffed. "But how is that going to get you out of that cell?"

Because after she escaped, would she be able to free Amara? "You never know which piece of information will be helpful. You just have to keep asking questions." Amara was a college professor. "You must have to pour over book after book, searching for that one piece of information that will tell you what you need to know."

"I suppose." Amara sighed, shifting against the pallet.

It moved slightly.

Kenna frowned. "Hey, Amara. Do me a favor." She got to her feet. "Back up from my side, away from the wall between us."

"Okay."

Kenna gave her a second, then kicked at the pallet. It didn't give way at first. She kept kicking. Wood splintered, her boot making a hole big enough for her foot to go through. She lowered her foot and looked in the hole at a cell the same as hers. "I think I can break this down."

She stepped back and adjusted her stance. It might not get them out of here unless she could get into a cell with an open door, but at least they wouldn't be separated.

Someone stepped into view beyond the gate.

Kenna turned and found Daniel, the reverend's son. A man who had murdered his adoptive mother wouldn't show any sympathy to her.

He stared at her. "What do you think you're doing?"

She stared right back. "Trying to escape. Obviously."

Across the aisle, Elijah Thomson woke up screaming.

Chapter Thirty-One

Dusk turned the sky an odd blue-green color.

Kenna found it compelling. Better than thinking about anything else going on right now. Like the persistent ache in her legs that made her muscles shake any time she managed to stop. Or the pounding in her head. Her nose was most likely broken, and her face probably looked like a total mess. All thanks to her comment back in the cell and what happened right after.

She hadn't caught a mirror as they shoved her out of the cell and up to the surface, but everyone with a broken nose she'd ever seen had bruises and a messed-up bridge.

"Keep. Moving."

She didn't look back at the man behind her, who jabbed the gun in her back to punctuate each word. Same way she didn't breathe through her nose, at least not after the first attempt.

Ouch.

The bleeding had stopped, but it was all down her chin and the front of her shirt. She'd felt her nose for as long as she could stand and found a cut and a lump. She wanted to sniff, but that would probably have her on the floor.

Kenna looked again at the sky. Not at the front of her shirt, or the fact her hands were bound with rope in front of her. The woman ahead, Amara, also with her hands tied. Ron Arnold walked behind her—behind the guy with the gun. They'd separated the three of them after she tried to help him stand.

An evening breeze ruffled the trees. A bird flew overhead.

If she strained around Amara, she could see the two men carrying Elijah Thomson on a stretcher. They'd given him an injection to knock him back out. She'd objected to that strenuously.

Daniel had punched her in the face.

They'd done it anyway.

She tried not to consider how this whole thing might go. If they ever quit walking.

It had taken about an hour, she guessed, to get to the entrance of the mine they'd been in. Two hours later they were still walking. Her head pounded too much to do the math on how far they were likely to have traveled or where that might put them now.

After all, since they'd been tranqed she had no idea where they started. Now wasn't the time to check if the tracker had fallen out of her shoe or if it was still there. But if they were nowhere near a cell tower, it was as good as a souvenir token from a slot machine at a gift shop.

Amara stumbled in front of her.

Kenna caught her elbow. "Are you okay?"

The professor nodded. So far she'd been left alone, which was good.

Kenna didn't want her on the receiving end of anyone's

frustration or anger. She'd rather it was directed at her not Amara.

As if Kenna would stand by and do nothing while a kid was shot up with who-knew-what.

"Walk."

She let Amara go and turned back to Mark. He might have a rifle over one shoulder, his finger close to the trigger, but she didn't think he'd be able to knock over a fly without the weapon. "Are you feeling okay?"

His face was far too pale. His skin was almost green around the edges. Hopefully, he wouldn't puke on her—or in her direction.

Or anywhere she could hear it.

"You shot me. What do *you* think?"

"That graze on your arm?" She blinked. "Did you get it looked at? 'Cause it might be infected."

"Let's go into the woods. I'll show you."

Kenna turned back forward and heard his low chuckle.

Ron yelped and fell with a thud.

Kenna stepped out of line.

Mark stopped her with the gun but grunted. Sweat rolled down his flushed face.

"Let me help him." She lifted her chin toward Ron. "The same way I'd help you if you needed it." She needed someone on her side. Out of the group—she couldn't count because she couldn't see the front of the train of people walking—there had to be someone sympathetic to her. She hoped.

Ron was on his knees. He lifted his head. "I can't walk any farther."

She grabbed his arm and turned with it over her shoulder. "Let's go." Then she levered him up to standing before he could object. Clenching her teeth as the move shot pain through her face that was worse than her arms.

She made an O with her mouth and breathed. Swallowed back acid and the last thing she ate. Which wasn't much. Sometimes she fasted for a day or two, or even three—though doing that was rare—just so that if she ever got kidnapped again, her body wouldn't freak out about not eating and being so hungry she couldn't think straight. She could use some water, though.

Her arms shook.

She turned her head to Ron, their faces close together. "We need to walk."

"I don't think I can."

Kenna let go of his hand and let his arm slip off her shoulder. "But you're going to anyway." She stayed beside him, keeping pace.

Mark took position behind them.

Ron said, "How much farther is it?" Talking to no one in particular. "Until we get to where we're going?"

Mark only said, "If you want to get there instead of die here in the dirt, then shut up."

"Who is that guy?" Ron asked.

"The reverend's son." Kenna shrugged one shoulder because being cavalier was better than crying. "He's mad 'cause I shot him. But he killed his mother, so you could say he deserved it. Or you could say I was doing a public service. Or it was self-defense, maybe part of another citizen's arrest. Whatever floats your boat."

"I think I'll get a boat." Ron looked up, catching her drift about acting like none of this bothered them. "In Fort Lauderdale, or somewhere else that's nice down in Florida. Where there's no Bigfoot sightings. No bears."

"You've gotta contend with gators though, and those lizards that are everywhere." She shivered. "One of them was in my room once. When you pick them up the tail falls off, so the lizard lands back on the floor, and you're standing there holding the tail."

Ron turned to her, a frown pulling those bushy gray brows together. "That's nasty."

She shrugged again. "That's Florida. I'm sure there's good stuff I can enjoy. In winter. Maybe I'll make a trip this fall. Find some good fried gator."

"I'm thinking Texas now."

Kenna would've laughed at any other time, but she caught sight of Elijah on that stretcher being carried by two men. Unaware of what was happening, or where they were going.

Her humor bled away like the stuff that had poured from her nose. What a fun experience. Who knew breaking your nose could be so gross? Maybe it wasn't that hard to guess, but she'd never had it happen, or seen it, so she hadn't thought about it.

Kenna watched the ocean-blue sky for a while. They were presumably going to get where they were going by sundown. Walking in the dark would be considerably more difficult, even following the trail of people.

Up ahead, the path they were on bent to the left.

She watched person after person disappear into the trees, then scanned the woods to the right, on Ron's side, unsure what she was looking for. When she turned to the left side, she spotted a flash of shadow. Which was gone far too quickly.

All manner of predators lived out here, under the stars. The question was whether those predators walked on two legs or four.

She walked a little farther, closing in on the bend in the path. Ron stumbled some more. He wasn't kidding that they needed to get there soon. Her head hurt so much that shadows danced in front of her eyes. Seeing what wasn't there.

Like that, deep in the trees. Just a shift of movement.

"What?" Mark said. "What do you keep looking at?" He walked in front of Ron so close he had to pull up short to keep from colliding.

Kenna hissed out a breath. "I don't know what I saw. Maybe it was nothing. My head is pounding thanks to your brother."

"And my arm is gonna fall off thanks to you." He shoved her with his good shoulder.

Kenna tried not to grit her teeth. It hurt her nose. But it was that, or tackle the guy out of pure frustration, and what good would that do?

He turned his head to call over to his brother. "I'm checking something out!"

Kenna stepped around him to keep going with the others while he did that.

Mark twisted around and grabbed her arm before she could move past him. "Let's go." He shoved her in front of him.

Kenna hissed out a breath. Then lifted her hands to her nose and caught herself right before she rubbed it. "Where to?"

"You tell me. You're the one who saw something."

Great. A detour then?

She angled them toward the right and stepped through the brush and thorny bushes. Tromped along, picking her way. Mostly trying not to fall so she wouldn't jar her head. Daniel could have punched her in a hundred places, but he'd intentionally targeted her nose.

"You guys killed your mom, you know that?" She circled around a tree and glanced back at him. "Clipped her in the neck with one of your bullets. She bled out on the living room rug." With Kenna's hands over the wound, feeling the hot blood pump out between her fingers.

"Not the old man as well?" Mark asked, as if disappointed.

"They didn't treat you well, your parents?"

"They aren't our family. The Children of the Morning are."

Right. "There's nothing out here. We should head back." They could continue north from here and catch up to the train of people farther up the trail.

"Why would we do that when we can make the time out here worthwhile?"

Kenna just stared at him.

They were out of earshot of anyone on the trail unless she yelled. And who would come running? Ron would be killed if he intervened.

If there was a God and He was in control, He could cover this. But awful things happened every day, and she would need to figure out why some people were saved and others weren't. Even with his evil intentions, Mark, had just as much free will as she did. If God intervened, that would violate Mark's free will. Which might satisfy some, but it wouldn't be just.

Instead, she moved closer to him. Only so he would struggle to fire that rifle at her from such close range and she'd be within range to use the weapons she had at her disposal.

Kenna lifted her arms, eased forward so their bodies were touching, and slid her bound hands over his head. She held on to the back of his neck.

A fission of something roiled through him. What should've been instinct—warning—was also excitement over what was about to happen. She saw it spark in his eyes, and he said, "You shot me. Seems like you owe me somethin'."

She tried not to look like she was about to barf. "Is that right?"

He lifted his chin, a tiny motion. A nod.

As if she would kiss him—plus whatever else he thought was about to happen—with her nose broken? Talk about ouch.

Kenna bent her knees, her feet spread. It wasn't perfect with her hands bound. She didn't have one arm under his for the normal body lock, but this would work if she went smooth and fast. She lowered her hands down his back, getting her arms around his waist so she could pull his hips in.

He put his arms over hers, his hands on her shoulders.

She planted one foot behind his left, got her head against his chest, and pushed his upper body back so he was bent but they were both still hip to hip, then dropped to her knees.

He hit the ground, her fingers under his back. She grimaced and pressed her weight to his chest, her shoulder against his throat, and levered all her weight against him so that he was pinned.

His legs flailed and he gasped, realizing what she'd done in the space of two seconds. The rifle jabbed against her hip, but with it trapped between them, there was nothing he could do to retrieve it. In only a few minutes, oxygen deprivation to the brain would make him pass out.

The train of people walking erupted, and someone ran over.

A punishing grasp hauled her off Mark and up to her feet.

He coughed, rolled over, and gasped.

She turned to the man behind him. "He wanted me to give him what I owed him. So I did." And whoever was out here—they hadn't been discovered. "I guess it's time to get back to walking now."

She faced him as she walked away. No way she'd give him her back—an invitation for someone to come at her from behind, where she wouldn't be able to see it until it was too late.

Beyond where Mark and the guy who'd dragged her up stood having a vicious-but-whispered-so-she-couldn't-hear-it conversation, she spotted that dark shape in the woods. Just a slight movement.

Could be a bear—or Bigfoot.

It could also be something else entirely.

"Let's go." The guy who'd hauled her up strode to her, grabbed her arm, and started walking her to the path. "You cost us five men. You're gonna pay."

He didn't let go.

Kenna pressed her lips together. They rounded the bend in the trail, and the landscape opened up as the mountains descended into a valley that had been cleared of trees except at the edges. In the center was a stone construction that looked like an altar.

Not good.

Kenna's stomach clenched. There were too many of them to fight. Too many innocents to protect, and she couldn't even see where Amara and Ron had gone—they were up ahead too far.

"No," Ron called out. "No, don't!"

After a second, she saw two men dragging him along to that altar in the clearing.

Where was Elijah?

Kenna scanned and scanned. She spotted him on one side, the fabric-and-frame stretcher on the ground now. He remained unconscious, thankfully.

"You betrayed us." The man with Ron shoved him toward the stone altar. "That means you're the first to die!"

Ron crumpled to the ground, his back against the stone, sobbing. The men around him laughed, the sound rippling through the group. There had to be twenty at least—small numbers if there were supposed to be eighty-eight in their ranks.

The guy holding her arm chuckled.

Mark clipped her shoulder on purpose as he passed her and strode to the middle.

Kenna looked around, trying to figure out how on earth they were going to get out of this.

"This is where it ends," the man beside her said. "For you at least. But you get to watch everything before you die."

Chapter Thirty-Two

Kenna started counting heads, trying to figure out how many there were. Like counting sheep to fall asleep—except this wasn't a bed, and four of the men had surrounded Ron Arnold. Kicking him. Yelling at him.

A tear rolled down her cheek.

There were too many for her to face, no matter which way she added it up.

She had no options left aside from refusing to watch what was happening.

The sky had darkened from the ocean-blue color it had been, and the first of the stars now peeked through. Ron had gone silent.

"Get him up."

Kenna's head whipped around so hard pain thrummed through her nose. Amara.

The history professor no longer had her hands bound. She strode to the altar. "Get the old man out of here and get the kid up. It's time to begin."

Amara was the caretaker.

Kenna's instincts had her moving through armed men to

the altar where she stood. When she realized what she was doing, she diverted and caught Ron with her bound hands.

"Easy," Kenna said. Judging by the looks on these men's faces, they'd have discarded Ron to die somewhere from the internal bleeding he no doubt had from the beating they'd given him. "I've got him."

As they walked away from the altar, she whispered, "Did you know Amara Denhill was the caretaker?"

Ron shook his head. He walked stiffly.

She couldn't take too much of his weight but got him over to the trees where he could lean against a thick trunk and close his eyes.

As she turned and sat, a lone man raced out from the trail they'd traversed to get here.

"Enough!" The reverend fast walked toward the gathered crowd of armed men at the altar with no visible weapon. They'd have shot him if he'd been carrying. They probably still would.

Two men dumped Elijah on the altar. Everyone turned to Jim.

Had God sent this man to be His emissary tonight, or was this only the pursuit of a grieving husband whose sons had killed his wife?

"You're not doing this. Destroying lives?" The reverend's face reddened, and he gestured wildly. "You people are *done*. Daniel and Mark? You are no longer my sons. You are criminals and murderers, and you will be stopped. I cannot stand by and say nothing when I have done everything right. I will not be silent!"

Daniel took two steps toward the man who was supposed to be his father. "You'll be silenced is what you'll be." He whipped his gun up and squeezed the trigger.

The sound echoed through the valley.

The reverend's body jerked and fell to the ground.

"Get the child ready!" Amara called out to the group, and everyone sprang into action.

Where before they had seemed to act of their own accord, now it seemed she controlled them like a queen bee with all her worker bees to do her bidding.

"Bring me the wine!" she yelled. "And we will drink together at last."

Ron grunted beside Kenna. "That stuff."

She glanced at him. "You took it...before?"

"Makes you see sparkles. I passed out before they could cut into my friend."

"Why do they do this?"

"To mark their new leader." He pushed out a breath that seemed painful. "Then she raises him at a new compound. When he comes of age, they begin recruiting in full force. When there are eighty-eight members, the cleansing happens." He winced. "I got your father in before that could take place."

"So they build a cult with every new generation."

"And when she dies, the successor will take over." That was probably supposed to have been Jolene, but it seemed more that she rejected the heritage she'd been born with.

"Why the children? The cold cases." She shifted around to face Ron. "The ones who were taken and killed, or never found."

"There will be a burial place around here somewhere." He pointed at the clearing where the cult members were staking torches into the ground. When it was fully dark, those lights would make it look like the picture she'd found. "And they'll put Elijah there too, if he doesn't survive tonight."

"I have to stop them." Somehow.

She stared at the reverend's discarded body. She would end up that same way if she tried.

There was no way to tell if Maizie had been able to track her.

"You think I haven't been trying to figure out who the caretaker was for years. Where they were holing up. Or who was involved." Ron grunted. "No one believed me, and I did what I could. I thought for a while the coroner might be involved. That he was misidentifying bodies that were discovered. Or covering up deaths."

"But he wasn't?" She probably would have thought the same if she were living in town trying to uncover a group of cult members.

"He was replaced. The mayor brought in this guy from Spokane. No way would they have been able to get anything past that guy."

"What about the mayor?" Kenna pointed out a guy. "Isn't that his son, the one Chief Hutton was looking for?"

Ron nodded. "One of them, but we can't take down this many ourselves. That boy is going to die...or be forever changed by what happens here."

Kenna squeezed her eyes shut.

Okay, Lord. I get it. I have zero control here. These people will do whatever they want unless someone stops them, and it doesn't seem like it's going to be me. Maizie might've tracked me, or this thing hidden in my shoe isn't connecting to anything and she has no idea where I am. Or there's help on the way, and they'll get here too late to—

"State police!"

"Hands up!"

"Guns down, hands up! No one move."

Kenna stared at the ocean of people who swarmed out of the trees and surrounded the Children of the Morning.

Someone fired a gun.

Kenna pulled Ron over to lie on the ground and covered his head with her body. The police officers responded to the threat.

Two different men screamed as though they'd been hit.

Kenna turned her head to look.

Several cops shoved cult members onto the ground, pulling hands behind their backs and securing them with cuffs while others watched their backs.

"Ron! Kenna!" Chief Hutton jogged over, followed closely by Jolene.

"Chief." Kenna grabbed his hand, and he hauled her to her feet. She nearly slammed into Jolene but clasped the other woman's elbows. "There's something you should know."

Jolene shook her head. "My mother. When Derek told me you were meeting her, I knew it wouldn't be what you thought." She glanced over at the crowd of cops and cult members.

One cop yelled back, "I need a medic! The kid's alive!"

Someone ran over with a medical bag, but they looked like a cop in tactical uniform. Some of the officers wore that, while others had on their normal uniforms with bulletproof vests.

Jolene continued, "I've suspected the worst for a long time. After I didn't measure up, she kicked me out. I put myself through college and moved here to do what I could to put a stop to her. I hope it's not too late."

Kenna squeezed her hand. "You were all right on time." She turned to Hutton, assessing Ron. "How is he?"

Hutton's expression darkened, and he pulled the radio off his belt. "This is Chief Hutton requesting medical transport at my location." When confirmation came back, he lowered the radio. "We have a helicopter in the county. They'll get

Ron and Elijah to the hospital." He reached back with a pocketknife he handed to Jolene.

They blushed at each other, then Jolene motioned to Kenna's hands. "Let me."

Kenna held up her wrists, and Jolene cut her free. "Thanks." She ran her fingers over her wrists, trying to smooth out some of the rawness. She inhaled through her nose and recalled quickly why that would be a bad idea. With a wince that also hurt, she reached up and ran her fingers down her nose gently. It still hurt, even being careful. "Ack."

Jolene tugged Kenna's hands down. "Don't touch it."

Kenna glanced at Ron, pale and lying on the ground.

Over by the altar, officers were aiding Elijah. Others were arresting suspects.

Kenna didn't see Amara anywhere. She frowned. "Where did your mom go?"

"She's not my mother. Not after this."

Kenna started toward the altar, Jolene beside her. She called out to the closest officer, "Did anyone see a woman?"

He shook his head. "We arrested all the cult members that were here."

"Okay, so where is she?"

He blinked and stared at her like she had no clue she was female and standing beside another woman. "Who?"

One of the other cops said, "You should get medical attention. Your face could use some ice and tape strips."

Kenna sighed. "We need to find the caretaker. The woman in charge of all this."

"What woman?" Daniel smirked at her. "There's no woman. I'm in charge of the Children of the Morning."

"No, I am."

A third cult member said, "I'm the leader."

Kenna pointed at the reverend, dead on the ground. "This

man"—she pointed at Daniel—"killed the reverend. I saw it. And there's a woman in charge."

"Maybe you hit your head." One of the cops stepped closer to Kenna. "Because I don't see a woman here."

"She adopted me," Jolene said. "And she's here somewhere."

The cops mostly just smirked and got on with rounding up suspects, cuffing them, and having them sit on the grass in a group.

"Let's go look for her."

Kenna glanced around. "She must have run off." Amara couldn't have gotten too far. But anywhere out of view was far enough she could hide and escape.

The helicopter crested the mountain, and the local nonprofit ambulance touched down.

She went back to Hutton. "I need a weapon, just in case."

He eyed her for a second, then had to get out of the way of running medics. He bent for his ankle, then handed her a revolver. "Don't lose it."

"Copy that."

"And if Jolene is going with you, then I'm coming, too." He went ahead of her.

Okay, then. Kenna followed.

They walked a circuit around the altar and all the people standing around.

She spotted a trail at the north end of the clearing. "Maybe she ran off during the commotion and went this way?"

"Let's check it out." Hutton went first, which put Jolene between them—the civilian protected.

The police chief picked up the pace quickly, and the teacher must work out because she didn't miss a stride.

Kenna focused on her footfalls and her breathing, trying

to ignore the fact her face felt like she had the worst head cold coupled with a migraine. At least her legs worked fine.

"I see her." Hutton lifted his gun. "Amara, put it down! It's over."

She fired a shot. Hutton ducked, dragging Jolene off the side of the path with him.

Kenna went the other direction and sought cover to the left of the trail. She lifted the chief's revolver and found Amara with her aim.

She sat on the ground with a rifle on her lap. Face pale.

Kenna frowned. "Amara, throw the gun away from you!" She used her former-FBI agent voice. "Do it! Now!"

Hutton shifted and said, "Jolene. Don't," his voice low.

The teacher stepped out from behind him into the trail. "Mom, you need to listen to me."

The older woman grimaced. Blood tinged her lips. "You never listened to *me*."

"I don't want your life. But that doesn't mean I don't love you." Jolene lifted her hands and stepped toward her mother.

Kenna watched indecision war on Hutton's face, then he backtracked through the woods to take a flanking position. So he could cover Jolene? Kenna could help with that. She stepped out behind the other woman, so they approached Amara together. She held the revolver ready.

"Mom, you need to put the gun away from you." Jolene kept her voice soft.

"I should've drowned you the first time you told me you wanted nothing to do with them."

Kenna winced. She didn't know her own mother, but that definitely wasn't what a mom should say—or threaten to do.

"We're not doing this," Jolene said. "Just give it up."

Amara shifted the gun on her lap, revealing blood on her thigh. Yet she'd tried to run.

Jolene gasped. "You've been shot. Let us help you!"

She lifted the gun and it flopped to the side, but she didn't get her finger on the trigger.

Kenna yelled, "Don't, or I'll have to shoot!" Amara was going to shoot off her own foot in an attempt to shoot Jolene—or Kenna. She wound her arm around Jolene's waist. "Take cover."

Jolene stumbled off the side of the trail, Kenna moved with her.

"Put the gun down." Hutton's voice echoed. "Now."

A shot cracked off, followed by another one.

Kenna made sure Jolene wasn't hit, then turned back to look at Chief Hutton.

Amara's head flopped to the side, blood on her forehead. He stood over her, breathing hard. Then he turned to Kenna. "Clear."

She echoed his call, then said, "Jolene?"

The teacher lifted wide eyes to her. "Is it over?"

Hutton strode toward them, stowing his gun. "It's over." He slid his hands into her hair, touching his palms to her cheeks and kissed her full on the mouth.

Kenna turned away. Her cheeks heated, and despite the situation she could smile.

The helicopter lifted above the trees overhead and flew toward the local medical center.

Kenna said a prayer for Ron and Elijah.

Chapter Thirty-Three

Kenna stood with Jolene while the chief explained what had just happened with Amara. The sound of gunshots had brought several state police officers running. One glanced over at Kenna now, a disapproving expression on his face. The chief said something to the officer that seemed to satisfy him, until the officer made a comment.

Kenna's head thrummed with pain. She turned to Jolene. The woman had just lost the only mother she'd ever known, and yet she only looked similarly disappointed.

"How did the two of you find me?" Kenna figured talking about something else could be a good distraction. "And how did you know to bring the state police?"

"When we didn't find you at the compound, Derek called that number you gave him." Jolene smiled gently and glanced at the police chief. "He spoke to whoever answered, and they said they could track you. They gave us the coordinates, and Derek had to call them in with the location. Since we're outside Helson. Way far outside."

"So. You and Derek. How long has that been going on?" Kenna said.

Jolene blushed, a tiny smile on her face. "We talk at church sometimes, and he comes to the school to do the safety talks with the kids personally."

"Right. The kids." Definitely the reason he did that, rather than passing the duty off to one of his officers. Kenna squeezed Jolene's shoulder. "Hang close to him. Don't let something like that slip through your fingers."

The other woman smiled. "Not now it's finally something, I won't." She sighed. "I want to be happy that he actually kissed me, but..."

Kenna nodded. "Stick with it. There will be plenty of things to celebrate."

Jolene would need the budding relationship in the coming weeks and months, when grief threatened to swallow her. The teacher was the kind of person who deserved good in her life.

And yet, so often, it seemed like life didn't work that way.

Perhaps this time it should.

"Thank you for coming here, and for making taking down the Children of the Morning such a priority." Jolene sniffed. "I just wanted to say that before you get shuttled off to get your nose looked at. I might not see you again before you leave."

Kenna nodded.

"I wanted to stop them, but even my mother was a force to be reckoned with. Adding all those men? I had no chance."

"But you stood up when it counted. You didn't stay silent."

"If we do nothing, evil wins," Jolene said. "And I stayed quiet for long enough."

Kenna couldn't help thinking about Michael Rushman. She'd done what she could to help Maizie, and the girl had saved herself in the end—Kenna just helped. But the people still associated with Rushman, even after his death, might continue operating in the darkness if she didn't explain every-thing she knew. The FBI might not uncover every hidden connection, exposing that darkness to the light. The truth about the FBI director could remain buried.

"I need to go to DC," Kenna said.

Hutton strode over. "Not until you get your face looked at." He winced, like Jolene had.

"Great." She must look a mess for them both to react to her nose like that. "I don't have a car anywhere near here."

Hers had been totaled, and Dixie's SUV was at the compound. "Where are we, anyway?"

"Far enough out of Helson I have to defer jurisdiction to the state police." He didn't know Jolene had already told her that part. He added, "We're in danger of running into the RCMP."

"Don't the Mounties ride horses?" Kenna asked. "That would be cool to see."

Jolene chuckled.

Hutton didn't look so amused. "I'm glad you can make light of this."

"It's done, right?" Except for a few loose ends.

Jolene said, "I intend to make sure the Children of the Morning never exist ever again."

He nodded. "I'll help."

Kenna looked around, wondering who was going to give her a ride back to town. They'd probably want her to go to the hospital, and to be fair that was probably a good idea. Maybe there was a low-key place, like a medical center where she could get checked out, where it wouldn't feel so much like a hospital.

And yet, even with this over, it still wasn't. There were more loose ends, and victims to find. Bodies to discover. Cold cases they could close now.

Her mind decided to remind her then that Ron Arnold had told her they would be buried nearby. Children who had not survived the ceremony to be the new leader were close.

She started walking.

The clearing where the altar stood still hummed with officers and cuffed suspects. She wanted to know how far it was to their vehicles, and which way they'd come, but not enough to flag one down and ask.

"Where are we going, Kenna?" Chief Hutton said her name quietly. "What are you chasing now?"

"Just a hunch." She passed two officers, guys who'd told her there was no woman in charge. Hopefully now they knew about Amara Dunhill, they would see that they'd been wrong. A cop who didn't think past his own preconceived notions wasn't the kind who should be on active duty. Guys like that needed to be behind a desk or retired.

She glanced at the chief. "Did you tell them they were wrong?"

He nodded. "And I told them I'd explain in writing myself, plus provide a witness written statement."

"More than one, with me and Jolene."

"I figured with the name thing, you might not want to be on record."

Yes, things would get sticky if she had to use a fake name in an official capacity. "I figured I can put my real name and then split town right before reality catches up." She glanced over again. "I'm going to head to DC and testify. Give a statement about what happened with the FBI director."

He nodded. "Good idea. What are we looking for here?"

Kenna slowed. Off to the side of the clearing, she spotted an expanse. There wasn't even really anything she could've said that gave her the impression this was where the victims of the ceremony had been buried. Just a sense.

Hutton stopped. "Whoa."

Instinct had dialed him into what was happening, and what this spot might be.

"We need Forensics out here." Probably even ground-penetrating radar. She stared at the uneven patches of grass. "I'm hoping I'll be able to tell William Farmington Junior's parents that they can lay him to rest."

"If we can do that, I can justify your presence here a whole lot more easily," Chief Hutton said. "Not that helping you evade the feds is what we're about. But it gives some credence to who you are. What you're about."

"I know what I'm about," Kenna said. "I don't love having to convince other people, but it's time to do what's right."

"You do that in every other thing you do. Why change now?"

Kenna absorbed those words with a warmth she hadn't been expecting. She smiled at Jolene, and the chief reached over to take her hand. "I need a ride to town."

It took a couple of hours, but she managed to get to Helson and check into the medical center. They had brought Elijah and Ron here so that the child could be close to his parents.

Kenna hadn't been able to get any information on them since she wasn't family, but as soon as this doctor quit touching her nose, she planned to.

Her body flushed, and her stomach flipped over. "Are you done?"

The doctor's brows lifted.

"Sorry."

She chuckled. "Do you want something for the pain?"

"Not if it's going to make me loopy or sleepy."

"Seems like you maybe could use a few hours of rest."

Kenna didn't close her eyes, even though she wanted to. This wasn't the most comfortable bed. The one at the rental house was better. But she could sleep here probably, and the doctor wasn't wrong.

And like the car trip here, as soon as she closed her eyes, she would immediately be assailed by the memory of waking up in that cell. Being a captive again, when she desperately needed to keep that from happening again—which, to be fair, if she was serious about that, she should get one of those regular jobs. She didn't want to think about Amara being the caretaker.

Elijah screaming.

"I'll live." Kenna turned so she could put her feet on the floor. "I have people I need to talk to. Here and on the phone."

With no idea where her cell phone was, or if it had been destroyed. Even the keys to the vacation rental were in Bianca's car at the compound.

Kenna sighed.

"You really should sleep." The doctor squinted at her. "But I can get you a phone to use."

Kenna turned again, straightening her legs on the covers, and lay back on the bed. Her body sank into the mattress. "I really need that phone." Her eyes wouldn't open.

The doctor patted her shoulder. "It can wait."

Sometime later, she became aware she wasn't alone. Kenna sucked in a breath through her nose and immediately groaned.

"Yeah, don't do that."

She fought against the fog of sleep and blinked her eyes open.

Ron Arnold sat beside the bed in a wheelchair, an IV bag tucked against the wheel that connected to his arm.

Kenna took inventory of herself. Then she sat up. "How long have I been asleep?"

"I was admitted fourteen hours ago," he said. "But you didn't show up until later."

"I got a whole night's sleep." She didn't need to look at the clock. She'd been here for hours.

"Your face doesn't look so good."

Kenna gingerly touched the edges of the bandages. "I need a phone." She could barely think straight, see straight, or talk.

His lips twitched. "Not bad work. For a civilian."

Kenna said, "Did you know Jolene wanted them taken down?"

Ron's expression lost its humor. "And her mom was the caretaker?" His tone held a sardonic note.

"You should talk to her. I think you two have a lot in common." Kenna wanted to add, *Besides, she'll need someone to walk her down the aisle.* But she refrained from saying that. It was early days yet.

Ron glanced aside.

"Just give her a shot. She didn't ask to be born one of them." Then she said, "Tell me how you are."

"I didn't need surgery, but I do have cracked ribs. They won't let me sit here long." He gave her a kind of eye roll. "Elijah was treated for whatever they shot him up with. Should be fine, physically at least."

"And Steve Thomson?"

"The detective's prognosis is still uncertain. Bianca came to see me, but I think she just wanted a change of scenery. She told me, 'Thanks for being there.'"

Kenna imagined the woman was probably getting a little stir-crazy.

"I'm going to have my daughter drive me to the coroner's

office when I leave here. Then I can identify Reverend Jim, so he can be laid to rest beside Clarissa."

"That's a nice idea," Kenna said. "Does the department have any idea who killed Annabelle, or Ben—Robert?" Both had been stabbed.

He nodded. "Chief Hutton came by while you were sleeping. They brought in the mayor's son. He made a full confession."

"Good."

Since Ben Landry was dead, unless she found what she was looking for in his house, she wasn't going to get answers about the missing pages in her dad's journal.

If she testified in DC, the FBI would get what they needed. Kenna would be able to rest assured they were going to prosecute anyone involved in Rushman's business. At least as much as anyone could trust the government to follow through. Though, with Jax there she had more faith in them.

"You know," Ron began, "when I met your father for the first time, he said to me that we do the right thing whether people will believe it or not. He knew no one would trust me after it came out that I was once one of the Children of the Morning. He knew exactly what would happen to my career, and how I'd have to claw back every inch of respect I'd earned. He even wanted to nominate me for a commendation."

"But he didn't?"

"I told him not to." Ron glanced aside. "I told him I'd kept my mouth shut so long I deserved it. The way I deserved you doubting me."

"Look, I'm sorry—"

He lifted his hand. "Don't be. You were right to question it."

"Didn't do us a whole lot of good." They had still been duped.

"We all do the best we can. The best we know how to do for the people we are charged with caring for. God knows what He is asking of us." Ron paused. "It's up to us to ask Him for wisdom."

Kenna figured she would need a lot of that with Maizie, and for herself as well.

"Time's up, Ron." The nurse knocked on the doorframe, then came in and wheeled him to the door.

"Take care, Kenna."

"You too, Chief."

He shot her a smile.

Kenna didn't even have time to reach for the phone before someone else knocked. She tried not to be grumpy, but she really needed to get to call Maizie.

She glanced over at the doorway and straightened when she realized it was William Farmington Senior and his wife, Irene. "Hi." She didn't know what else to say.

"We won't take up much of your time." He held out his hand, and Kenna gave it a squeeze. "We just wanted to say thank you."

Kenna frowned.

"Our William came home this morning," Irene said. "Bill and I finally get to lay him to rest, and that's thanks to you."

Kenna's eyes burned with hot tears and her sinuses blocked, which made her nose hurt. But she did not touch her face. She held out her hand to the little boy's mom. "I'm really sorry for your loss."

"Thanks to you," the dad said, "it won't happen to anyone else's child. Not ever again."

Kenna nodded. "The chief and Ms. Dunhill are going to ensure that."

Bill swallowed. Dipped his chin.

"Helson is going to be free of this. Finally."

Irene sniffed. "Yes, finally."

Bill shook her hand.

Irene gave Kenna a gentle hug, and another whispered, "Thank you."

Then they were gone, and Kenna was alone again. She lay back in the bed and stared at the ceiling. So much loss of life, but it was over now. There would always be crime in Helson, just like there was everywhere. But a threat had been eliminated. Just like in Vegas.

The people who lived here would finally be able to move on.

Chapter Thirty-Four

Kenna held the phone to her ear and stood beside the corner chairs in the waiting room, feeling the need to get out of here. But unlike with a cell phone, she was currently tethered to the base of the phone on the wall beside the chairs.

"That was when we realized it was Amara who was the caretaker." She explained how she'd gone with Chief Hutton and Jolene to chase after the older woman.

On the other end of the line, Kenna heard a crackle like someone shifting. Maizie had put her on speaker, with Stairns and Elizabeth there listening. The connection wasn't great, but she needed to check in with them.

"Now we don't have to worry about the Children of the Morning."

A woman a few seats down sucked in a tight breath and glanced at Kenna, outraged she'd say the name out loud. Kenna wanted to shift the phone away from her mouth and say, *I killed half of them. The other half are in jail.* Her dad might have saved a group of children, but Kenna had brought the lost home.

They both did the right thing, saving lives and bringing their brand of justice.

"That's good," Elizabeth said. The counselor was soft-spoken, her tone gentle and reassuring, which was probably good for her line of work.

"Yeah, it is," Maizie echoed. "I'm glad you finished it."

"Me, too." Kenna focused on the base of the phone. "Even if it wasn't why I came here, they're done." She'd finished what her dad started. "Derek and Jolene will make sure no one continues their work."

"The ones that were arrested will keep believing, though." Maizie sounded almost nervous. "They could start it up again."

She heard Stairns say, "They are all going to be in prison for a long time."

Kenna said, "We can't police what people believe, but they won't go free. The line of caretakers died with Amara, and without their leader it will hopefully dampen any attempts to restart it later. If Amara has anything, it will be destroyed."

She figured someone would head back to the Gathering Place and take a sledgehammer to that altar. Destroy it down to rubble. She would do it herself, if she lived locally.

Maizie said, "The news story about her death and the whole Children of the Morning thing broke. It's been playing all day so far. Her colleagues are all coming out of the wood-work, talking about how they knew she wasn't quite right in the head."

"So they're throwing her under the bus?" Kenna placed her palm against the wall. The doctor had given her a couple of pain pills, so she felt better. And she'd slept. But she still felt like she'd been hit by a truck.

"Completely," Maizie said.

Stairns chuckled. "A few of them are even saying she approached them, wanting to know if they'd join her secret society." He sighed. "Sounds like she was fully engaged in recruiting."

"The state police and the chief here in Helson can find out how far it spread, but that's concerning." Kenna paused. "I wonder what she was doing here locally before I called her." Amara had probably been holed up with her people, though. Conniving. Getting ready for the ceremony.

"So they're going to do there what we did with Ben?" Maizie said.

"At least we know now he wasn't connected..." To Rushman. "I'll see if Dixie can go through his things before she sells his house." It would take a few weeks, since the Realtor was here with her family, but Kenna could wait. And Bianca Wynn would get a payday out of it.

"We still need to find the older guy." Maizie paused. "All I've got is a conspiracy theory website no one has updated in months, and a cold trail. He's disappeared."

Kenna didn't figure it was because of a connection to Rushman, but another reason they hadn't seen the last member of Intellectus since Vegas. "Keep looking."

It was a long shot that the guy was part of it, but they needed to know. All the i's need to be dotted, and the t's crossed.

No loose ends. That would keep Maizie safe in the long run.

"I will," Maizie said. "That sheriff in Colorado has disappeared as well. He was going live on social media nearly every day, calling for the police to turn you over to his county for trespassing and conspiracy to commit murder."

She'd tangled with that guy before she went to Las Vegas a couple of months ago. At least, she'd set free the people his rancher brother had held captive, reuniting a young man with the young woman he loved.

She and Jax had even seen them get married in Vegas.

Certainly she could understand a man being angry and grief-stricken over his brother's death, but as a sheriff he should've arrested the guy. Instead of targeting the people who ended his reign of terror over those captives.

"Right." Kenna frowned, which made her nose hurt. "Because the fact his brother was keeping itinerant workers as prisoners isn't relevant here?" It was good he'd gone quiet. She had some things to say to him if he did show up.

"Maybe he gave up."

"I hope so," Kenna said. "Maze, I need a phone. I also need a car so I can go pack up the vacation rental. And I need a plane ticket to DC."

Maizie whimpered.

Stairns said, "I thought you were dead set on not telling them about Maizie."

"I'm going to testify about the director." It was the right thing to do. Kenna knew that. "And help the FBI bring down the web that was built. Every piece of it gets broken." Rushman's organization would be ended like the Children of the Morning. "That's not all, but it's enough. And it's what I need to do."

She heard a bunch of shuffling on the other end of the line.

Maizie leaving?

Kenna said, "Maizie, listen to me."

"I'm here." Her voice sounded thin.

"They aren't going to know you. They aren't going to hear your name, or where you are, or what you're doing. None of it." Kenna checked no one was listening, then said, "I promised I'd keep you safe, right?"

"Yes."

"God willing, that's exactly what I'm gonna do." Kenna paused a second. "You get me?"

She heard something that sounded like Stairns' chuckle.

Maizie said, "Yes, I get you."

"Good." Kenna smiled to herself.

"I'll have a courier deliver a phone and get you a rental car. And a plane ticket."

"I appreciate it." Kenna winced, realizing something. "I also need somewhere I can put my guns while I travel." No airline wanted the arsenal she carried on a plane with them.

"I'm on it," Stairns said.

"Thanks, guys." Kenna spotted Dixie—Bianca—at the far end of the waiting room. "Gotta go."

"I'll get you what you need."

"Thanks, Maze." Kenna hung up and went to meet her friend at the other end of the waiting room.

Bianca looked like she hadn't slept in three days, dark circles under her eyes. Her makeup had faded. Her hair didn't have all of its usual volume.

"Hey, how is everything?" Kenna asked. "How are you feeling?"

Bianca tipped her head to the side in a tiny shrug. She turned, and they started walking back the way she'd come. "Elijah is doing fine. His grandparents are sitting with him, but I think he's mostly just anxious to go home."

"Do you need someone to fix the front window?"

"Chief Hutton already called. He said he's taking care of that for us."

"Good." Kenna nodded. Elijah didn't need to see the mess when he got home. "How is your son?"

"He'll get there. He's still pretty scared." Bianca led her toward the intensive care unit, where her husband had been admitted. "I imagine it will take a long time, but Steve and I will both hopefully be there to help him through it."

Kenna squeezed the smaller woman's shoulder. "That's what I'll be praying for."

Bianca eyed her.

"Don't ask. It's new, but it's a thing."

Bianca chuckled.

"Tell me how Steve is."

She opened the door to the room, and Kenna entered behind her, where she found Detective Thomson in the bed, hooked up to all kinds of wires and monitors. His chest rose and fell of its own accord.

As Kenna watched, his eyes opened, "Tell her how I am, dear."

Kenna chuckled. "I guess that answers my question."

Bianca grinned.

"You let me think he was still in that coma?"

Bianca moved to her husband's side, and took his hand, chuckling. "Everyone is safe, and alive. On the mend, and ready to get back to our lives. Thanks to you."

Kenna shook her head. "I was there. I thought I had the house secure, and I still didn't manage to stop them from taking Elijah. Or hurting you."

Thomson stared at her for a few seconds. "And you got yourself kidnapped, too, by the sound of it. And yet, you acted quickly with me. You kept everyone safe, and you kept everyone alive."

Kenna's stomach flipped over. "Not a great result."

"But it isn't a bad one, either." Bianca glanced over at Kenna. "So thank you for coming here. This never would've been over if you hadn't. The Children of the Morning would have continued to operate, and Elijah would have been either killed, or forever lost to us. Thanks to you, I have my family still and this town has a shot at freedom."

"You're both very welcome," Kenna said.

She couldn't even claim full credit for how things turned out. After all, she'd been in the thick of it with no idea how to take them all down. She'd prayed for God to intervene. He'd used a number of things, including the GPS tracker Maizie made Kenna keep in her shoe. It all could have easily gone wrong, and there would have been nothing she could do about it.

The death of Reverend Jim and his wife, Clarissa, would be a note of grief for the town. The result hadn't been a win on every level, but hopefully a man who had a faith relationship with God, and his wife the same, had made peace with the end of their lives. She would never know, but she liked to trust in the midst of the tragedy.

"And in case you wanted to know, I told Steve all about Dixie Cabrera."

"And Tilly?" Kenna asked, grinning.

"Yes." She smiled back.

Thomson said, "I don't want a dog."

Kenna chuckled. "Don't tell me you're a cat person."

"Dixie isn't."

Thomson grinned. He tugged his wife down and kissed her. "It doesn't matter to me who you were, just who you are now."

Kenna loved that for them. She couldn't help being happy for Dixie—Bianca—and how things had worked out well. Their family would heal. Life would go on.

Kenna would find a new case after she testified about Rushman and the FBI director.

Hopefully, Jax would be involved with whatever she did

next. Wherever she went, and whatever case she decided to solve.

Her work here in Helson was done.

Someone knocked on the door. Kenna turned to see a nurse, who said, "Kenna Banbury?"

She nodded.

"There's a courier out here with a package for you." She said it like a question.

"Thanks." Kenna held out her hand to Thomson, then gave his wife a hug. "Stay out of trouble."

"I don't make promises I can't keep."

Kenna left the room, chuckling.

An hour later, she had the phone all set up and her things packed. The rental car had been delivered after the courier dropped off the phone and instructions. It was parked in the driveway. And she had a plane ticket. Her flight left Seattle later tonight, getting her to Ronald Regan International Airport early the next morning.

The call connected, and Maizie said, "Everything good?"

Kenna angled her head toward the phone, lying on the counter. "Yeah, thanks for everything."

"No problem."

"But is it really what you want to do with your life?" Kenna frowned, an odd note of worry in her chest. "Don't you want to...go to school?"

Maizie was quiet for a second. "I've been talking to Elizabeth. I think I might enroll in something online for the fall semester."

"Computer science?"

Maizie snorted. "Maybe criminal justice."

"Now that would be a thing." Still, she could see Maizie excelling at forensic analysis, or even forensic accounting. "Lots of options for what you can do."

"I'll figure out what I want to study," she said. "For now, I'm just going to take a couple of classes and see how it goes."

Kenna had zero clue how much education the girl had. Obviously she was literate, and on certain things she would test at a genius level. But that didn't mean she understood everything about the world. Most of her learning would likely be social, even with online classes. She'd have to tread carefully.

"I know you'll do great," Kenna zipped up her duffel. Stairns was going to have her park the rental in the airport long stay, and he would drive over from Colorado, get the weapons, and then return the car to the company. "It might be rocky, but you've done harder than this."

Maizie was quiet for a second.

"When I get to DC, I'll check in, but then I might not call for a few days."

"Okay."

Kenna took the call off speaker and said, "Turn on your video."

"I'm in the trailer."

"I know." Kenna had figured she was. "I want to see what you see."

Maizie's face loaded on the phone screen, and she was frowning.

"Go over to the table and duck your head under."

Maizie turned, and the view moved so fast Kenna nearly got motion sickness. "What am I looking at?"

"The panel on the floor." It hadn't been replaced. "Pull it away from the wall, beside the rear-facing chair first and then going toward the back. There's something behind it."

"Looks like a box."

"It's a metal tin. I bought it at an army surplus store."

Maizie flipped her camera and lifted the lid. Kenna saw

all her childhood keepsakes inside—movie ticket stubs, receipts, yellowed photos. A ribbon from a county fair, for a painting she'd done just by squeezing paint down a fold and pressing two sides of the paper together, making a sort of butterfly with the dry paint. Apparently, she'd won.

"You see the necklace?"

"Got it." Maizie pulled out her fingers, a silver chain dangling down. On the end was a yellow flower.

"My dad gave that to me on my sixteenth birthday."

"Wow." Maizie's voice sounded thick with emotion. For all the things she'd never had?

"I'm giving it to you."

Maizie slipped the chain over her head, and the call ended.

Kenna stared at the screen of the phone. A second later she got a text.

> Thank you

She stowed the phone in her pocket and headed to the airport.

Chapter Thirty-Five

Kenna stepped onto the top of the escalator. It crested the edge and headed down to the bottom. She caught sight of him standing at the bottom. No one could miss the handsome man in a well-fitting suit. The short dark-blond hair that was tight on the sides but a little more unruly on top.

Jax pushed off the wall, smiling as he headed for her. "Your nose does not look good. Looks like it hurts."

Kenna looked down at her jeans, beat-up Converse, and the T-shirt she'd been wearing all night on the plane. At least she'd showered before she left. Her broken nose, she couldn't do anything about. If the FBI wanted to see her, she wasn't going to pretend she was something she wasn't.

He chuckled as she stepped off the bottom of the escalator. "You look great. Don't worry."

She wasn't a fed and didn't plan to be one ever again. She stopped in front of him and lifted her chin because he was four inches taller than her. "It's good to see you."

Jax traced his thumb across her cheek, avoiding the sore spots. "Yeah, it is." He said the words softly, then leaned in and touched his lips to hers. They hadn't exactly settled into a familiar comfort with kissing, but they would get there. If they could spend more than a few hours together at a time. Still, it felt good. Peaceful.

"I have a duffel." She wanted to touch her face but kept her hands away from accidentally jogging her nose.

"Let's go get it off the conveyor." He snagged her hand in his and headed for the direction the sign indicated she could find her checked luggage.

"I'm surprised I wasn't met by a full detail of FBI agents."

He slowed by the glass door and motioned. "They're waiting outside at the curb."

"You persuaded them to hold off?" She'd figured they would want to secure her, at least. Make sure she didn't balk at the last minute and change her mind.

"I told them I wanted to see you first." He squeezed her hand. "Without an audience."

"So they all know..."

"...we're *together*?" He shot her a smile that looked more cunning than anything else.

"I don't know if I'd say 'together' when it's more like, 'long distance slash seeing how things go' with a side of 'where are you moving now' and 'I'm busy taking down a dangerous cult.'"

"I heard that was a teacher. Not you." He chuckled. "Her mom was the leader?"

"It was a complex situation with a lot of moving parts."

"I'll get a pizza," he said. "You can tell me the whole story."

She winked. "Now you're speaking my language."

They didn't have to wait long for her duffel. Jax hefted it over his shoulder, and they headed for the curb outside. She wiggled her hand out of his before the automatic doors slid open.

Two FBI agents broke off their group conversation. In all she spotted three, one in the driver's seat. The SUV would be full if there weren't any other vehicles to make them a convoy. She shifted her foot so she could feel the GPS button device that had saved her life before. There was only a small chance these agents would dump her in a secret prison for killing their boss a couple of months ago, so she probably didn't need to worry about that.

"Ms. Banbury."

Kenna nodded. "Yep."

"This way, please." He motioned to the vehicle, and she climbed in the back row just so they'd all have to twist around if they wanted to talk to her. Jax got in and sat beside her. They treated him with respect, which was good because if they hadn't she'd have kicked up a fuss.

She belted up, and he leaned over to whisper, "I'm due in New York to join a drug taskforce first thing Monday."

"That's great." She squeezed his hand.

"Yeah, it is."

She didn't know how long he would be there, but she could get over her dislike of mega cities and come visit. Plus, he would get vacation days. Maybe he would want to show up where she was and help her work a case. Unofficially, of course.

She would spring for the pizza.

"My mom loves the idea." He grinned. "She's already planning on flying over from San Diego for a shopping trip. My dad will probably stay at whatever hotel they book and watch TV while she's spending all their money." He paused. "How's your family?"

She loved that he worded it that way, even if it was only so he could ask without alerting the agents listening that they were talking about Maizie and Stairns. "They're good. I'm sure I need to check in soon, make sure nothing is on fire." She shrugged one shoulder. "But I have time."

He squeezed her hand.

"I guess I also have to call Ryson and tell him he was right about that fruit thing." She hadn't exactly come to fully upending her entire life for a relationship with God, but she'd begun to take the steps. Like a flower bending toward the sun, a little at a time. Maybe it was her history, but she needed to go slow. Build trust.

Jax frowned. "What fruit thing?"

"I'll tell you later."

She'd felt the peace of God in that clearing when there had been no hope and no way out. That was how she knew she could do this—she could testify as to Michael Rushman's organization and the intricate web of exploitation he'd constructed over years. The fact Maizie had been at the epicenter of it might come up. But as far as Kenna knew, the girl might have been around at some point in Vegas but she wasn't there now. She didn't plan to lie and say she had no idea where the teen was. She would do everything she could to keep Maizie safe.

The SUV slowed in a line of traffic, unsurprising in this city. The agent driving hit the turn signal and pulled out of the line onto the sidewalk for a few feet before he turned right down a side street.

Up ahead, a trash truck pulled up to block their way.

The driver of their SUV hit the brakes and swore. "What on earth..." He turned to look behind them.

At the same time, a man jumped out of the trash truck driver's seat with a grenade launcher, which looked like a chunky rifle.

The passenger shoved his door open.

The trash guy fired. A grenade hurtled its way to the SUV and under the engine.

"Down." Jax pulled her head down and covered her with his body.

Her face smashed the seat as the SUV exploded. The front end lifted, and the whole vehicle flipped over. Another explosion rocked them, and the vehicle spun.

Agents screamed.

Kenna gripped Jax's hand and held on.

Until everything went black.

Chapter Thirty-Six

Kenna coughed out a mouthful of sand. Her whole body hurt still. She rolled over and sat up, the room almost pitch-black.

In the distance, out a tiny window at the top of the wall that streamed in sunlight like a spotlight, she could hear mariachi music playing from a stereo. She'd heard car engines, and a small airplane. Down the hall she'd heard people screaming. But no one had come for them.

Yet.

She crawled across the room to where Jax sat with his back to the wall. She patted his shirt, which she'd torn into strips and tied around his ribs.

His hand caught hers. "I know you need me to not lose hope..." She heard his unspoken *but*.

"We're going to get out of here." She tucked her knees in close, her bare feet sliding across the sandy dirt under them. When she'd lost her shoes—and the tracker—she didn't know.

Where exactly they were, she didn't know.

All she recalled were snatches in the back of a truck, after they'd been dragged out of that government SUV. After all the agents had been shot.

On a small plane.

Another vehicle.

Sounds. Smells.

Kenna slid her hand up so she could touch his face, even though she could barely make it out in the dim afternoon light. "I'm gonna get us out of here."

She touched her forehead to his and held on.

Help us, Lord.

Also by Lisa Phillips

Find out more about Brand of Justice at my website:

https://authorlisaphillips.com/brand-of-justice

Book 1: Cold Dead Night (Aug 2022)

Book 2: Burn the Dawn (Nov 2022)

Book 3: Quick and Dead (Feb 2023)

Book 4: Over the Limit (June 2023)

Book 5: Skin and Bone (August 2023)

———

For Lovers of Romantic Suspense check out

-Benson First Responders-

———

Other series by Lisa:

Last Chance Downrange

Chevalier Protection Specialists

Last Chance County

Northwest Counter-Terrorism Taskforce

Double Down

WITSEC Town (Sanctuary)

———

For other titles including several with Love Inspired Suspense, you can find the complete list here:

https://authorlisaphillips.com/full-book-list